Freddie Stockdale was born [...] read law at Cambridge. He [...] and daughter in London, a[...] marriage. He also farms in [...] Opera; and is the author of [...] *Bridgwater Sale* and *Crimin[...]* by Black Swan. He is also the author of two books about opera, *The Opera Guide* and *Figaro Here, Figaro There*.

Praise for Freddie Stockdale:

The Bridgwater Sale

'A witty and well-shaped plot leads us into the highest of comedies. A top-class début'
David Hughes, *Mail on Sunday*

'Full of good jokes and sharp insights, with an affectionate picture of English country, "county" life . . . I enjoyed it very much indeed'
Jessica Mann, *Sunday Telegraph*

'Spiced with wit and charm'
Sarah Broadhurst, *The Bookseller*

'The novel's combination of technical detail and emotional charge might suggest Jilly Cooper, with a *Polo*-like mixture of hanky-panky and rumpy-pumpy between gavel and rostrum'
Literary Review

Criminal Conversations

'A delightful story . . . Entertaining reading with lots of legal fun and sex in between'
Publishing News

'Mr Stockdale writes in an admirably plain, racy style which is touched with a bawdy, 18th-century sense of humour. It is hard to close his book once opened . . . Deliciously cynical'
Country Life

'A sure talent to amuse'
The Lady

Also by Freddie Stockdale

THE BRIDGWATER SALE
CRIMINAL CONVERSATIONS

and published by Black Swan

Affairs of State

Freddie Stockdale

BLACK SWAN

**AFFAIRS OF STATE
A BLACK SWAN BOOK : 0 552 99625 4**

Originally published in Great Britain by Doubleday,
a division of Transworld Publishers Ltd

PRINTING HISTORY
Doubleday edition published 1995
Black Swan edition published 1996

Copyright © Freddie Stockdale 1995

The right of Freddie Stockdale to be identified as the author of
this work has been asserted in accordance with sections 77 and
78 of the Copyright Designs and Patents Act 1988.

All the characters in this book are fictitious
and any resemblance to actual persons, living or dead,
is purely coincidental.

Condition of Sale
This book is sold subject to the condition that it shall not,
by way of trade or otherwise, be lent, re-sold, hired out or
otherwise circulated in any form of binding or cover other than
that in which it is published and without a similar condition
including this condition being imposed on the subsequent
purchaser.

Black Swan Books are published by Transworld Publishers Ltd,
61–63 Uxbridge Road, London W5 5SA,
in Australia by Transworld Publishers (Australia) Pty Ltd,
15–25 Helles Avenue, Moorebank, NSW 2170
and in New Zealand by Transworld Publishers (NZ) Ltd,
3 William Pickering Drive, Albany, Auckland.

Reproduced, printed and bound in Great Britain by
Cox & Wyman Ltd, Reading, Berks.

Affairs of State

Part One

May

Chapter One

'Order! Order!' Thursday the twelfth of May, and the whole Chamber was in turmoil. Red-faced men were waving sheets of paper, stout women were bellowing to make themselves heard above the din. In short, the House of Commons was conducting the nation's affairs in its usual manner.

'Order!' The Speaker had risen in his chair, his ancient face disfigured with rage, 'Order!' The hubbub gradually subsided. 'The Honourable Member must withdraw those words immediately.'

All eyes turned towards a pigeon-chested little man with a black toothbrush moustache and red-rimmed eyes who was standing in the third row behind the Government front bench. He bowed awkwardly towards the Speaker. 'I will withdraw "deceitful" and "blackguardly",' he said, 'but I do *not* withdraw the word "toad". If ever a man embodied the basic ingredients of toadishness, being indeed the apotheosis of slimy, pop-eyed and amphibian reptility, it is my Right Honourable colleague, the Member for Market Plumby.' The House erupted again, those around him shouting out protests, while those on the opposition benches, two sword-lengths across the green-carpeted gangway, matched them with delighted support.

Alone in his Olympian disregard for the chaos around him, James Hepburn, the youthful Member for Glenbuchat, continued to study his wife's letter. It was the first for some time. *'The crocuses on the broad walk have just come out, a carpet of yellow that reminds me how late everything is up here. Darling, the tower roof has been leaking again, and water has poured through into the tartan room,'* he read. *'Sandy has won a star for his arithmetic, but Jennie will not concentrate on her scales.'* He was a tall man, just past thirty, with the pale skin that goes with dark red hair, and the bloodshot eyes and nagging headache that go with drinking too much whisky the night before.

'The Prime Minister!'

Below James, the squat round figure of his leader rose from the front bench with a sheaf of papers in one hand, and his familiar pebble-lensed spectacles, boon to the nation's cartoonists, in the other. He cleared his throat and placed the papers carefully on the despatch box.

'My Honourable friend and colleague, the Member for Berington,' (some shouts), 'and so I shall continue to refer to him despite his characteristically colourful references to myself, disagrees with his own party's policy on steel closures. That is his absolute right, and I would be the last person to complain of his resolute support for his constituents, the employees of the Berington steel works. He is however wrong on two points.' The huge chamber of the Commons, brilliantly lit by the television lights, was hushed as the crowded Members waited while he fiddled with his glasses, first wiping them with a spotted red silk handkerchief and then spinning them expertly round before balancing them on his stubby nose. 'In the first place, we gave no assurance on the renewing of the contract for sheet steel, NO!' He had to raise his voice above an incipient growling from the Labour benches opposite. 'I repeat, *no assurances whatever*! In the second place, my wife *does* assure me that I do not, whatever my Honourable friend's asseverations to the contrary, look like a toad.' (Prolonged cheers.)

'Number four, sir!' Prime Minister's Question Time, that regular Thursday afternoon rendezvous, was in full swing. However much the legislative power might have passed in substance to Brussels, its soul remained firmly within the Palace of Westminster. There, among the gothic nostalgia of Pugin's pinnacles, the residual heirs of William Pitt and Charles James Fox traded insubstantial insults in place of noble oratory.

'Poor old Mrs Ogilvie has had another operation at the infirmary,' read James, turning the closely written page. *'She's still got ridiculously high blood pressure and may not be coming back for months. So I have started a new girl, who answers to the name Lucy. She's not very bright, of course, but at least she can cook, thank God! You'd laugh like a drain if you could see her efforts to lay the table for dinner.'* There was an eruption of shouting beside him, and he folded away the letter and put it in his pocket.

'Siddown and shuddup!' His neighbour, a fat young man of the same age but with wavy black hair and scarlet cheeks, was roaring at their gleeful opponents across the gangway.

'Resign! Resign!' came back the raucous chorus of voices, all of them conscious of the television cameras relaying their efforts back to their admiring constituents.

'Really!' James's neighbour, Nick Boynton, flung himself back onto the green leather bench, wiping his forehead with a white silk handkerchief. 'What absolute *turds*!'

'They're enjoying themselves,' said James. 'And so are you!'

His neighbour grinned at him, and then gave an apoplectic snort. 'Bastards,' he muttered. 'As for Paine there, he ought to be SHOT!' He glared down at the little man from their own benches who had started all the trouble. Then with a heave of his shoulders, he resumed his lounging position, masking his moist brown eyes behind their heavy lids.

'He has to consider his constituents, Nick,' said James soothingly. 'He only had a majority of three hundred.'

'How many steel-workers vote Tory?' scoffed the other without turning his head. 'Socialists one and all, I should say. Or National Front. The sooner we send them back up north, the better.'

James stared at him. 'You can't be serious.'

'Oh, not all the way up to you, old boy,' Nick yawned peaceably. 'Just as far as Tyneside or wherever all the other steelies come from. Are you dining with us tonight?'

James shook his head. 'Not tonight,' he said. Nick, his neighbour on the Conservative benches, was Chairman of the 'Unmentionables', a small group of ten young MPs who had set themselves up after the last election ostensibly to promote a radical reorganization of the state education and health services. This, the copybook approach to self-promotion, had already shown encouraging signs of success with the promotion of Nick to act as Parliamentary Private Secretary to the Arts Minister. No matter that this involved little beyond acting as the great man's bag-carrier and informal ambassador to the back benches; it was a palpable first step up that rickety ladder towards their mutual goal: a seat at the Cabinet table, the minimum criterion of success in a political career. Once let a politician slide his or her legs beneath that, and whatever humiliations follow, they may always claim that their and their family's sacrifices, of time, privacy and freedom, have been on the noble altar of the public good, and that all the years of swallowing insults and squabbling for place have been justified by their demonstrable success.

James had only joined the group because Nick was a good friend from school and university where they had both studied Art History. Nevertheless, he was no more immune to the lure of advancement than any other young politician in his first Parliament. With a working majority of only seven, and with two years still to run, this Tory administration was remarkably tender in its treatment of its back-benchers, the foot-soldiers who kept their grandees in power by dutifully tramping to and fro, as instructed, through the Government lobby. So long as they charged obediently through the correct defile, they might reason why for as long and as loud as they liked. And no-one listened to their most casual opinions with a greater show of benign interest than the Rt Hon Leader of the Conservative and Unionist Party, Prime Minister of Great Britain and Northern Ireland, and Member of Parliament for the Midlands constituency of Market Plumby. Indeed, as James paused beneath the massive bronze statue of Winston Churchill on emerging from the Chamber an hour later, it was the panjandrum himself who laid an affectionate hand on his shoulder.

'My dear James,' he murmured. 'Thank you for your support this afternoon.'

'But I did nothing, Prime Minister.'

'Under present circumstances, that may be considered the most active support!' laughed the other, screwing his eyes into strange polygonal creases of mirth. 'I'm coming to dine with your group next Tuesday. I hope there will be a most stimulating exchange of views.' He moved away, slipping his arm expertly through that of a passing Secretary of State. James watched the two men walking down the Commons' corridor before wheeling right, and out of sight, towards St Stephen's Hall. Other Members were milling around him, some of the men, like Nick Boynton, consciously traditional in starched white collars and pin-striped trousers, others, like Iain Mackenzie, the Scottish Labour Member for the industrial town of Newtown Strathurquhart just across the river from

James's constituency, were as conscious of striking a blow for sartorial secession with their creased blue jeans and knotted shoelace ties.

The women too paraded their affiliations, here a Tory dame in purple velvet, her doughty throat straining at three colossal ropes of cultured pearls, there a slim young Labour delegate from the inner cities, her dark eyes flashing from between suspiciously long lashes, her svelte figure burdened with an ingenious cradle of straps ready to receive the baby currently confined within the Commons' crèche.

Seventy-five feet above James's head towered Pugin's great vaulted ceiling, elaborately painted with the emblems of Parliament and its constituent countries. Above and around him stood the statues in bronze and marble, on plinths and in niches, of men celebrated for their leadership in a thousand years of island history. The vast multi-storeyed chandelier glittered with Gothic menace above the heedless chattering crowd who represented their nations' citizens in this, the supposed focus of law-giving. James could not suppress a great surge of pride at belonging, at the age of thirty-two, in such a glorious setting, the theoretical and highly decorated hub of government, where every wall and every ceiling proclaimed their lineage of power.

His father had represented the Glenbuchat constituency for more than thirty years until his sudden death in the middle of a General Election three years before. The Glenbuchat Conservatives, with two days to go before the closing date for nominations, had unanimously turned to his only son. James, contentedly settled in Battersea with a young wife and two tiny children, had made a snap emotional decision to shelve his career as a London banker and return to Scotland and fight for his father's party and constituency.

'But, my darling! You've always supported the Social Democrats,' Susie had said, running in out of the rain, with the children squealing with delight behind her. 'And you've just been promoted.'

'I know,' he had smiled ruefully at her. 'But it's what my father always wanted. And I feel I understand Glenbuchat. I know the people, and I know what they want. The political label somehow seems less important. It will give us a real reason to move into Hepburnstoun.'

'If it's what you want.' Had he realized then that this prospect might hold less allure for her than for him? The whole period had seemed crowded with urgency, the funeral, the campaign, being elected, and leaving his job, which of course meant less money to redecorate the big house. And now, here he was, the standard bearer of the last Conservative stronghold north of the Tay!

Tearing himself away from the colourful throng, he took the Members' lift down to the car park and drove out into Parliament Square past the crisp salute of the elderly constable on duty. He had decided to buy Susie a present before returning home on the evening shuttle.

Chapter Two

'More tea?' The Prime Minister's study on the first floor of Number Ten, Downing Street, had only just been redecorated. Gone were his predecessor's dun-coloured flock-paper and the modest watercolours of the Potteries. Now the tall room sparkled with light reflected from the massive pair of gilded Chippendale mirrors that flanked the fireplace above which Sargent's bravura portrait of Arthur Balfour raised its languid brows in patrician hauteur. A lush new crimson silk lined the walls, punctuated with an ingeniously rococo silver fillet, and Lord Curzon's massive bureau plat, supported by its swirling dragons, filled the bay with metallic splendour.

The view outside, half-veiled by spiked security bars, across Horseguards' Parade to the creamy terraces of Carlton House Terrace, was at its most beguiling, with the flowering cherries (St James's Park enjoying a balmier climate than the chilly mountain setting of James's Highland constituency in Glenbuchat) fully out, and the distant thump of a military band added pomp to the circumstance. But the three people seated there that same evening were oblivious to anything beyond the piece of paper beside the teapot.

'No thank you, my dear.' This was his second term as Prime Minister, a role he had long taught himself to accept as the perquisite of other, abler men. Clearly intended by providence for the role of Minister of State, he had found himself propelled delightfully upwards as a direct result of his party's Balkan disasters. First Home Secretary and then, in a sudden dog-fight of labyrinthine treachery between the mandarins of his generation, he had emerged, once the fog of battle had cleared, as the only eligible survivor.

'Good old Toady, a safe pair of hands. Time we had an old-Harrovian in charge again.' His unpromising appearance disguised an adequate intellect and some capacity for hard work. It also explained his frantic anxiety to be liked. His wife, a slender little birdlike brunette, her pale angular face glazed with the effect of too much powder, her sunken eyes darting out strange glances of uneasy malice before crinkling up into a poor pastiche of good humour on either side of her beak, paid no attention. She refilled her husband's cup with the pale aromatic tisane, and put the pot down with a clatter.

'He'll have to go.' She said this almost as a challenge to their companion, an elderly man with wisps of gingery hair, who was sucking noisily at his pipe. They all looked again at the piece of paper. It was headed, in longhand, 'Memo to PM'.

'It has come to my attention that someone, presumably your "Political" Secretary, gave an unattributable briefing yesterday (Wednesday) to The Sunday Times. *The substance of this was that I was secretly working to reintroduce the death penalty for terrorist offences against your wishes, and, more damagingly, against the clear consensus opinion of Cabinet. I would be grateful if you could (a) confirm to the Editor that this is wholly untrue, and (b) give your aide clearer guidance on what his job does (and indeed does not) entail. I have had quite enough of this backstairs loutishness. Any more and I shall be unable to continue in your administration further.'* It was signed by David Brotherton, the Home Secretary.

'"More damagingly"! What does he mean: "*More* damagingly"?' she demanded with an angry look at her husband.

'He means,' suggested their guest, 'that going against our Prime Minister here is less of a sin than going against his colleagues.'

'It's an insult,' she cried. 'A blatant declaration of war. The man's power-*mad*!'

'Six,' murmured their elderly guest, tapping his pipe on the table. Husband and wife stared at him. 'Six,' he repeated, and took out a battered leather tobacco pouch. Walter Meyrick had been Chief Whip to three Conservative Prime Ministers in the last five years, and handled each one differently. Against this woman's over-mighty protection of her husband's ragamuffin dignity, he had found that common sense served as a healthy antidote. 'To put it another way,' he said thoughtfully, 'if David went so far as to start voting against us out of pique, your majority would be down to five. He's an independent sod, always has been. I couldn't promise to deliver on that basis. We have two men due to go into hospital at the moment, and you saw this afternoon how unreliable Paine is becoming.'

'Time to get down to business,' groaned the Prime Minister. 'You'll have to leave us, my dear. Thank you for the excellent tea.' There! He had managed it without his customary apology. He had asked, told, his wife to depart without even a stammer. Perhaps she would eventually learn to leave him to do his job unaided. Casting a malevolent glance at the little heap of ash the Chief Whip had deposited on his saucer, his wife collected her novel from the window-sill and left the room in silence. And if, as she passed through the long panelled dining-room on her way to her own little nest of gold, the green boudoir, with its Turner cowscapes and slanting view across the garden to the Cenotaph, she was observed by the portraits to be muttering angrily under her breath, surely they could not have heard the words, *'Bloody men!'*

'My dear Walter! So good of you to come,' said the Prime Minister.

'I've come every Thursday afternoon since you re-appointed me,' said Meyrick. 'In case you're interested, I thought Cabinet this morning was a total disaster.'

'Because?' Thank God she'd gone quietly.

'Because unless you can stop your senior ministers squabbling like fractious children, this atmosphere of indiscipline will destroy your Government. Good God! You had Brotherton up on his hind legs bellowing like a bull, the Foreign Secretary giggles like a schoolgirl, and *then* we had Dutton bursting into tears. It's my job to get your Bills through on time. How can I do that when the place is like a bear garden?'

'What should I do?'

'If you mean about Brotherton, do as he suggests. You really cannot risk his going just now.'

'Because of the steel closures?'

Meyrick chuckled. 'I heard old Paine's harangue,' he said. 'He's just a whingeing old woman. No, I'll get that through for you safe enough. By the way, I'd like to promote young Hepburn to the vacant Whip's post. He's been a steady support and I think there's potential there.'

'Have anyone you like, Walter. So long as you get the Bills through.' It really had come to that. No doubt the Prime Minister, as a decent, eager young barrister fresh from National Service, had entered politics full of genuine if pliable ambitions to promote the welfare of his country. One nation! Fair dos! (And keep the lid on income tax.) But somewhere along the twisting path that had led him up the yellow staircase of Number Ten, past those dreary mezzotints of Disraeli, Churchill, Major and the rest, that section of his soul had perished. Perhaps it had always been a modest section, or perhaps the shock of discovering that his most savage political foes were more generally to be found among his fellow-Conservatives, had undermined his youthful enthusiasm. Whatever the reason, domestic peace, meaning nothing more ambitious than good relations with his own wife, was all that survived of his original goal of peace and prosperity for all mankind. Given a quiet home, he was quite content to leave the governance of the country to his barons, being the senior Cabinet departmental heads and their civil servants. And content also, to leave the governance of these barons to Walter Meyrick.

'The one I *am* worried about,' said Meyrick, 'is the *Miscellaneous Provisions No. 4 Enabling* Bill on the eleventh of July.'

'The what?' The Prime Minister stared at him. 'I've never even heard of it!'

Meyrick, who had been patiently refilling his pipe, struck a match and applied it carefully to the new mixture. Now in his late sixties, he was at least ten years older than his leader. He had just bought a small château near Antibes, and the sooner he could retire there, the happier he knew he'd be. A couple more years, and he could slip quietly away with the regulation peerage. His stern pale face, and rigid military bearing was, also, the husk of that idealistic young man who, encouraged by his father, one of Churchill's wartime Cabinet, had picked up the Tory colours in the wake of the Suez débâcle. He had seen those ideals failing miserably under Heath and then mercilessly trampled in the Thatcher years. Worse, he had been forced to see how empty and self-regarding those ideals had been. And when faith has gone, what is there left for a man of action but the orderly administration of such power as he had, meantime, accumulated? Neither of these men were wicked, but neither of them possessed, let alone shared, a vision. Each day was but the orderly progression of their work. Fate makes one pair of men into labourers, and another pair into Prime Minister and Chief Whip. Let others incubate ideas. Their lot was to police the nation's orderly progress. What they did share was a complete though unconscious indifference as to direction. Form had long since conquered content.

Meyrick sighed. Had his father had to cope with this sort of thing too? Had Churchill forgotten from time to time who was fighting whom, and why? 'If you remember, Prime Minister,' he said calmly, 'it's one of poor Anstruther's leftovers. As you know,' he permitted himself an ironical smile, 'he died before he could get all his bits and pieces tied up. I explained it to you; it should give you a much easier time in the Commons.'

'Oh, that one. Bypassing the bloody lot! Or something of the sort. Surely we've had the second reading?'

'Ye-es.'

'And it got safely through the committee stage, didn't it?'

'*Just.*'

'So it should be plain sailing now.'

'Yes and no. His department is frantic to get it on the statute book as soon as possible. Apparently all his other legislation hangs on it for efficient implementation. But the Lords don't like it either.'

'So what's their problem?' The Prime Minister, though the nephew of a peer himself, had less patience for the Upper House than for the back-benchers on whom his position now depended. After all, he had despatched quite a few from the back benches to the Lords himself.

Meyrick sucked thoughtfully at his pipe. 'Well,' he said. 'No-one seems quite able to explain what the beastly thing says, which is just as well, perhaps. And one group is busy going round saying it should be thrown out unless the Government gives way on milk quotas.'

The Prime Minister stood up abruptly. 'Whatever else this Government gives way on,' he exclaimed, 'it will NOT be on those bloody milk quotas. I spent six months getting that through the House. I'd rather resign.'

The Chief Whip gave a snort. He knew the wounds in the party were too deep to allow any of the factional warlords to command support. Like it or not, he was stuck with his current chief, the only man too insignificant to have made many enemies in the struggles of the recent past. 'Margaret's supporting him,' he murmured. 'And John. *And* dear Teddie.'

The Prime Minister dredged up a laugh. 'In that case,' he said, 'you ought to be sure of a vast majority. You've got two months to wangle it, when all's said and done. Sometimes I wonder why we don't shoot ex-Prime Ministers instead of sending them to the Lords.'

'A brave statement,' murmured Meyrick, 'considering your own position if we lose the vote.' There was an awkward silence. 'I must say that there've been rumblings about *No. 4* all round the House. It's very obscurely phrased.'

'Who's handling it?'

Meyrick stared. 'If you remember, Prime Minister,' he repeated, 'you appointed Ralph Dutton to replace the late if unlamented Anstruther.'

'Why on earth did I do that?'

'I seem to recall,' replied Meyrick imperturbably, 'that you did it to ensure his support for the new *Licensing Hours* Bill.'

'What? Chancellor of the Duchy just to get him to vote for his own party?' The Prime Minister was in a puckish mood. It was nearly six o'clock.

Meyrick sighed. 'At least he's stayed loyal to you

ever since. You'd better ring *The Sunday Times* and get David sorted. He's safer in than out.'

'Let's have a drink first,' said his host, crossing the room to press a button beside the fireplace. 'I want to hear more about poor Dutton. Is it true his wife's run off with their chauffeur?' When the butler brought in the drinks tray, he found the two politicians laughing uproariously about the gossip of the day.

Chapter Three

'It's charming.' Susie Hepburn held up the blue silk scarf James had bought her, and examined it against the light. 'Very spoiling!'

'Do you really like it?' Her hair was blonde and glossy, and smelt of orange blossom.

'Yes, darling. So useful.'

His plane had been on time, as it usually was on a Thursday, but the three-hour drive, winding through the Perthshire glens and then up into the Highlands had tired him. 'Is there any ice?'

'Oh God, that girl!' She crossed to the open door and shouted down the stairwell. 'Lucy! Are you there?' There was an indistinct answer from some distant corridor. 'Mr Hepburn would like some ice in the drawing-room. I did tell you.' Another indistinct response. 'Just do it, will you?' She came back scowling. 'That girl's too cheeky by half.'

'I said I'd go and read to Sandy,' James said.

'It's far too late for that. I've turned his light off. Please don't encourage him.'

'But I haven't seen him all week!'

'And whose fault is that?' she suddenly snapped. 'If you must maroon us up here in this freezing awful barracks while you swan around the House of Commons, the least you can do is support me in dealing with the children. He really must go to bed at the proper time, otherwise I get no time to myself at all. Now, darling!' She flashed him a deliberately charming smile. 'Be a poppet and go and make yourself a cooling drink while I have my bath. You must be utterly worn out.'

Not for the first time, James reflected ruefully on the contrast between his wife's letters, in which he seemed to enjoy at least some small degree of affection and confidence, as opposed to when they were together, when he seemed relegated to those who needed strict guidance. Walking slowly down the broad staircase, he had to force himself to ignore the little voice that called out to him from the floor above. He loved this house, with its familiar smells and childhood memories, the dark hiding-place behind the library bookcase, the dusty glory-hole at the top of the tower, even the dank and now deserted cellar corridors filled with two centuries-worth of discarded junk.

But he could also see that it was hardly ideal for Susie, whose pride in the immaculate state of their compact London home could find little to satisfy it in the gaunt rooms crowded with heavy mahogany under the empty gaze of his grandfather's collection of stuffed heads. There were rows of red deer around the hall and stairs, wildebeeste and zebra in the library, which also boasted two full tiger skins on the floor complete with snarling teeth and tongues of pink pumice, a moose in the kitchen corridor, and, more controversially, their drawing-room was punctuated by a set of six lion heads, one symmetrically placed above each of the Raeburn portraits. Sometimes he felt Susie would mind less if these last heads were not in the habit of shedding a monthly dandruff of infinitesimal hairs onto the polished parquet. Only the crocodiles in his study escaped her criticism, since this was the one room into which she never came, taking a fierce pride, rather, in according him, as her mother had to her father, the right to one secure male bastion in an otherwise matriarchal household.

'Dinner will be in twenty minutes.' For a moment he was unsure where the voice came from. 'Is that all right?'

Looking round, he saw a young woman with long dark hair standing in the shadows beside the gathered velvet curtains that masked the kitchen corridor.

'Yes,' he said absent-mindedly. 'That's fine.' The indistinct figure turned away. He found a glass mixing-bowl piled high with ice placed beside the drinks tray in the drawing-room. Pouring himself a generous measure from the whisky decanter, he filled the tumbler up with ice cubes and settled himself down on a sofa. It was good to be home. He must have dozed off, because the next sound he was conscious of was the dull booming of the gong. It rose to a crescendo, seeming to signal some portentous heathen rite, and then abruptly died away.

'God almighty!' Susie, luscious in a pink silk kimono, swept into the room. 'Doesn't she know what an *ice-bucket* looks like?'

He stared at her. Everything was in its proper place, hair that sparkled like spun gold, the tresses now drawn up into a tiny bun before cascading over her slender curving shoulders, full rosebud lips, black eyes with irises of crushed mulberry, a snub nose of delicate construction, little pink ears, a discreet bosom – and yet, and yet – there was an icy managerial glint and a sarcastic slant to the eyebrows that he could not admire. Moreover she had, to a rare degree, that quality of self-absorption which is so conducive to one's own comfort, though less so to that of others. Had it always been so, or had he dried up her softer side by uprooting her from the fertile suburbs and transplanting the family into the Highlands' thinner soil? It was difficult to remember. Had they ever been truly happy together? He supposed so. There was such a secure cocoon of tradition woven round their marriage, with Hepburnstoun, the children and his job, that the starker questions of life seldom intruded. But seeing her conceited scowl now, he could not help feel his heart shrinking at the prospect of an evening alone with her, let alone the night. There was an austere, brittle air about her which gave to the normal physical ease of marital sex the repellent air of a society hostess reluctantly dispensing hospitality to the local vagrant.

'What are we having?' He made a conscious effort to put some warmth into the question.

She shrugged. 'Hare soup, haddock soufflé and what's left of Mrs Ogilvie's home-made blackberry ice-cream.'

'Sounds wonderful!'

They ate in silence, appreciating the food which Lucy, the young woman he had seen earlier, pushed through the hatch. She had a dark shapely face with high cheek-bones and bright enquiring eyes, and she appeared, from what he could see of her, to be wearing a white smock over a green woollen sweater.

'This soufflé is excellent,' he said to Susie, heaping some more onto his plate.

'I'm coming down to London with you,' she said abruptly.

He stared at her. 'Splendid,' he said, adding after a moment's thought, 'but what about the children?'

'They'll be fine here. Mrs Granville says she'll come and look after them.'

'I thought she had her hands full with her mother-in-law?'

Susie sighed. 'You can always find objections to everything,' she said. 'I've spoken to Granville, and he says he can manage perfectly well for a month.'

'A *month*?'

'Anyone would think you weren't pleased that I want to be with you.'

He walked back to the table. 'Of course I'm delighted,' he said. 'It's an excellent idea. I was just worried about Sandy, that's all.'

She shrugged. 'He'll cope. It's good for children to get used to surviving without their parents' constant supervision. I'm coming back with you on Sunday night. Angus and Mary have asked us to dine on Wednesday.'

'That's nice,' he said between mouthfuls. 'I can do Wednesday.'

'I think I'll wear my gold moiré dress. You'll have to be a darling and get my diamonds from Coutts. Just look at these spoons! Bloody girl, she really hasn't the faintest idea.'

Over her shoulder, James was embarrassed to see the young woman's face leaning through the hatch to reclaim the soufflé dish. To his surprise, she held his glance and winked.

Chapter Four

'There's disloyalty everywhere, and it's serious.' The Chief Whip's office was a large room just off King Arthur's corridor, and overlooking the now twilit Thames. The following Tuesday, Walter Meyrick stood staring out at the mysterious surface of the great river which sparkled with myriad reflections, while its smooth ripples gave little indication of the churning currents underneath. An only child, he had been born on the banks of this same river, in the little manor house which he, in his turn, now occupied, almost a hundred miles upstream. But there, among the water meadows of Shotesbury, it was no wider than a horse could jump, a clear-flowing stream with none of this metropolitan subterfuge.

His office had one way in, through the main Whips' office and the waiting-room dominated by his secretary's broad desk with its formidable array of telephones and electronic equipment. But it had two ways out: back the same way, or, for visitors too distraught to face the satirical glances of the waiting queue, there was a locked side door on to a narrow spiral staircase through which he might, whether out of kindness or discretion, allow them to slip away to lick their wounds.

Walter Meyrick was accustomed to difficult interviews. After all, his coded files held the deepest secrets of his party's members while he himself held their careers, or the hopes thereof, firmly in his grasp. These varied from something as sad and insubstantial as one Member's comic inability to make the simplest speech without his knees shaking to, in two cases, one being of ministerial level, the very real suspicion of murder. That was the fun of the thing, that was what was left to him once the glory of idealistic visions had departed. And, to be truthful, it was quite a substantial legacy. A man might be a lion in the daily press, but he could be little other than a mouse in the office of the Chief Whip. Red despatch boxes, punctual chauffeur-driven limousines, little trips to exotic far-flung places, convenient offices within the Commons, and then, as the shadows lengthened, that final accolade, a seat in the Lords (or at the very least a knighthood) – all these colourful candies were bottled on Walter Meyrick's shelves, out of reach but plainly visible to the aspiring Members.

'First things first.' His companion, Ralph Dutton, Chancellor of the Duchy of Lancaster and Member of Parliament for West Cumberland was a thickset man with heavy black brows, the rings under his eyes made darker, no doubt, by his current domestic difficulties. He pulled out a cigarette case and extracted a thin blue cylinder which he tapped lightly on the table before lighting it with a paper match. 'What are you going to do about Paine and his steel contracts?' He exhaled a thick cloud of smoke.

'Nothing.'

'Nothing? He's stirring others up as well, you know. Even some of the peers, and that takes a bit of doing.'

Meyrick smiled, pointing to a grey folder on his desk. 'The higher his profile now, the bigger the stir when he comes back to roost!'

'You've got him taped?'

'Trussed up and ready for market!' Somewhere a telephone rang, followed by a discreet knock on the door. 'Yes, Joan?' A fat anxious face had appeared, a face that seemed to expect, even invite, rejection. 'What is it?'

'I'm terribly sorry to interrupt . . .'

'And yet it seems that you have.'

'It's Mr Paine. He sounds very upset.' The two men glanced at each other and grinned.

'Oh *dear*!' said Meyrick with heavy sarcasm. 'Tell him I will see him at . . .' He examined his watch, 'ten-thirty tonight.'

'He's hoping you will see him now.'

'It'll be one a.m. if he argues. In fact, tell him midnight, by which time I shall have gone home. Let the bugger sweat!' The woman withdrew. 'You see?'

'How did the press get on to the Dublin fiasco?'

'Who knows?'

'I suppose Toady told his wife as usual? That woman is impossible.'

'He says not. He's beginning to learn. Slowly.'

Dutton sighed. He had told his wife everything, a confidence which she had evidently not reciprocated. He was due back at his empty home for dinner, and he needed a drink. No wife to warm his bed, and no man to clean his shoes. It wasn't easy to calculate which was the greater loss. 'I'll put out some feelers,' he said. 'My clerk knows everything that goes on.' At least he still had someone to confide in. 'You know,' he continued, his voice rising into a whine, 'it's very hard . . .'

'My dear Ralph! Will you forgive me? I have to see rather a lot of people this evening.'

'Oh? Of course. I'm sorry. It's just . . .'

'Good *night*, Ralph.'

After Dutton had left, Meyrick stayed very still for a few minutes, reflecting. Then he stretched out his hand, and depressed a button of the intercom on his desk. 'Send Commander Trent in, would you, Joan?'

The man who entered was a trim square man in his middle fifties. There was nothing exceptional about him, except perhaps that he gave off an air of violence, very imperfectly suppressed. He had massive shoulders, a jutting jaw, and angry eyes. Watching him with a proprietorial pride, Meyrick decided he was the perfect British bulldog, whom no-one in their right mind would allow anywhere near their throat.

'How are the men in tights?'

'Who?' The Commander stared at Meyrick.

'Your underlings. The Serjeant-at-Arms and his merry men!'

'They don't like it.'

'Having you in charge? I bet they don't. But that's progress. It makes the rest of us feel a sight safer.' The Commander nodded. 'The Prime Minister is anxious to show he is trying to stem the leaks, but not so anxious as actually to do so. You understand me?' The Commander showed his teeth. 'You may be working in tandem with my new young Whip, once I've appointed him. He's called James Hepburn. He's very eager, and very inexperienced. You won't have any difficulties there. All we want is a peaceful Palace of Westminster where we can get on with our various tasks without undue interference. You're doing a great job.' If the Commander had had a tail, no doubt he would have wagged it.

It was nearly eight on Tuesday evening. On the floor below, James and Nick Boynton were checking the table in the private room booked on different days each week by the 'Unmentionables' for their little dinners. There was a crisp white tablecloth, crested Commons cutlery and, to mark them out from humbler groups, a vast silver centre-piece lent (rather reluctantly) by Nick's elder brother. Tonight the crystal saucers which balanced on its upturned arms held marrons glacés, chocolate truffles and, piled high on the larger central bowl, a glutinous heap of sugared plums from Fortnum's.

'Have you done the *placement*?'

Nick nodded. 'Toady's on my right, you're on his other side, and the others arranged as usual.'

'The wine?'

'Crozes-Hermitage '87 with the turbot, Château Palmer '59 with the tournedos, and a '62 Yquem with the bombe glacé.'

'He ought to be happy with that.'

'Quite!'

James watched him tinkering with the table, swapping a spoon here, straightening a napkin there. Even Susie could hardly have shown greater commitment to the minutiae of presentation. Perhaps bachelors took more interest in this sort of thing, having as yet no other to do it for them. Certainly Nick had been just the same at school, physically assaulting anyone rash enough to disturb the symmetry of his beautifully decorated room.

'They're saying that outburst over steel has cost Paine his knighthood,' murmured Nick over his shoulder, as he gave the cloth a final tweak. 'That's what I call hitting where it hurts!'

'I wouldn't have thought he'd mind that much,' said James.

Nick laughed. Relaxed, he had a soft, even cherubic face, and his immaculate clothes reinforced the impression of a man entirely at ease with, indeed in control of, his surroundings. Member of Parliament for the busy East End seat of Spitalfields, he combined an aggressive rumbustiousness in the House with dedicated hard work in his troubled constituency. This was an inspired combination for his voters, who enjoyed his shouting matches on the television screen, and appreciated his genuine efforts for racial harmony and industrial investment. They even respected his forthright distaste for the humbug of egalitarianism. 'We're all equal before God,' he liked to assert, 'and before our doctor. Passive we are indisputably equal, but don't let anyone fool you that it goes further than that. To schoolteachers and employers, we're each as good as the effort we're prepared to make. When we're active, it's every man and woman for themselves.' And if alcohol already seemed to play too prominent a role in his life, that served only to make him seem more human, more at one with his community, a considerable proportion of whom invested what little they had been able to earn or otherwise acquire during the day in cloaking their evenings under an agreeable and comforting haze. 'What a simpleton you are,' he said, patting James's arm. 'It's not old Paine who'll mind. That old bat Thora Paine's hung on for years to be a Lady. She'd have bolted ages ago but for that. She'll be tearing up the carpet!'

Half a dozen other youngish men, all plump and noisy in their crisp white shirts and smartly tailored dinner-jackets, crowded into the room, almost immediately followed by the leaden figure of the Prime Minister.

'Welcome!' cried Nick, bustling forward and brushing his wayward hair out of his eyes.

'I'm very honoured to be here,' replied their guest, putting on a broad smile and taking the chair indicated to him. 'How are you, Nick? James? Why, Robert! Henry! John! And Gerald too. *And* my old friend Rupert.' He made himself very pleasant to each of them, nodding and beaming like a marionette, gobbling down the food and managing to drink very little. Ten years ago, none of them would even have acknowledged him in the corridor, but then ten years ago none of this crew had even been in the House. They wouldn't remember him in his third-rate days, fifteen years on the back benches and a couple of years as his uncle's Minister of State in return for sorting out a family trust. Yet here he was now, Toady the Magnificent, master of all, fêted by his colleagues and handing out bishoprics and Garters like there was no tomorrow! If the holding of such power wasn't worth a few smiles, even to young idiots such as these, he asked himself, what in Heaven's name was?

'We want to bowl you a googly, Prime Minister.' They could lob him a pterodactyl for all he cared! He was just finishing the ice-cream, and was allowing himself a second thimbleful of their honeyed wine.

'Come on then,' he said, beaming happily at their flushed young respectful faces. 'I expect you want to hear about Gibraltar?'

'Well, no,' said Rupert Pilkington, a fleshy but fastidious Welsh Member who sported an embroidered waistcoat held in by a heavy gold chain. 'It's this *Miscellaneous Provisions No. 4* thing we don't quite understand . . .'

The Prime Minister stared at him. How could anyone have so many pulsing blue veins visible in one face, and at that age? At least young Hepburn, the red-haired one tagged for promotion, *looked* normal. He even had quite an attractive line in serious smiles, and the sort of face people would instinctively trust in a politician, however mistakenly. He looked . . . well . . . electable. Whereas *Pilkington* . . . 'Ah!' replied the Prime Minister, deciding to play for time. 'That.'

'Yes.'

He sniffed his glass, closing his eyes and assuming an air of ecstatic concentration. 'This is superb wine.'

'Thank you, Prime Minister,' said Nick, who as chairman of the club was accustomed to fielding the compliments. 'We lay down a little each session.'

'To comfort those whom promotion eludes,' added John Pope in a sly voice at the end of the table. No-one laughed. His face was against him in comedy, being too lopsided to carry much consequence.

'About *No. 4*?' prompted James, who was genuinely interested. 'The wording is very obscure.'

'Tell me why you're agin it?' replied his leader, having decided that attack might buy time.

James looked at Nick, who gazed thoughtfully at his plate. 'Well,' he said, 'we're none of us quite sure what it *means*.'

'But as Conservatives elected on a shared manifesto, are you not committed to support your Government?' A fervent rumble of 'Hear, hear' passed round the table. 'Nick here is your chairman, and indeed, I may say, a not inconsiderable member of my administration. What do you say, Nick?'

'Oh well,' replied the stout young legislator, agreeably conscious of the burdens of office, 'if you put it like that, Prime Minister, it goes without saying that you can count on us. A toast!' They rose as one. 'The Queen! Coupled with the name of her Prime Minister!'

'The Queen! The Prime Minister! God bless them!'

'Gracious me!' muttered one of the elderly waitresses outside, patiently preparing their coffee and liqueurs. 'What can be the matter?'

'Perhaps they're murdering the old bugger,' said her sister hopefully, as she took a gulp from the bottle of crème de menthe.

The head waitress shook her head. 'Not bloody likely,' she said. 'They need him as much as he needs them. Here! Take in that tray. I'm not waiting here all night. I've got better things to do!'

Chapter Five

'Grow up!'

'What did you say?'

'Oh, I'm so sorry. I know I don't always express myself with total clarity.' Nick Boynton, the following morning, his cheeks an ominous purple from the evening's entertainments, moved closer to Paine, the recalcitrant Member for Berington, and thrust his face down to the shorter man's level. 'What I was trying to get across, in my admittedly rather obscure way, was just this . . . you're supposed to be a Conservative, not a one-man bloody Job Centre. You can't make steel no-one wants to buy, at a price they wouldn't pay for gold bars and still expect tax cuts. Do try and see some sense.' He turned on his heel and strode off down the Commons' corridor.

'What's his problem?' Paine, at the end of a long and undistinguished parliamentary career, was genuinely puzzled. He had represented Berington, the town of his birth, since 1959. He had supported his party on all major national issues, and had exercised his own judgment on all local issues, and had been praised for doing so by colleagues and opponents alike. No less a Prime Minister than Harold Macmillan had personally congratulated him for passing through the noes lobby in total if ineffectual conflict with the latter's policy.

'Well done, Baine,' he had said, shaking the young man's hand. 'Stuck to your principles. Nothing wrong with that.' But Paine had been passed over for promotion then, and indeed had been passed over ever since.

'He thinks you should support us on steel, and on this *No. 4* business,' said James who was standing nearby with a colleague. 'And he's got a hangover.'

'He's very young,' said Paine patiently.

'And very intemperate,' put in another passing Member. 'He really should be politer to senior Members like old Paine here.' The latter bowed with mock gratitude at the back-handed compliment. 'Hello! Here comes trouble!'

Down the corridor towards them could be seen advancing the menacing figure of the Chief Whip, immaculate in morning dress, complete with gold watch-chain and white gardenia.

'Good morning, Paine,' he said. 'So sorry I had to cancel our meeting again last night. Urgent government business.'

'I really am most awfully anxious to speak to you.'

'And here I am!' Meyrick put a wealth of sarcasm into his expansive gesture, throwing open his arms and bowing very low.

'I mean,' said the other, 'in private.'

'Talk to Mrs Davies. She'll fix it up. Now, James. I want a word with you. Can you spare five minutes?'

'Of course.' James, after first straightening his tie, hurried after the Chief Whip, noticing, not for the first time, the deference with which Meyrick's progress was met as he stalked the Commons' tributaries, one eye ever cocked to catch any sign of incipient rebellion against his master.

'Gin and tonic?' They had reached the Portcullis Bar, which even at eleven-thirty was doing a decent trade.

'Whisky, please.' James felt a sudden need to show some independence, however trivial.

'A large whisky for my friend here, please, John. We'll have them by the window.' They settled themselves down beside a stout little table already equipped with peanuts, green olives and two notepads with pencils attached. 'I won't beat about the bush, Hepburn. The Prime Minister's asked me to offer you a job as junior Whip.'

James felt his cheeks burning. 'Why? I mean . . . how?'

'You mean who's gone?'

'Well — yes.'

Meyrick grinned and pulling out his pipe, began to stuff it with tobacco from his leathern pouch. 'Buxton.'

'Buxton?'

'Yes. He wanted to spend more time with someone else's family.' The older man paused to put a match to the tobacco. 'We've had our eyes on you for some time. You've given plenty of discreet support at times when it's been most needed, and what you say when you speak makes sense. And, to be candid,' he sucked in noisily and blew out a choking gust of smoke and ash, 'I need vigorous reinforcements. I need a young man on the team.'

James, trying hard not to cough, gave what he hoped was an intelligent nod. 'I see.' He could not help thinking that he had leap-frogged over Nick in a highly gratifying way. He had not begrudged his friend his first step up, and was entirely confident that Nick would feel the same way about this advance. After all, it had been the same at school, with Nick getting elected to the House Library first, on the strength of his prowess at games, while James had beaten him to House Captain.

The difference between them now was that Nick was wholly professional in seeking promotion, whereas James, an involuntary recruit, tended to let the beguiling world of parliament drift round him. He was always determined to do the best he could, and knew that he had been effective in working both for his constituency and on his various committees, but he had not as yet been infected with an all-consuming urge to exercise power over others.

'Well, that's settled then,' said Meyrick with a complacent smile. 'Enjoy your drink, and report to my office at one-thirty for a briefing. I'm not worried about steel, but I am worried about this pestilential *No. 4* business.' He stood up as the barman limped over with their drinks.

'Thank you,' said James.

Meyrick raised his glass and drained it in one. 'The pleasure is all mine,' he said. 'It's like awarding House Colours at school. I like to see a young man making his mark. Congratulations!'

'Can I ask . . . ?'

If Meyrick felt impatience, he masked it. 'Please.'

'Of course I understand the basic requirements, but . . .'

'It's very simple,' said Meyrick, with a conspiratorial smile. 'You'll have a block of about thirty Members you have to keep in constant touch with. Ostensibly this is to listen to their views, arrange their pairing, and generally overwhelm them with tender loving care, in return for their rewarding you by voting the way they said they would at the election. But, *entre nous*, it also includes keeping a discreet eye open for sexual or financial misdemeanours. We'd rather know before the reptiles do. That way we can take evasive action before it gets vomited all over the front pages. You will also come to enjoy the seductively murky world of carrot and stick, by which your fellow Whips keep their charges in order. Remember,' said Meyrick gleefully, 'you have plenty of goodies up your sleeve: free trips to the South Seas on *parliamentary business*, flattering photocalls with visiting statesmen, favoured 'pairing' for long weekends. Best of all (for the really well-behaved) is the reward of promotion up the government ladder and the promise of a 'K', or even a peerage, at the end of the road. You'll find they lap that side up like there's no tomorrow. *But!*' Meyrick raised a single portentous finger. 'Any symptoms of recalcitrance among the "rank and vile" we meet with an entirely different treatment: no pairing equals no nights off, no free trips, no invitations to Number Ten, a positive block on promotion prospects and, finally, if the patient proves terminally obstreperous, a quiet word with the constituency chairman. All you need say is that honours that might have been available within the constituency (i.e. the chairman's own knighthood) cannot be considered while the present Member fails to support the party line, and things begin to hum! It's truly remarkable how swiftly the threat of deselection, being thrown out on their ear, brings Members into line! The black arts of the Whips' office have had three hundred years of parliamentary democracy in which to be refined. It is much our greatest contribution to *democracy*.'

And if, thought James, their object was to frustrate that very freedom that Parliament was ostensibly formed to promote – to vote according to conscience – who was he, the newest recruit on the greasy pole of promotion, to complain? This was power.

'Don't look so worried,' said Meyrick, rising. 'You'll enjoy every minute of it. You'll see what I mean at one-thirty.' And with that, he left.

Punctually at one-thirty, James presented himself outside Meyrick's door. Mrs Davies, the unlovely secretary, let him in with a welcoming smile. 'Hello, dear. We're going to be seeing a lot more of you, I gather.'

'Yes, Mrs Davies.'

'Mr Meyrick wants you to sit in on his interview with Mr Paine in five minutes. In the meantime, settle yourself down over there on the sofa and read these notes on the steel contracts.'

He had only just started on the typewritten notes, a detailed analysis of the voting patterns of Paine and half a dozen other dissenters, when there was a knock on the door and Paine himself looked round the door, his moustache twitching uncomfortably.

'Am I expected?' he said. 'Oh, hello, Hepburn. Are you in the queue too?' He sat down on the sofa. 'This sort of thing terrifies me; what about you?' James wasn't quite sure how to answer this, but was saved from doing so by Meyrick himself throwing open the inner door and advancing towards them.

'There you are! Splendid! I'm so pleased you could fit us in. I expect you've heard that James here has joined the home team. He's taken over your area,' James was conscious of an uneasy atmosphere blowing his way from the other end of the sofa, 'so naturally he'll be sitting in on our little chat.'

'But . . .'

'Come in, both of you. That's if you really do have time, old boy?'

'Oh, all right then,' sighed the poor supplicant. 'I don't suppose I have a choice.' But when James made to let him pass in ahead, he angrily gestured to the new Whip to go first.

A low chair was placed in front of Meyrick's desk, with another higher one by the window. James was shown to the latter, while Paine found himself perched on the former, some eighteen inches below Meyrick's chilly stare.

'So?' The Chief Whip's voice was gently inquisitive.

'So?'

'What can we do for you?' Paine looked anxiously at Meyrick, then at the floor, then at the ceiling, pointedly ignoring James. '*You* asked for this meeting, not me.'

Paine sighed again. 'I know,' he said. 'I've been a Conservative Member for nearly forty years.'

'Wonderful!' said Meyrick in a neutral tone.

'And I've given good service!'

'You're famous for it.'

Paine stared at him. 'You've only got eleven Members with longer service.'

'Eleven?' mused Meyrick. 'Is it really eleven?'

'You know damn well it is,' said Paine.

'And?' Meyrick shot a quick, amused glance at James, who was feeling increasingly uncomfortable.

'Vanderbank and Gottlieb weren't elected till '64.'

'So?'

'Don't play with me, Walter. You know they both got their Ks in the last Birthday Honours.'

Meyrick raised his eyebrows unnaturally high. 'Oh?' he breathed. 'You're worried about a *knighthood*? Is *that* it?'

Paine stood up in his agitation. 'You know I don't want one for my own sake.'

'No-one ever does, as far as I can tell.'

'Do you deny that I'm due one?'

'Well,' Meyrick lounged back in his chair and gazed out of the window. The Thames was a dirty grey today, undulating sluggishly and carrying an apparently inexhaustible flotilla of filth towards the unsuspecting sea. Was his whole life to be mirrored in this river, born at the source, educated downstream, and now working at its most public confluence? Perhaps he'd end up as one of those doddering has-beens at Greenwich? He sighed and turned back to the quivering Paine. 'I'm not sure that anybody is ever exactly *due* one,' he murmured. 'But I think I could put forward a case on your behalf.'

'PUT FORWARD A CASE! I'm the only long-serving Member in the party without one. Why should I be different?'

'We . . . ell,' Meyrick turned to James who was quite beside himself with embarrassment at the way the interview was going. 'What do you think qualifies a man for the ancient order of knighthood?'

'Me?' James was acutely conscious of Paine's smouldering glare.

'Yes, if you would.'

He shrugged. 'Half a million in used notes to Central Office?'

'I like a man who enjoys a joke,' said the Chief Whip drily, 'but I think the real answer to Paine's question is this: your colleagues aren't biting the hand that feeds them.'

'The rumour is that I'm to be denied my knighthood if I vote against the Steel Bill.' Paine was staring at Meyrick with an expression of awful fascination, half-fear, half-enslavement.

'*Your* knighthood?'

'All right. *A* knighthood then.'

'And whence comes this sinister rumour?'

'Right where you're standing if I know anything about this bloody place!'

'Well,' drawled Meyrick, 'it is *rather* difficult to imagine the Prime Minister putting your name forward to Her Majesty at the same time as he goes to tell her his Government has fallen.'

'But my wife . . .'

'Ah! The *delectable* Thora!' Meyrick's ill-natured sneer was so offensive that Paine leapt out of his seat and might have struck his torturer had James not quickly interposed himself. 'Let me be frank,' said Meyrick, tiring of his sport. 'You cannot please both your steel-workers and your wife. I don't see why I shouldn't tell you straight. Unless you withdraw your opposition to this Bill and intend to speak in favour tonight, I personally shall block any recommendation for an honour now, and in the future.'

Paine stared at him in appalled silence. Then he said slowly, 'And if I do support it?'

A genial smile spread across Meyrick's face. 'Ah, then,' he said. 'I will certainly raise the issue at the next meeting of the honours board. It does seem somewhat overdue, doesn't it? I'm sure they could be persuaded to see the merits of your case.'

'You promise?'

'My *dear* Gerry! Word of honour.'

After Paine had slunk out, nothing was said while the Chief Whip relit his pipe and his new subordinate gazed unhappily out of the window.

'That's how it has to be done,' said the senior man at last. 'There ain't no other way.'

'Will he support us?' asked James gloomily, half-hoping for the answer no.

'Oh yes! That sort *always* do.'

'So he'll get his knighthood?'

Meyrick stared at the young man before him with narrowed eyes, as if sizing up James's ability to cope with the unpalatable sides of life. Whatever he saw made him grin. 'Not if I have anything to do with it!' he said. 'Come on, we'd better be getting to the Chamber in time for prayers. Then I've got to try to sort out our eminent Home Secretary who's belly-aching again!' And if, in observing James's confused expression, Meyrick caught a rueful glimpse of his own shattered illusions, he could not have acknowledged this, least of all to himself.

When, thanks to Meyrick, the two senior members of the Cabinet met later that day, it was hard to imagine a greater contrast between the squat, homely figure of the Prime Minister, and David Brotherton, his tall, grey, patrician Home Secretary, an elderly voluptuary, whose angry hawk-like profile peered beakily down at the shorter man, like a heron inspecting an unsavoury specimen of flotsam.

Meyrick, joining them in the former's office, found them already arguing over a leader in the morning's *Daily Telegraph*.

'I supported your standing as PM only because I

believed you would support me on tougher immigration,' Brotherton was saying, his voice grating with unconcealed anger.

'No, you didn't,' interrupted Meyrick, pulling up a chair. 'You supported him because you couldn't bear the thought of Jennings at Number Ten.'

'Jennings! There was never the slightest chance of *Jennings*. Look at him now. Fiddling about in Brussels, so fat he can hardly walk through the door without a couple of builders in tow to make good the damage.'

'David, *listen* to me.' The Prime Minister had switched to his wheedling tone. 'We need you.'

'*You* need me. That's what you mean. But why the hell should I put up with all this crap from your kitchen Cabinet? Look at this leader. "Home Secretary must go the extra mile for child brides" for Christ's sake. That comes straight from your ghastly pouting Mrs Afterbirth.'

'Mrs *Afterbirth*?'

'The Home Secretary means Mrs Arthingworth, Prime Minister.'

'Child brides indeed,' spat Brotherton. 'Dirty little prostitutes more like. What her interest in them is, I dread to think.'

'Mrs Arthingworth is a very able adviser and a very distinguished *thinker*. She spent several years with the Joseph Institute.'

'More fool she. I'm telling you straight. Any more of this and I shall resign.'

'My dear David . . .'

'Don't dear David me. I'm saying this as plainly as I know how. I've been on the front bench for nearly twenty years, which is a sight longer than you have, and I have a better idea of what Conservative policy should be than a whole truckload of "very able advisers". I'm not having my department thrown off course by some unelected frump. Nor do I like being sniped at under cover of the Tory press.'

'We *all* understand,' said Meyrick soothingly. 'It must be very annoying. But are you sure you don't take too much notice of the papers? *The Sunday Times* one day, the *Telegraph* the next. Commander Trent is personally spearheading a comprehensive investigation into these alleged leaks. What does it really matter? After all, you *are* the Home Secretary.'

'It matters,' said Brotherton angrily, 'because it is perceived as weakening my position. I have enough trouble with my junior ministers and civil servants as it is, without them thinking Downing Street is against me.'

'But we're not,' said the Prime Minister, wondering whether he dared pat his enraged colleague on the sleeve, and swiftly deciding against it. 'Witness the fact that you are very much in charge.'

'Try telling that to your women!'

If the Prime Minister recognized that as including his wife, he chose not to take issue with it, contenting himself with a neutral smile. 'I hear everything you're saying, David. I do need you, and you have, as always, my unwavering support.'

Brotherton looked him up and down in a most insulting fashion. 'Whatever that's worth. Good day, Walter.' He turned on his heel and left the room.

'Phew!' The Prime Minister sat down heavily and blew his nose.

'We need him on board.'

'Thank God they aren't all like him. Haven't you got anything in your closet you could use to restrain him?'

Meyrick shook his head, regretfully. Brotherton, a junior minister under Margaret Thatcher, and subsequently Secretary of State for Education and then Defence under the succeeding administrations, was a very rich man in his own right, having inherited substantial commercial property from his mother. A bachelor, he had never shown any sign of the weaknesses so convenient to an aggressive Chief Whip, and his yacht, kept fully crewed and operational in the Mediterranean, had given him the extra political clout of being able to entertain his potential supporters in a style to which decreasingly few of them had ever been accustomed. 'I'm working on it,' he said. 'But no. I think we've just got to grin and bear it. It's only because you didn't give him the Foreign Office in January.'

'*The Foreign Office!*' The Prime Minister's voice was almost a squeak. 'How could I move Roger? He's frantic for an earldom, but he's only got a majority of a few hundred. We'd lose the seat and then where would we be?'

'Precisely where we'll be if you don't stop your people getting at Brotherton.'

'He should follow agreed policy.'

'I agree. But your majority is very slender.'

'So tell me about your new recruit.'

'James Hepburn.'

'Yes, I was watching him. Bit like his father. Excellent presentation, possibly a bit too *nice*? Is he really going to be tough enough for what you want?'

'It's surprising what a taste of power can do for a man,' said Meyrick without discernible irony. 'He's certainly the brightest of his vintage. His bank was furious about losing him. In a way he's perfect: plenty of money so there's no risk of services-for-sale, settled home life so no risk of Tory-sauna-scandal . . .'

'That sort's often the worst,' grumbled the Prime Minister with evident feeling.

'Not Hepburn,' said Meyrick with a confident shake of the head. 'He's almost too straight. I'm not sure I don't feel safer with the riskier ones. Talking of which, you ought to bring Boynton in soon. He's a conceited ass, but he's desperate for recognition, and he's good in front of the cameras.'

'What a help you are, Walter.'

'I do my best.'

Just the other side of the Abbey, James and Susie were getting ready to go out for dinner when the telephone rang.

'Hello?'

'James, congratulations!' It was Nick Boynton.

'Thanks. It is exciting.'

'More than that. It's the start of a great career. We're all thrilled.'

'Oh yeah?'

His friend laughed. 'Well, Paine is a bit put out. And Rupert's spitting tin-tacks. But who cares about them? I think it's absolutely splendid. You won't start bullying your old friends, I hope?'

'Not so long as you all do your duty and vote for idiotic measures like this *No. 4* just because I tell you to.'

'I can see you're a natural Whip already!' The next call was from Meyrick. 'I'm calling an emergency meeting of all Whips in forty-five minutes. Be there.' Short and to the point.

'Susie?'

'Don't bother me, darling. I'm trying to do my face.'

'I'm afraid I can't come.'

'What do you mean?'

'I've been called back to the House. Some sort of crisis.'

'God, what a *bore*! You'll have to ring Angus and Mary yourself. They'll think it very rude. And you can call me a taxi.' She returned to her task.

When he reached the House half an hour later, he found his eleven new colleagues all assembled in Meyrick's office. 'There's a distinct possibility,' said their chief crisply, 'that Brotherton will go tonight.' There was a collective intake of breath. 'There's been rather an unfortunate satirical piece in the *Evening Standard* suggesting Number Ten don't think much of him, which, coming on top of other things, may, just *may*, tip him over the edge.'

'Will he vote against us?' asked someone.

'I can't think that's likely,' said Meyrick. 'But he's always been a loose cannon. And it's possible. I want you all out there, keeping an eye on things. Any sign of recalcitrance and you bring them here to me. Carry them if you have to. If necessary, I'll get Mrs Davies to lock them in the bog till after the vote. I want no slip-ups. So get on with it!'

In the Chamber, James found that Nick was on his feet. 'And so, let me say this.' Nick, despite his volatile temperament, was a popular figure on all sides of the House, attracting sympathy through his human foibles as well as respect for his hard work, and was invariably listened to with interest, 'While respecting the views of my Honourable friend, the Member for Newcastle South East, I do feel that it is in the best interests of the steel-workers concerned that their many talents should be redeployed into work which, by generating profit, is by its nature more reliable for them and their families, than that they should be turned into a subsidized peep-show of *"What our forefathers did"*. Why should these technically advanced craftsmen be confined to an arid museum existence rather than allowed to enrich themselves and their nation by confidently adapting to the new trading conditions of today?'

'BLOODY RUBBISH!' Iain Mackenzie, James's Labour pair and Scottish neighbour, was on his feet, hair everywhere, and waving his order paper.

'After such a graceful request,' smiled Nick, 'who could resist giving way to the blandishments of my Honourable friend, the Member for Newtown

Strathurquhart?' He temporarily took his seat, acknowledging the ripple of laughter behind him.

'This measure,' proclaimed the successful interloper, 'is as cynical a slice of Tory treachery as ever slithered out of the mouth of that serpent wallowing on the front bench opposite, I REFER,' he shouted over the cries of syntactical outrage, 'TO THE PRESIDENT OF THE BOARD OF TRADE. WHAT HAPPENED TO TRADE, I ASK? WHAT HAPPENED? WHAT HAPPENED? THERE IS NO TRADE! THE PRESIDENT CLOSED IT DOWN!' He sat down to a thunder of jeers and counter-jeers.

'Well!' said Nick, back on his feet. 'That was a really helpful addition to this serious problem. The steel-workers in Berington must feel a very *Solomon* has come to their aid. Thoughtful argument, cunningly phrased, clearly presented. An unanswerable case, I should have thought,' he looked across at the fuming Mackenzie and smiled, 'for the IMMEDIATE REPATRIATION OF THAT LUDICROUS REPRESENTATIVE OF MINDLESS REACTION!' He had sucked in enough air to swell his voice into a reverberating bellow and the Labour benches erupted into volcanic complaint which just as suddenly died away. The Commons clock had reached the hour, the television arc lights had instantly dimmed, and everyone sat back and began to relax. Mackenzie himself, straightening his tie and turning down the collar of his coat, shook a friendly fist at Nick, who grinned back, coughing after the exertion. He couldn't help congratulating himself that in pubs all through the East End, his supporters would be waving their tankards in triumph, cheered on by his boisterous performance. But it was over now, and he and his colleagues could all relax until the cameras started again to beam their antics to the outside world.

He's quite a showman, thought James, who had been used to Nick's tantrums from school. At least he can laugh at himself, even when it's not put on, like now. Several Members, including the Prime Minister, walked out, but there was no sign yet of Brotherton. Then suddenly tension returned. The Deputy Speaker had called 'the Honourable Member for Berington' and Paine, squinting down through his moustache at a crumpled page of notes, was the object of universal attention.

'When this measure was first brought before the House . . .' he began.

Nick's mouth fell. He leant across to James. 'He's going to *recant*!' he whispered. James nodded. 'What a scrotally-challenged little creep!'

'But this morning you said . . .'

Nick giggled. 'Oh that? I just needed to let off a bit of steam. Everyone's entitled to their principles. It's just that Paine wouldn't recognize one if it walked in and sat down on his lap. If I deeply disagreed with the Government, I hope it would take more than Walter Meyrick to make me recant!' And indeed James himself was still uncertain whether to admire the well-oiled workings of parliamentary patronage, or to regret the human failings of yet another politician for whom preferment mattered more than constituency. But then, perhaps Nick was right? Should these steel-workers be kept uneconomically slaving over their furnaces, churning out a product for which there was no market, for no better reason than that they were used to doing so, like so many social dinosaurs in a theme park?

'The last temptation is the greatest treason, to do the right thing for the wrong reason.' Paine, his head held awkwardly high, went on, 'During these past days, I have asked myself whether resisting this measure was truly in the long-term interests of my constituents . . .'

'What did he promise you? A baronetcy?' shouted out Mackenzie.

'With the immediate threats to their income, these men could be forgiven for not taking the long view . . .'

'Or did you hold out for a peerage? That would be as long a view as any!'

'I'd be grateful if the Honourable Member would allow me to finish.'

'One thing's certain,' shouted back the irrepressible Scotsman. 'You'll be finished in Berington!'

And so it went on. At nine o'clock James and Nick slipped downstairs to the restaurant, only to find it seething with the shocking (to those not already forewarned) news that David Brotherton, the Home Secretary, had abruptly resigned.

'Aha! Space at the top,' chuckled Nick. 'Room for one more on the gravy train. The "Unmentionables" seem to be in fashion. Who shall we nominate for a leg-up?'

'But what about the majority?' James was already mentally reviewing the various Members said to be ill or out of reach.

'You Whips! That's all you ever think about. Old Brotherton's a sound chap. He'll go on voting with us. It's definitely gravy up for grabs.'

'There won't be much gravy if the Government falls.'

Nick nodded reluctantly, his thoughts full, perhaps, of vacant ministries with four-litre Daimlers attached. 'Look! There he is.' They looked across to where, at the very next table, the tall beaky figure of the former Home Secretary, was enjoying a quiet glass of claret with a friend.

'You're a bloody disgrace!' Nick shouted at the startled old man.

'You're not on television now, Boynton. You know nothing about it,' replied Brotherton quietly. 'I have been continually provoked by Downing Street. Perhaps you didn't see this evening's *Standard*? Another set of insults, clearly originating from them.'

'I know enough to know you shouldn't be upsetting the Government out of poncy self-importance.' Nick winked at James.

The tall man turned to his companion wearily. 'This is Mr Boynton, a young man with more volume than courtesy,' he explained with a wry smile. 'It is not a species that welcomes explanation. Mere facts get in the way of prejudice.'

'I . . .' Nick's face had suddenly turned scarlet.

The others rose and left.

'Really, Nick,' said James softly. 'You do sometimes go over the top, you know.'

'I know. I do know.' Nick wiped his forehead. 'It's just . . .'

'Just . . . ?'

Nick closed his eyelids, and then opened one a fraction, revealing a narrow glinting slit of an eye. 'You wouldn't understand. It'll be all right when I get high office.'

James watched him covertly as Nick again wiped his streaming forehead. He must be at least three stone overweight, he who had been the picture of boyhood athleticism, Boynton the legendary star of the Eleven, Boynton the nonpareil stroke of the Eight, the envy of lesser creatures. Perhaps it was a pity he had thrown up the unexpected offer of a Fellowship of their old college to seek political power. At only thirty-three, his features were already beginning to coarsen, stretched by the accumulating fat. The long hours at Westminster, waiting for votes, listening to interminable speeches, were only tolerable if spent in good company, with good wine. Even so . . .

'Are you all right?' James asked, suddenly and genuinely anxious about his old friend. 'I mean, you're happy, aren't you? You chose this life. You do a first-class job. Everyone says so. Your mother must be very proud of what you've already achieved.'

Nick grimaced. 'Happy?' he echoed. 'What a deep, deep question. Or do I mean shallow? I wonder you don't ask yourself that before dissecting other people? But who's happy anyway? Not Toady with that termagant for a wife, not Dutton all abandoned on his own, and definitely not Paine, or even bloody old Brotherton with his yacht and what have you. No principles and no sense of duty. What a pair! Oh yes!' A sudden thought brought a bitter smile to his face. 'I'll tell you who's happy: Walter Meyrick. That's one man who's in his element. His is the only power left in Westminster, the power to make us poor puppets dance on his strings! He's *really* happy.'

A bell began to ring insistently, and all through the restaurant the diners began to drain their glasses and fold away their napkins. 'Come on, that must be the *vote* . . .'

The Steel Bill was passed with the Government's majority reduced to six, the former Home Secretary having vehemently declined to register his support for the administration of which, until just half an hour before, he had been the most vociferous partisan.

Chapter Six

'So how was dinner?'

'Fine. You'd have enjoyed it too, if you hadn't been stuck with your dreary politics.' Susie had been asleep when James had got in the night before, and had already gone out before he woke the next morning. 'They were very good about it, but it made us thirteen at table.'

'I know. I'm very sorry,' he said. 'Who else was there with you?'

She paused to light a cigarette from the green onyx box on her desk. It was eight o'clock the following evening and she was already late for dressing for another dinner party. 'Oh, just the usual crowd, you know, the Monteviots, old Tommy Tenterden, the Dorsets, Mary Griffin, she's on her own again, poor darling, those dreary Websters with her awful brother . . . and Fred Tevis.'

'Ah!'

'And what's that supposed to mean?'

'I thought he was in New York.'

'No,' she said nonchalantly. 'He's back. They've made him head of Schumann and Goldwater after poor old Siegfried got kicked out.'

'Looking well, I trust?' No wonder she was in London!

'James.' She stubbed out the cigarette with an angry movement. 'Please don't be silly. That was over years ago.'

He turned away, angry with himself for showing such obvious resentment.

'I'm sorry,' he said, turning back and trying a smile. 'It *is* silly of me. Who did you sit next to?'

'I had Angus on one side, and Henry Dorset on the other. Satisfied?'

'I keep meaning to tell you. I've got promoted!'

'Tell me about it in my bath. I must rush. I'm dining with the Schombergs. Be an absolute cherub and fetch me that old pink thing you gave me last Christmas.'

She was already deep in violet-scented bubbles when he returned.

'Is this it?'

'You are a marvel. Could you put it on my bed?'

They had let the house in Battersea, and the flat James was renting in Tothill Mansions offered nothing more romantic than a twin-bedded bedroom, with a low sitting-room, a little office, plus kitchen and bathroom.

'Now come and tell me about your sparkling career!' She ducked her head under the bubbles.

'Well,' he said, balancing awkwardly on the lavatory, and waiting for her to emerge. 'They've made me a Whip.'

'Gosh! Is that good?' She scrubbed her hair with a thick lather of shampoo.

'It's not bad for a start.'

'Where's the towel? Christ! Look at the time! You'll have to leave me to get ready. They'll kill me!'

Obediently he went and sat quietly in his office, leafing idly through the fresh pile of constituency letters. He knew that as Member for his homeland, the farms scattered among the great mountains and the little towns nestling in the glens, he had an easy time of it. Nick, with his teeming streets crammed with shops, and his borough councillors at each other's throats, kept a full-time office and a staff of four. James, whose constituency chairman had promised him a quiet life, was often disappointed at how prescient the old doctor had proved to be.

'Dear Mr Hepburn,

When is this Government going to do something about those poor children in Bulawayo? Is this a Christian country or is it not? How can you personally sit back and ignore starving babies when your own children lead a privileged and well-fed existence in a house large enough for twenty families?

Whilst writing, may I remind you that your subscription to the Glenbuchat Ladies Luncheon Guild falls due next month. And we shall be expecting you at 1 p.m. sharp on Sunday 3rd July as usual.

Yours aye,

Helen McPherson'

The address was given as The Manse, Glenbuchat, NB. There were six other letters asking him to attend or send donations to similar functions, and a letter in green ink from a woman who had discovered that her neighbours were planning to kill her with cyanide gas. He could hardly complain. His life as a Member of Parliament held few enough such distractions, thanks to a well-run local council, and an efficient constituency agent of the old school, who believed in a decent measure of respect and privacy for a Member who actually lived within the community he represented. His monthly surgery, conducted within the antlered austerity of the Hepburnstoun estate office, rarely produced more than a couple of anxious businessmen eager for guidance on the minutiae of trading overseas, and of course old Doddie Gordon, who really just came along for a chat over the quarter bottle of Johnnie Walker which he invariably brought with him.

A swirling cloud of pink chiffon and Chanel announced the imminent departure of his other half. Few marriages had begun with less auspicious omens. No sooner had he begun to love Susie, then a modestly successful model based in Paris, than she had run off to Los Angeles with a fashion photographer to the great relief of James's father, who had taken an instantaneous dislike to her icy glamour. Once that was over, she had turned up one morning at James's office, bearing apologies, flowers and two tickets for the Battersea 'Boners', his much-prized local football team. It was on again, and indeed a proposal was imminent when she had met Fred Tevis, a rising partner in Kleinwort Benson. James met him twice, and had to concede that his curly-haired rival was both charming and amusing, offensive only in his gift for attracting Susie's affectionate interest. It wasn't long before kind friends (and his own sense of smell) alerted him to the fact that she was cheerfully sleeping with both men. Because he loved her, and perhaps also because he enjoyed her sense of adventure in bed, James managed to swallow his jealousy enough to pretend not to notice. Thus Susie became accustomed to his complaisance, while he became accustomed to her exercising a right to stray. Then, one April, Fred was recalled to New York. In May, despite his father's anxious pleading, James proposed, and by the end of September, Susie had become Mrs James Hepburn of 146, Prince of Wales Grove, London SW11 and of The Mains, Hepburnstoun, Glenbuchat in the county of Duffshire. Had she been unfaithful during their eight years of marriage? James had tried not to speculate. Indeed there had been times when he had benefited from some sudden new attention she had, perhaps absent-mindedly, bestowed upon him in bed. If others might have found the contrast between her chummy letters and abrasive presence hard to take, James, a quiet man, chose to make the best of both. 'After all,' he had reflected, 'it was I who taught her that I was willing to overlook a multiple approach. If anyone should be blamed, it's me.' It was easier to blame himself, since that entailed no extra strife.

'I thought you didn't like the Schombergs?' he said, looking up at her glossy hair.

'I don't. But it's better than sitting in front of the television watching *Good for a Chuckle* with that ghastly man with no teeth! How do I look?'

'Gorgeous!' It was true.

She stared at him. 'Are you being sarcastic?'

'No!' He rose hurriedly to reassure her.

'Please not,' she said. 'You mustn't smudge my lipstick. Have you rung the children?'

'I just missed them this morning. Mrs Granville says they're fine.'

'Oh, good. Don't disturb them tonight, but you can send them my love when you ring tomorrow. Bye!' She had gone, mercifully without his yielding to the almost overwhelming temptation to ask whether this sudden interest in the Schombergs had any connection with her host being Fred Tevis's new colleague.

Chapter Seven

'When are Mummy and Daddy coming back?' Sandy Hepburn was sitting on a stool beside the kitchen table, staring up at Lucy, who was skinning a rabbit. Having reached the age of seven years and fifty-seven days, he was very aware of being master of the household in his father's absence.

'You'll have to ask Mrs Granville,' she said with a smile. 'She knows more about their plans than I do. But today is Friday, and your father often has the weekend off, doesn't he?'

'Don't you mind all that blood?' Sandy's wide dark eyes, twin mirrors of his mother's, gazed awestruck at her crimsoned fingers.

'Not at all,' she replied. 'It'll make fine rich gravy.'

'You've got even bigger boobs than our teacher.'

Lucy looked at him gravely. 'Is that meant to be a compliment, Sandy?'

He looked momentarily nonplussed. Had he overstepped one of those invisible lines that grown-ups set? 'Oh yes,' he said at last. 'They're MEGA!'

'Mine or your teacher's?'

'Both,' he said cosily and came round the corner of the table for a cuddle.

'G'morning, Master Sandy!' Jock the postman had a thirty-mile round on his bicycle, but the reason it took all day was that he stopped at each of the seventeen houses on his beat for a gossip and some form of refreshment. Now he rested his cheerful face, pink with the exertion of pushing his bike up and over the little footbridge below the house, on the window-sill and looked imploringly at Lucy.

'I suppose it's a dram you're after?'

He grinned. 'It's after eleven!'

'Come on then.' She was almost laughing. 'Back to the nursery, Sandy.'

'Can't I come with you?' He knew Lucy kept something for Jock in the stables.

She shook her head. 'If you're good,' she whispered, 'and I mean very good . . .'

'What?' He stuck his tongue into the corner of his cheek.

'I'll let you help me make the whisky cake for tea!'

'Oh Lucy,' he yelped, 'do you promise, really?'

'Off you go then,' shouted Jock. 'She'll be back for you shortly.'

In the nursery, he found the solid Mrs Granville, a severe woman in her late fifties, delivering a stern rebuke to his sister Jennie for colouring in the new wallpaper.

'But it looks pretty!' she was wailing.

'That's not the point, young lady, as well you know. What your mother will say, I daren't begin to guess.'

'You are a tit, Jennie!' said Sandy, only to find himself in the eye of a second storm.

'I thought you were supposed to be with Lucy,' said Mrs Granville when she had calmed down. 'I'll be glad when school starts again next week.'

'She's taken Postie over to the stables,' explained Sandy. Mrs Granville pursed her lips and said nothing. 'She's very kind, isn't she?' he went on.

'Kinder than Mrs Ogilvie,' added his sister who was now in a mutinous mood, and knew that Mrs Granville doted on her elderly friend, their ailing housekeeper.

'There's kindness, and kindness,' muttered Mrs Granville, picking up her knitting. 'Now why don't you both have a nice game of Ludo?'

'Will you play?' asked Sandy.

'Oh do! Oh do please, kind sweet Mrs Granville,' chimed in Jennie. 'We'll love you for ever if you do!' She took the older woman's hand and stroked it beseechingly.

'Cupboard love!' But she put down her knitting and went to get the box.

Hepburnstoun was a tall square house perched on a knoll by a bend of the river Buchat where three small valleys met, and despite its sparkling white harl, it still had a distinct air of menace with its dark little windows and sinister curtain wall. Of the old tower house held by the Hepburns as fiefs of the Frasers of Buchat, little remained. Burnt to the ground by marauding rivals, only a vaulted cellar and a mysterious cylindrical stone hole masked by an iron grating testified to its medieval origins. But the uneasy peace enforced after Culloden by General Wade's redcoats gave the Hepburn of the day, a prudent supporter of King George for all that his youngest son fell in the cause of the Stuarts at the Bridge of Mar, sufficient confidence to build in the new style.

The tall entrance tower with its alarming machicolations and beetling balustrades had been commissioned from Bryce by a descendant, whose son, James's grandfather, had then employed Lorimer to design the new billiards room overlooking the river and the stable block among the stunted trees above the house.

It was there, in an unoccupied room above the old carriage-house, that a naked Lucy, straddling the handsome postman with cheerful abandon, was administering energetic refreshment to that fortunate young man.

'There,' she said, when at last he had given up craning forwards to kiss her breasts and laid back his head with a deep sigh on the musty sacks that covered the floor. 'Are you all done?'

'Oh, Lucy,' he whispered. 'Why won't you marry me?'

'Marry you?' She cocked her head at him. 'And what would your Meg have to say about that?' He had a fine set of teeth and full high-coloured lips. 'No you don't!' His energy was astounding.

'LUCY! LU . . . CY!'

'Bloody children!' Jock wriggled away from under her as she jumped off him and frantically pulled on her few clothes at the sound of Jennie calling for her from the stable courtyard below.

'Coming!' She risked a glance through the cobwebs of the window. Jennie was standing just below, but looking towards the house. 'Hurry up, man!' she whispered. 'Your fly's wide open.' Clattering down the wooden staircase, she suddenly stopped at its foot, brushed back her hair and walked slowly out into the sunshine.

'*There* you are,' said Jennie. 'Mrs Granville was worried about you.'

'That was kind of her,' said Lucy.

'Hello, Jock!' said Jennie, noticing the postman's awkward stance in the doorway. 'Has Lucy given you a drink?'

'Yes thank you, Miss Jennie,' he said, licking his lips.

'Whose house do you go to next?'

'Old Mrs McCleod and her sister Miss Jean up at Inchnabo.'

'Do you get the same there?'

'Not quite,' he said, walking over to where his bright red bicycle was propped against the harled stone wall.

'That's a shame,' said Jennie seriously.

'Just as well,' laughed Lucy, taking the girl's arm. 'He's got work to do, and so have we!'

They walked hand in hand down the pink tarmac road that led to the back door of the house. There was still a chill in the air, despite a bright sun, and the clouds were thick and grey, threatening rain before evening.

'Look!' cried Jennie. 'What's that?' A great bird was flapping its way slowly up the river, its heavy wingbeats seemingly insufficient to keep it aloft.

'Why, that's the heron Mr Granville was telling us about. It's nesting up by the loch. He says it's ten years since they last nested there.'

'Can we go and see the babies?'

'Not yet.'

'Please, Lucy! Please say we can.'

Lucy laughed again. 'I don't suppose they've even laid an egg yet,' she said. 'Give them time, poor things!'

'Does it take so long?' whispered Jennie. 'To lay an egg, I mean?'

Lucy shrugged. 'Yes, I think so.'

Jennie stared up at her. 'Lucy,' she said after a long pause. 'Have you ever laid an egg?'

Lucy looked down at the tense little face. 'No,' she replied. 'No, not yet. Not the way you mean.'

Nor was Jock's red bicycle the only strand that bound together the isolated dwellings scattered up and down the glen. This day being Friday, it also brought Mr Sandars' van to the kitchen door. This, a battered green van of indeterminate vintage, a sort of reduced removals lorry, held two tiers of household goods, from cooking pots to stock cubes, and all brought to their very doors, for sale, once a week, by Mr Sandars, while his wife and daughter minded the dark little shop in Glenbuchat, with its seaside postcards, boiled sweets, and bargain bags of anthracite.

Sandy was up the steps of the van almost before Mr Sandars had had time to move back from the driving seat and take his place behind the home-made counter of pinewood trimmed with linoleum.

'Hello, Mr Sandars!' he cried. 'Can I have some chutney, please.'

Mr Sandars looked down at the child. A very tall man, with a high domed forehead, bright mischievous eyes, and a ready, conspiratorial smile, he radiated an air of kindly grandeur despite his long coat of faded beige alpaca. 'I thought your mother said you shouldn't have any more,' he said gently.

Sandy stared up at him. 'My mother's gone . . .' he said, and then his voice suddenly failed him.

Mr Sandars fulfilled many roles in the valley. He registered the marriages and then the births, even those births without preceding marriages. Also he supplied the necessities of daily subsistence, and functioned as an unpaid social worker, listening to the joys and woes of his customers, some of whom existed in very lonely circumstances indeed. As he steered his rickety van through the fords and over the cattlegrids of the fifty-odd farmsteads of his patch, he had come to accumulate a vast knowledge of the vicissitudes of human life. Was he not also the registrar of their deaths and, thanks to the old Nissen hut behind his shop, their undertaker as well?

And it occurred to him now, not for the first time, that the happiness of a household could often be calculated in inverse proportion to its disposable income. This was not an inflexible rule, yet how could he avoid contrasting Sandy's transparent misery, here in the midst of his father's beautiful estate, compared, say, with the guileless happiness of the Cheyne boys, fighting cheerfully over their only toy, the wreckage of their sister's old pram!

'Well then . . .' he beamed down at Sandy from his great height. 'If your mother's no here, I think I can find what you're after . . . !' and, with a flourish worthy of a great conjuror, he produced a bottle of ripe reddish chutney, emblazoned with a green and gold label, which, to Sandy, being gloriously redolent of carefree nursery days, held more charm and glamour than the most expensive box from Harrods. 'If only all heartaches could be solved as simply,' mused the St Bernard of the glens, as he watched the little boy run gleefully into the kitchen. Next he had to visit old Ruthie Farquhar up at her half-ruined farmhouse named Badachurn, and then her two deaf and dumb neighbours at Inchmore, less of a steading now than four bare stone walls supporting a rotting thatch of dead reeds bound with a flourishing yellow moss.

It wouldn't be long now, perhaps, before both the latter dwellings would fall terminally vacant, to be reclaimed by the jealous winds blowing down from the high stones of Ben Gierach. And before then, he himself would have delivered the three old bodies into the frosted burial ground behind Glenbuchat kirk. Anyone knowing his towering figure, with its undeniable air of patient majesty, and seeing him now searching his great key-ring to lock up the van before continuing on his solitary round, might be forgiven for seeing him less as St Bernard than as St Peter himself, kindly keeper of the great ascent.

Chapter Eight

That same day found Nick Boynton agreeably engaged in that most seductive of political pastimes, plotting the course of his own advancement.

'I expect you were surprised to get my note?' David Brotherton, erstwhile Home Secretary and now reverted to the role of a humble back-bencher in the Conservative interest, maintained a neat little Georgian house off Smith Square, within easy walking distance of the Palace of Westminster.

Nick, who prided himself on being able to cope with most situations, had indeed been startled to receive a cordial invitation to drop in for a drink before lunch with the old grandee. Nevertheless, he knew how vital the support of all sections of the party was for serious promotion, and if Brotherton could forget their row the other night, so could he. He made himself give a confident smile. 'Always pleased to hear views from on high.'

'Hmmm.' Brotherton leant back in his chair and stared hard at his guest. He had chosen carefully, after spending a day at his desk with the parliamentary list, and various other notebooks he had himself compiled in latter years. 'What I have to say must be treated as strictly confidential. Are you willing to abide by that?'

'Of course.'

'Some more sherry?'

'Please.'

Brotherton passed him the decanter, and watched Nick's eager movements in filling his glass. 'Why do you think I resigned one of the great offices of state?'

'Because you were being undermined by the Downing Street mafia.'

'A smokescreen, dear boy. When you reach my age,' he reached out to help himself to a cigar, 'you learn to put up with the pinpricks of little men like Toady. *No!*' He leant forward, assuming a grave and confidential air. 'I'm afraid I couldn't condone being a party to this infamous *No. 4* legislation!'

'*No. 4?*' Nick laughed out loud. 'If you know what it means, you're way out in front of the rest of us.'

'It's no laughing matter,' said Brotherton portentously. 'Oh, I know it's very cleverly worded, and I don't believe for a moment old Anstruther understood what he was letting loose on an unsuspecting world. But you and I,' he let the flattery hang in the air like a precious perfume, 'we're too spry to let the wool be pulled over our eyes. It's got to be stopped.'

'Because . . . ?'

'Here, a drop more?'

'Thank you.'

'Because it will lead ineluctably to nothing less serious than the total emasculation of parliamentary scrutiny. You have another look at it. I'm nearly seventy, and anything I say will be put down to personal pique. But a rising young chap like you . . . well, you could make all the difference if you chose. We don't have too many what I call "conviction politicians" left any more. Most of the ones I admired left the House after the Balkan row. All we're left with now are the *apparatchiks*, men like *Dutton*. We need more like you.'

Nick stared at him. 'I've been meaning to say how very sorry I was to have been so discourteous the other night.'

'My dear fellow,' Brotherton waved a languid hand, 'think nothing about it. I've always enjoyed your style of cut and thrust. It's why you'd be such a very valuable ally in blocking this.'

'It shouldn't be difficult, with such a slender majority.'

'Indeed not. But this is the key to what I want to ask you. There's quite a number of us, including some very senior figures indeed, who won't vote on the night, but we're all, for one reason or another, rather vulnerable to dear Walter Meyrick's kindly attentions. We need someone of indisputable integrity to stand out as a standard-bearer. We'll stay under the parapet until the last moment. That way they'll waste all their ammunition on you, and we can make them drop it.'

'I'd be honoured.'

'I must warn you, you'll come under a lot of pressure.'

'I think I can deal with that.'

'Your young friend Hepburn won't be pleased.'

'I can rely on James. He's my best friend.'

'They're sometimes the worst.' Brotherton nodded solemnly. 'You realize you'll be seen as a very high-flyer when this is done?' Nick smirked. 'No, I'm serious. We chose you because of your remarkable reputation. I don't think I'm letting any serious secrets out of the bag when I say you're already earmarked for promotion.' Had he gone too far? He paused to light his cigar. He mustn't overdo it. But if ever he'd seen a young Member positively thirsting for power and recognition, it was this one. More vanity than sense, too. Not a unique prescription, he had noted, over the years. And if he himself was now too old to be listened to, and Brotherton ruefully admitted that that probably was true, so be it. But not, as he had so recently discovered, too old to ache for revenge. There was a true conviction! It filled his mind, he could taste it through the acrid tang of the smoke in his throat. Toady must fall, and if that meant bringing in Labour, why, then the whole lot of them, his erstwhile colleagues, would become as idle as he now saw his future was likely to be. 'Read the damned thing,' he said, summoning up a companionable chuckle. 'Then make up your own mind. You'll see what I mean.'

Chapter Nine

'So you're Lucy.' James, back for his May surgery and for constituency consultations with his chairman, had walked over to the stables after a late breakfast and had come face to face with her in a doorway. She looked flustered and was brushing her damp hair out of her eyes.

'Yes,' she said, with an awkward smile. She had had plenty of opportunities to observe him during his previous visit, but supposed she herself had been rendered invisible to him by the magical veil imposed by household service.

'Have you been seeing to the pony?' She really was very red in the face.

She smiled again. 'No, I was just looking for Sandy.'

'I think I saw him up by the walled garden.'

'Thank you,' she said, making no move to let him through the door. After a pause she said, 'Could you come with me? There's something I want him to tell you.'

'Of course.' Together they walked out of the arch, past a bright red bicycle leaning against a post, and across the rough lawn that led up to the high brick wall that had once protected innumerable vegetables from the prevailing blast and now served only to hide the tangled undergrowth and gnarled fruit-trees.

Once through the rotting door, they found Sandy crouching over a dead hedgehog.

'Look!' he called out triumphantly. 'Real fleas!'

'Lucy says there's something you want to tell me.'

James smiled down proudly at his son. 'We'd better bury that poor fellow later.'

'It's not a fellow,' said Sandy. 'I can see its paps.'

'Sandy,' said Lucy. 'Tell your father about your dream.'

The little boy blushed. 'It's not important,' he said. 'Dad's here on business.'

'And to see you,' said James gently. The boy looked up at him with a clouded expression. 'Tell me about your dream.' Suddenly Sandy had flung himself sobbing into his father's arms. 'I dreamt that Mummy's never coming back,' he said between hiccups. 'I dreamt there was someone hateful in her place. With metal teeth.'

'She sent you lots of hugs,' said James desperately. 'I told you that last night.'

'But when's she coming back?' wailed Sandy, desperately clinging to James's legs. 'Why hasn't she written? She always writes.'

'She's been very busy,' he heard himself saying, and caught a flash of something satirical in Lucy's eyes. 'Anyway, I'm here, and you've got Lucy here and Mrs Granville.' Sandy gave a loud snort. 'And Jennie!'

'You're not wearing your bra,' said Sandy, suddenly turning an accusing eye towards Lucy. 'What have you done with it? You had it on at breakfast!' Poor Lucy flushed scarlet.

'Really, Sandy!' said his father, half-amused and half-angry. 'That's no way to be talking.' He couldn't help noticing that his son was undeniably right. 'Please apologize immediately.'

'Sorry, Lucy.' Sandy's head was bent very low.

'And look at her when you say it.'

He wrenched his head up, 'Sorry, Lucy.'

'That's quite all right.' She bent down and kissed him. 'If you come with me now, we'll see if we can find Jennie.'

'Has Jock gone?'

'Jock?' James was momentarily at a loss.

'The postman,' said Lucy over her shoulder, pushing Sandy before her.

'Oh yes, of course. Mrs Stewart's son. I wish I'd seen him.' But they were hurrying away.

The only constituent to approach his Westminster representative was a retired land-agent worried about his liabilities to a failed insurance company. Not even old Doddie had turned up on this occasion, so James, after waiting a further twenty minutes to salve his conscience, decided to walk down to the river. Behind the house, a bedraggled wood stood in for the once luxuriant Caledonian forest. Stunted pines and still-leafless birch trees punctuated the mounds of moss, and the damp corpses of rotten timber made his progress something of an obstacle course. By the middle of June, all this would be filling up with ferns and young foxgloves, but the last snows of May were still imminent and prudent Nature held herself in abeyance. The hurrying water was bright and clear, lit today with white flashes from the chilly sun, and the reeded banks were firm beneath his feet.

In the distance, he could see wisps of smoke drifting up from the hillside beyond the shale bank opposite, a moraine of compacted land where two glaciers had run together in their slow inexorable slide towards the sea. Crossing the river by the footbridge, a rickety construction of planks made grey by weather and lichen, he scrambled up an almost perpendicular path to the top of the moraine and was startled by a wild duck which flapped noisily across the surface of a little pond to his left, before climbing off into the sky and then wheeling back in a wide circle to see if the interloper intended to stay and deny it a peaceful return to its dreamy refuge. Smiling, he hurried through the spongy peat hags and across the heather to where he could see a stout man wielding a home-made flame-thrower, while two other gamekeepers were energetically beating out a fire which had spread further than intended higher up the slope.

'Good morning!' he shouted.

The stout man turned and waved a cheerful greeting before carefully extinguishing his strange contraption. Half an hour's chat with them, and James was off again, circling the hill and dropping down into a steep gully where two of the estate foresters were busy mending a deer fence, one of them the husband of the doughty Mrs Granville. It was nearly lunchtime and time to return to the house. 'Why did I ever leave?' was the thought that nagged him, but the answer was equally insistent: 'To earn a living.' This estate could no more pay its way than could the steel works in Berington. Both were part of the same legacy from the past. At least his museum was supported by his father's astute investment in supermarkets. There was no such easy option for the steel-workers, who had already received both their notice and their redundancy slips.

He took the higher sheep track across the heather back towards the house. In doing so, he had to skirt a small clump of stunted pines clinging to the side of the hill. A crow startled him, rising suddenly from among a patch of older heather. Something caught his eye, and he walked over to investigate.

'Damn!' He was looking down at a gin trap, its discoloured metal jaws, toothless as an old man's gums, clamped over a single limb. Part of it was already picked clean, but there was enough reddish hair still attached to identify it as the hind leg of a fox. How long had the poor creature lain there, struggling desperately in the metal's remorseless grip, before deciding to gnaw its way to freedom by amputating its own leg? He turned angrily back towards the men working on the opposite slope. These traps had been illegal for years, he had always argued with his father that they should not be used. But part of him knew that the keepers had a clearer sense than he of what the survival of their jobs entailed. It wasn't he who would be facing a jobless mountain winter without fuel if the shooting tenants decided the moor held more vermin than grouse. But why couldn't they at least visit the traps daily, to put their victims out of their misery? And all around him, the towering wasteland, in all its cruel immensity, rose up to mock such impractical idealism. This was the landscape of survival, and every creature, man, beast or bird, had to fight daily for its place to exist in so barren a wilderness.

His mind full of the fox's lonely vigil, James walked slowly on down the hillside.

'So that's the "Pride of Hepburnstoun"!'

He hadn't noticed Lucy coming to meet him. 'Yes,' he said. 'Planted in 1746. It'll start fruiting in August.' The magnificent rowan tree, chieftain of its race, stood forlornly in a little dell, sheltered by a thick belt of spruce trees, its trunk encircled within an iron paling lined with wire to protect it, as by a chastity belt, from the promiscuous advances of roedeer. 'They say there'll always be Hepburns at Hepburnstoun, as long as the "Pride" has its berries. Pretty absurd, really.'

'Jock forgot to give you this.' She handed him a crested envelope. 'He came back with it.'

'That was kind of him.' He slit it open. It held a single sheet of House of Commons paper, and read very simply: *'If your wife must screw around, at least tell her to be discreet about it.'* There was no signature.

Chapter Ten

'Minister! Can you tell us anything about the children?' The following Wednesday, Nick Boynton, newly-appointed Minister of State at the Home Office in the reshuffle following Brotherton's resignation, brushed past the reporters with practised ease.

'Later,' he said calmly. 'You all know the case is *sub judice* and that means I can't say anything at this time.'

'Is there blood on the carpet?'

'*Blood?*' laughed Nick. 'We've been wading knee-deep in the department's entrails! You'd have needed wellington boots in there.'

'Will the social worker be prosecuted?' A particularly nasty case of child abuse had cleared everything else from the morning's headlines.

'Come on, boys!' he said jovially, as he clambered into the maroon Ford Granada. 'I can't comment on that, now can I?' The car sped away from the curb, leaving the men with microphones still shouting their questions. Thirty-four and a minister! So all the hard work had not been in vain. Brotherton had been right. He was marked for power. He lay back in his seat, complacently watching his secretary's face relax as the traffic cleared, and their journey towards the motorway began to accelerate. She was a trim young woman with sharp features and watchful grey eyes. He yawned, having spent most of the previous night first trying to read the *No. 4* gobbledegook and then, having given that up, in catching up on the thick pile of official papers in his lacquered red box. Within a few minutes he was asleep.

James, by contrast, was spending the morning on his own affairs. When he had first moved to London, he had become friends with Houston Blake, a trainee solicitor, and when the latter had become a partner in Stirling, Gadsby and Chown, the mainstream Chancery experts, it had seemed only sensible to entrust his own affairs to them, including the various family trusts. Blake occupied an engagingly eccentric triangular space overlooking the Mansion House, and James leafed through the latest trust accounts, while the obligatory pot of office coffee was being poured.

'You're sure you won't have sugar?' Blake, a genial man with pale-blue eyes and slicked-down blond curls, was watching his client anxiously.

'No, thank you.' James shook his head. 'Too many late nights and too much booze! I'm cutting out sugar and cream.'

'Very sensible,' agreed his friend, reflecting that James was indeed showing signs of consolidation. 'You see that the fixed costs have doubled in three years?'

James gazed at the Hepburnstoun figures sadly. Yet there was no real problem. His income from his supermarket shares alone ran well into six figures, whereas Hepburnstoun in a bad year, and this was a bad year, only showed a loss of £67,560 after depreciation, although this ignored the long-running saga of the stables' roof.

'Can't you put the rents up?' Blake presumed that James's ambition was to run the estate at a profit. Why else would anyone own land? And yet . . .

'How can they pay more, when they're not making a profit themselves?'

'Perhaps', the lawyer narrowed his eyes, and sipped his coffee, 'they should consider a different occupation.

I mean,' he hurried on, seeing the flash of anger in his client's eyes, 'are you really doing them a favour, keeping them slaving away in all weathers, if they're not making money at the end of it? Amanda and I went to Skye last summer. A bleaker spot I've never seen. If you didn't provide the buildings and pay to keep the roof on, they'd be gone tomorrow.'

'A fat lot of rent I'd get then!'

'And a great deal of expense would be spared,' said Blake. 'Cigarette?'

'No.' James continued to stare at the figures. 'I just can't see where we can cut back.'

'Your children's trust accounts are far healthier.' Blake passed another set of papers over. 'It was very sensible to sell the Alma-Tadema when we did. Top of the market. Not only did we pay for cleaning the Raeburns, but we have paid off the tax bills and the overdraft and dealt with all the school fees at a very favourable rate.'

'I never liked it. All those bare bottoms.'

'Are you sure you want to saddle them with an estate that looks like losing more and more money every year?' This was the recurring theme of each of their meetings.

James leant back in his chair, and stared out at the people hurrying up the steps of the Royal Exchange. To the left rose the great wall of the Bank of England, to the right towered the delicate pediment of the Mansion House, all so redolent of the opulent splendour of Britain's imperial past. There had been bad times before, the Jacobite days, the Gordon riots, the Great Agricultural Depression which had lasted for nearly sixty years until Hitler's war, two years indeed when his grandfather had had to commute the rents altogether. In any failed endeavour, someone, at some time, has to call a halt. He just didn't want it to be him. If Sandy were one day to sell Hepburnstoun, all well and good. But he, James, wished to avoid the odium of being the generation that gave up. 'No,' he said, 'or rather, yes. I do want to pass it on to them, indeed I have passed it on to them.'

'Oh yes,' said the lawyer. 'You've passed the ultimate ownership on, but as life tenant of the whole, it's you who pays the bills. Without you, the trustees would have to sell up forthwith. Indeed, as one of them, I can tell you we view the future of the place with considerable unease. My questions to you are these: is it wise and is it genuinely worthwhile?'

'If you mean, would we rather have a centrally heated *bijou* residence on Jersey and four million in the bank, the answer is no! These things are cyclical. All we need is a small shift in the German market for venison and some decent weather for the hay. It's a paradise for the children. And it's home.'

'And a very expensive one! But you don't need to defend it to me,' laughed Blake, playing with his blotter. 'I'm not your accountant. Or your bank manager. I understand. All too well, as it happens. We're moving. The partnership, I mean. This old heap's coming down and we've got a purpose-built block going up in Tower Hamlets. At half the rent.' He leant back and laughed again. 'Actually it's a relief. One's got to move with the times. Shows we're not taking your money under false pretences.'

James drove back to the Commons and had just found a space in the underground car park when Nick's car pulled in beside him.

'Good morning, Minister of State!' called out James, grinning. 'You can't wobble on the *No. 4* Bill now, eh?'

'You mustn't park there, sir.' One of the guards had hurried over. 'That's the Chancellor's space.'

'I'm so sorry,' said James, turning back apologetically. 'I'll move it now.'

'No, no, Fanshawe,' interrupted Nick, handing his aide a great pile of grey folders. 'This is my friend Mr Hepburn. You give the dear Chancellor my compliments, and say he'll move it tomorrow! You can blame me.'

The guard laughed obligingly and turned away, raising his eyes in despair. Another five years and he could retire to real life in Epsom, away from all these overblown Parliamentarians with their Gilbert-and-Sullivan dialogue. For the tenth time that day, he checked his revolver, whistling an Italian tune he'd picked up on the radio. The office notice board had told him it was a red alert day, and he wasn't having his retirement ruined, not by some terrorist, and not by any plonking Lord Mucks either! He waved two more cars into their spaces, submitting to the condescending badinage from their self-conscious drivers. Chandelier socialists! They were the worst.

Fixing his face into the simpering smile he knew they liked, he bandied chummy jokes through clenched teeth. 'Ha, ha! Very good indeed, sir. Very droll.' Turning away, he permitted himself a wide vomiting grimace, drawing back his lips and rolling his eyes, before sauntering over to the radio desk for his hourly check.

'Members' car park,' he muttered into the transmitter. 'All clear.'

'Has the Prime Minister arrived?' The stilted voice of the Serjeant-at-Arms grated in his ear. Why was he up and about so early? They were all on tenterhooks with this new skinhead brought in over their heads.

'No, sir.'

'He's expected at any minute. Hang on! I can see them on the video screens. They're just coming up Birdcage Walk. On your marks!'

'Right!' He hurried back to the main gateway at the foot of the ramp just in time to see the first of the two police motorcyclists pulling up at the top of the slope. He stood smartly to attention and snapped off a regulation salute as the black Daimler sped into his lair. The Prime Minister gave no sign of noticing. He had just refused to tell his wife about the Birthday Honours. His face was dark with gloom and indigestion.

'Poor old sod!' thought Fanshawe, watching the round little man bustling towards the lift. 'Who ever would want that job?' And he walked back towards the office where a cup of tea would surely be awaiting him. He started to whistle again.

Chapter Eleven

'You know my husband, James?'

'Of course I do.' It was now Thursday the twenty-sixth of May, and Fred Tevis was all smiles, his eyes positively twinkling with assiduous benevolence. 'How are you, James?'

'Very well indeed.' James took the proffered hand, enduring its confident squeeze. Who knew where it had last been? Susie, always decorative at parties, seemed to have an extra glow that night. Her pretty face shone with animation, and there was something softer in her eyes that made her the focus of many admiring eyes.

'Good to have you both together.' Thursday night was traditionally a night off at the Commons, and the Meyricks were giving a large buffet evening in honour of a visiting senator from Washington. His host took James by the arm as he spoke and steered him away to a corner. 'And how are things at home?'

'At home?' James was momentarily thrown by the question.

'Glenbuchat. You've been up there recently, surely.'

'Oh yes, indeed.'

'I have a crucial question for you.' James held a steady expression, while inwardly panicking about how to deal with an enquiry about Susie. 'We're thinking of a small informal committee to take a look at security of information within the Palace of Westminster. Could you handle that?'

'If you'd like me to.'

'Excellent, because I want you to chair it.'

'My darling boy!' Meyrick's wife came bustling up to claim a kiss from James. 'Susie is the belle of the ball. You should never have locked her up in the wilds of Scotland like Bluebeard. She could be quite an asset to you on the political circuit. She's got the senator eating out of her hand!'

So long as that's all, thought James sourly, as he was led over to meet another guest, who was already talking to the ubiquitous Fred.

'Here's my good friend James!' the latter announced loudly. 'Come and tell us about your new job. James is a Whipper-in!'

'Really?' breathed his companion, a short over-painted blonde who travelled as the senator's aide. 'You look kind of young for that sort of thing.'

James smiled. 'I'd much rather hear how the senator got on in Brussels,' he said. 'We're very anxious about the trade agreements.'

'You politicians!' Fred exuded bonhomie. 'No time for small talk. I'm trying to persuade Susie to bring you up to Tring this weekend. I'm giving a proper English weekend party.'

'That sounds very nice,' said James politely. 'She hasn't mentioned it.'

'I'm sure she will,' grinned the other. 'Knowing Susie.' He laughed, quite loudly.

'No doubt.' James bowed stiffly and stalked over to where Nick was giggling at something Dutton had just said. Both fell silent and straightened their faces as they saw him.

'Walter tells me you've got another new job on the boil,' Nick said casually. James nodded unhappily. There was little joy to be gained from knowing himself to be the object of even his friend's derision.

'Going from strength to strength,' added Nick kindly, immediately sensing his friend's vulnerability. He took James's arm, and steered him over to a neutral corner, well-hidden from both Fred and Susie. 'Look,' he said, 'My mother's still got that house on the Loire. Why don't you just both disappear there for a few weeks, get away from all this? It'd be good for the two of you to have some time to yourselves. I know my new boss could get Toady to swing it with Walter, he owes us a favour or two. I mean it.' He was staring into James's eyes. 'I can see you're on edge.'

'Really?' James rather prided himself on maintaining an inscrutable façade, the prerequisite of privacy.

'Yes! Take her away for a bit. Recharge the batteries.'

'Well, you're wrong. But thank you,' he said, trying to smile warmly. 'Anyway,' he added, 'I couldn't bear to be away now that I've got a real job to do at last.'

'I gather we've been invited to Tring, wherever that may be,' James said as they drove slowly back through Mayfair.

'Mmm.' Susie was almost dozing, hunched against the door of the car.

'I'd hoped we might go home and see the children.'

'That would be nice too,' she said sleepily.

'Sandy misses you.' She gave no reply. 'I told you about his nightmare.'

'Mmm. Let's go the next weekend. I'd really like to go to Tring. It'll be fun.'

'What's the draw?' He was trying to sound noncommittal.

'Fred has taken over some stately home for the weekend. There's going to be dancing, and fireworks. He says he's even laid on clay-pigeon shooting specially for you.'

'How kind!' It was impossible to suppress the sarcasm, but again she ignored it.

'I really think you might put yourself out for me, just for once,' she muttered. 'It sounds wonderful.'

After that, they completed their journey in silence.

But going up in the lift, he said, 'You don't really want to go to bloody Tring, do you?'

She shrugged. 'Since when have my wishes been of any importance?'

'You've always hated country house jamborees. That's why we never see Tim or the Gaspards any more. You always say we never know anybody there.'

'He says he's asked the Dorsets.'

'*God!*'

Just as the lift halted at their floor, she turned and stared at him. It was a look so bleak, so chilling, that he suddenly felt sorry for her. 'All right,' he said. 'I'd like to take you if you think you'll enjoy it. We'll go.' But she was already hurrying away from him, down the darkened corridor, already just a blur.

But after a week that had been divided between coaxing unenthusiastic MPs into supporting a new schools curriculum and sitting in on a bored committee exploring the intricacies of animal rights, and with the prospect of a weekend with Fred Tevis as his host, it was almost a relief to James to get his constituency chairman's anxious call on the Friday morning, begging him to come north to address the management committee on the reasons for Brotherton's resignation. Susie had seemed scarcely to hear his excuses and had left for Tring that morning, smiling insouciantly and deftly ignoring his attempt to kiss her goodbye.

'They'll all be so sad to miss you, darling,' she had said as she left. 'But of course they'll understand.'

'What about the special clay-pigeon shooting?'

'Oh, I'm sure Fred will think of something. He's very resourceful.'

'I've never doubted it.' Still fuming, he watched her little sports car swing excitedly out of the underground garage and accelerate into the path of a taxi, Susie greeting the outraged hooting with a cheery wave. It wasn't, he thought, that he didn't care that the comfortable certainties of his marriage were being unravelled; it was really that he had never, in dealing with Susie, felt that he had any control or even influence over her caprices. At the beginning, he had persuaded himself that this was good, evidencing a lack of chauvinism and showing respect for her independence. It was only later, when a deadly indifference had quietly settled in, that he reflected that a little healthy bargaining might have established a firmer base for true mutual respect between adults. But it was precisely because he had seen her as a wilful child, and so humoured her, that he now felt so much less than might a man who placed a higher value on his partner's character. As for true respect, he realized that he felt none for her, now or ever. Moreover, he had come to believe that, in marrying a woman whom he had desired but did not esteem, it was he who had behaved the worse.

Now, five hours later, having collected a hire-car from the airport compound, he set off on the long haul over the Forth bridge and up past Perth into the hills. Already the summer grass was beginning to soften the harsh winter contours, and round the low white homesteads newly-born lambs greeted the evening with their plaintive cries. There was no wind, just the biting freshness of mountain air. London, and the sultry committee room, seemed just a fading nightmare.

By the time he reached Mrs Granville's grey cottage on the bend by the Hepburnstoun gates, he had forgotten everything except the joy of seeing his children. How absurd to think of uprooting them from this paradise. But as he rounded the last corner of the drive, the house seemed strangely deserted, the windows blank and unwelcoming. The front door was locked, an unknown phenomenon. Angrily, he tugged at the bell-handle, and heard the bell pealing eerily in the corridors beyond the hall. He had left his spare keys in London. Nothing happened. He tugged again.

Again there was no response. Surely they knew he was coming? Suddenly, unaccountably, he was terribly afraid. Were they ill? Kidnapped? Dead? His eyes misted with tears, he ran round to the back, cursing himself for neglecting his children, for leaving them unprotected from adult cruelties. The shuttered door resisted his frantic knocking.

A menacing silence enveloped the dank buildings and the dull lifeless hills around. He ran up to the stables and found the pony's stall empty, the door ajar. He ran back to the kitchen door. In thirty-three years, he had never known the house to be barred against intruders, least of all against himself. He was just preparing to break into the pantry window when the sound of laughter and a horse's hooves echoed across the river. And there, on the opposite bank, below the moraine's shingle banks, he could just make out four figures in the yellow cart, which was making slow progress down to the ford, with Muggy, the bedraggled pony, evidently making heavy work of its cheerful load.

As they splashed through the water, he could now see Jock the postman urging the pony on, with Sandy beside him, while Lucy held little Jennie on her lap behind.

'Where on earth have you all been?' He did his best to hide the anger he knew to be unreasonable. 'I was worried about you.'

'Muggy took us up to the loch!' shouted Sandy, his face shining with excitement. 'We saw the herons and their nest. It's very high!'

'In an old pine!' chimed in Jennie. 'The mother heron's sitting on her egg!'

'I hope you don't mind.' Lucy had slipped off the cart and hurried up to him. 'I should have checked with Mrs Granville, but I was afraid she'd say no.' Jock was silently unharnessing the pony, his face impassive.

'It must have been great fun,' said James with a smile. 'I wish I'd been with you myself.'

'We had a picnic,' said Jennie. 'Egg and bacon baps!'

'And treacle flapjacks!' shouted Sandy. 'Lucy kept one for you, but Jennie ate it on the way back.'

'Sneak!' The two children fell on each other with shrieks of rage turning to squeals of laughter.

'Come on,' said Lucy, 'or there'll be no more picnics. Up to the bathroom, double-quick.' They scampered off.

'Let me help you put that away.' James walked up to where the young postman was struggling to push the cart backwards into its shed in the out-buildings. 'Thank you for giving them such a nice time.'

The young man smiled shyly. 'It was my pleasure,' he said. 'Does them good to get up into the mountains.' Together they packed away the harness and then James led the pony back to its box, while Jock fetched it some fresh straw, and a couple of handfuls of hay. 'Poor old Muggy!' he said. 'She hasn't worked so hard for months.'

'Any signs of grouse?'

'Not that we saw. There are teal nesting on the loch, and Lucy thought she saw an otter by the weir.'

'She's wonderful with the children,' said James enthusiastically. 'And a very good cook.'

Whatever thoughts Jock may have had on this he kept to himself. 'I must get off home,' he said after a pause. 'I'll be late for my supper.'

'Is your mother keeping well?' asked James. 'I haven't seen her for ages.'

'Pretty fair,' was the wry response. 'As fierce as ever!' They both laughed. Jock's mother was a great Liberal, but that never stopped her inviting James in for tea whenever his canvassing took him up the little valley where her husband's croft fought a losing battle against the English landlord's encroaching forestry.

* * *

Climbing the stairs, James could hear the unmistakable sounds of a water fight in progress. Tactfully, he turned away into the upstairs nursery, a light airy room warmed now by an aromatic fire of spitting pine logs. The room had square barred windows with a good view of the mountains beyond the river. They rose stark and blue-hazed above the dun-coloured contours of the lower hills, and their jagged stone peaks were still white with snow. Some years it never left them. Lucy ran in, panting with laughter, and with a shock, he suddenly realized how beautiful she was. Her bare arms were a mass of soapy foam, and her tangled hair was frankly a mess. And yet! Her dark eyes sparkled with high spirits, and her sopping clothes revealed a figure of such ample allure that he had to make a conscious effort not to stare.

'Do you need any help?' he heard himself saying.

'No, they're fine.' Her mouth was wide, with full lips that now curved up into a delighted smile. 'They're so happy you're here. They're like different people.'

'They looked pretty happy coming down in the cart.'

'Yes,' she wiped her face on a towel. 'They did enjoy that. It was good of Jock to drive us.'

'He's a nice man.' He watched for her response, acutely conscious now of her closeness.

'Yes,' she said vaguely. 'Have you seen the Savlon? Jennie's got a raw patch on her arm. I think she grazed it on a boulder. Here it is.' She turned away, presenting a back view as enticing as the front. James smiled ruefully to himself and went to find a book. It seemed years since he had read to the children.

'*Peter Rabbit* all right?' he asked when two clean warm bodies had hurled themselves onto the sofa beside him.

'*Peter Rabbit*!' cried Sandy in disgust. 'I am nearly eight, you know.'

'What about *The Jungle Book*?'

'Try this,' said Lucy helpfully, passing him a slim book with the cartoon of a tall crocodile on the cover. 'This will keep them quiet. Mrs Granville will be back by now. She's been having her day off in Newtown Strathurquhart.'

Later, sitting alone in the dining-room, and eating the thick rich stew that Lucy had left for him on the hotplate, he reflected that she was already performing every function of a wife except the one that, to his dismay, he found he would most appreciate. For he had come to recognize in her something he had not experienced from his wife, an innate generosity of spirit, and a liveliness which made her, as a woman, painfully attractive to him as a man. The sooner she married Jock, the better, he decided, and poured himself another deep measure of whisky.

Chapter Twelve

'Let's go through the arithmetic again,' Walter Meyrick said in his most business-like voice. He had gathered his Whips around his table on the last Tuesday in May for their regular end of month assessment of the Government's progress. 'We have 335 Conservatives against 136 Labour, 134 Liberal Democrats, 43 British Nationalists, and the usual 15 odd-bods from Ulster and the like. We can assume they'll all combine as usual against the *Miscellaneous No. 4* third reading on the eleventh July, not that they know the first thing about it.'

'Any more than we do,' put in his deputy helpfully.

Meyrick glowered at him. 'So that gives us a base majority of seven.'

'If everyone falls into line.'

'Quite.' Meyrick took out his pipe. 'First, I'd like your individual reports.'

On becoming a Whip, James had been absurdly proud to be allocated his bloc of MPs. His responsibilities included vetting their voting intentions, and helping them to arrange pairs with Members of other parties to give opportunities for days off while maintaining the Government's majority. He also had to file regular reports on their success or failure in debates, their attendance record and, crucially, their particular problems and aspirations; the key, in fact, to their capacity to be *persuaded* should their intentions ever vary from those of the Chief Whip. This work he did carefully, though not without a certain misgiving about the manipulative nature of the job.

He was not, however, so naïve as to expect more than three hundred individuals, each one a highly ambitious and self-opinionated Conservative Member, humbly to follow their leaders' instructions without a certain amount of unambiguous arm-twisting. After all, each had their own constituency officers, party workers and plain old voters to placate, irrespective of Walter Meyrick and his minions.

One by one, the Whips gave thumbnail sketches of 'their' Members' intentions. When it came to James's turn, he said:

'Of my bunch, thirty-one present no problem including Gerry Paine who seems to have turned over a new leaf.' He caught Meyrick's mocking wink but did not respond to it. 'But John Pope and Nick Boynton are very uneasy because they say they don't understand what this measure actually means, and I'm afraid Sir Cuthbert Moore-Talbot is seriously ill again.'

'Could he die on us?' Meyrick frowned.

James nodded. 'I spoke to Lady Maud Moore-Talbot this morning. His specialist wants to move him into the Wellington, but Sir Cuthbert is refusing to be shifted.'

'What's the majority?'

'Over sixteen thousand.' If James had expected signs of relief, there were none. A general groan filled the room.

'Highly marginal!' grumbled Meyrick. 'Given Toady's current ratings.'

'He turned up for the steel vote,' said someone. 'I saw him on his stretcher afterwards.'

'Oh, yes,' sneered Meyrick. 'He's an example for us all. Never missed a vote, rarely made a speech, collected his knighthood . . . Let's hope he doesn't ruin it now by dropping dead just when we need him most.' James stared at him in angry surprise. Sir Cuthbert had been so courteous, and made himself so pleasant to James, that it seemed an outrage to hear his life dismissed so casually. Increasingly, he found himself disliking his Chief's casual malice.

By the time they had all made their reports, it had emerged that eighteen Members had admitted to growing reservations about supporting the *No. 4* measure, more than enough to ensure its failure.

'Why can't Dutton explain it to them?'

'Good *God*!' shouted the exasperated Meyrick. 'Hasn't he tried? We've had three meetings of the 1922 Committee. Every back-bencher in the land has questioned him about the bloody thing.'

'Do you understand it?' asked James quietly.

Meyrick turned a chilly eye towards his new recruit. 'Whips aren't paid to understand,' he said. 'Our job is to get the legislation through. As members of the administration, we may be assumed to support the Government's policy, whatever it is. If we don't, we shouldn't be holding office under it, should we?' There was a chorus of submissive assent. 'So?'

'Can we offer them a deal?' The Deputy Chief Whip, for all his grim appearance, was a man ever eager for peace.

'What sort of deal?'

'I think a bit of back-pedalling on milk quotas would please the Shire members, and . . .'

'No!' said Meyrick firmly. 'Anything but milk quotas. Toady is totally committed on that.'

'He was totally committed on pensions,' said someone, 'and look what happened to them!'

Even Meyrick laughed. 'Nevertheless,' he said, 'I do think he has dug himself in too deep over milk. What else?'

'An eighteen-man deputation to Barbados next winter,' suggested James, thawing. 'To study the voting patterns?'

Meyrick raised his eyebrows. 'Very good,' he said. 'I can see you're learning the ropes.' James shrugged.

He cared as little for compliments this morning as for brickbats. Why *should* their colleagues be dragooned into voting for a measure apparently so complex that it could not be explained? How could he defend that to Doddie Gordon and Jock the postman, or Mr Sandars, or Ruthie Farquhar up among her lonely foxgloves at Badachurn? His voters trusted him to do his best. They patiently tolerated the party squabbling as did most voters, from Truro to Lerwick. Not one in a hundred took any real ideological interest in that side of things. What James believed they did care about were the big issues, and, being pragmatic like all people living on the threshold of deprivation, they also cared how those issues affected their pocket. And why not? A healthy income did not prevent him from appreciating the insecurities of those without one.

Another hour of discussion, and the meeting broke up with little decided beyond an instruction to the relevant Whips to try to isolate and then win over their minority of dissenters. After all, there remained only six weeks before the crucial vote on the eleventh of July.

James meanwhile decided to take the rest of the morning off and drive to Bedfordshire to visit Sir Cuthbert. The old man's wife had repeatedly begged him to call in, and now seemed a good opportunity.

Groby, his destination, was well signposted off the A6, and Groby Place, a melancholy jumble of grey stone towers and pinnacles stood in a clearing beyond the church, in the shade of massed if bedraggled pine trees. It had clearly been raining there, although his drive out of London had been almost sunny. There were brown puddles in front of the porch, and large droplets ran down the back of his neck as he waited for some response after he had yanked at the rusted metal bell-pull.

'Yes, sir?' A very old man wearing a long white apron over immaculate black trousers stared blearily out at him.

'I'm James Hepburn,' he said. 'Lady Maud's expecting me.'

'Come in, sir.' The old servant's teeth were intermittent and yellow. 'She's on the lav.' He led James into a small sitting-room hung with political cartoons, all identically framed in gilded wood. 'Supermac' by Vicky, 'Churchill' by Low, and even 'Colonel Blimp' illustrated the length of Sir Cuthbert's service to his country. A major in the Scots Guards, he had been returned to Parliament for Bedfordshire (Woburn) in 1945 against the national swing. Crises, scandals, devaluations, referenda, come what might, Sir Cuthbert could be found on the fourth bench up, second seat from the corner, representing Bedfordshire (Woburn) with a silent but unwavering little smile. His heavy moustache had slowly turned from gold through grey to a snowy white. His eyebrows had sprouted strange wild projections, and the lines on his face had deepened into veritable canyons of jovial ruddy flesh. Old hands swore he had once spoken, very late at night, on a Bill about badgers, acting almost it had seemed as one of those quiet furry creatures himself, snuffling gently with some half-heard joke about 'being badgered'. Someone had laughed, perhaps out of sheer nerves, and Sir Cuthbert, secure in his reputation as a humorist, had rested on his laurels ever since. Not even the recent threat of burying nuclear waste on the very outskirts of Groby had elicited anything more than a knowing smile. 'But knowing what? That's the question!' Nick had grumbled in frustration, since he had led the campaign to have the waste dumped in a safe Labour stronghold instead. And yet here, in this room where the desk was overflowing with pictures of Sir Cuthbert bowing low over the Queen's hand,

Sir Cuthbert opening the new fen sluice, it was obvious the man took pride in his duty, meticulously if silently accomplished.

'I'm so sorry to keep you waiting.' Lady Maud Moore-Talbot was tiny. She had very little hair, all scraped up into a spidery web-like bun, but her eyes were blue and sharp. 'He's so pleased you've come. Shall we go straight up?'

The staircase smelt of dry rot and had tall heraldic beasts carved out of the bannister newels at every turn. The shields clutched by their wooden claws were innocent of heraldry, suggesting instead some sudden hiatus in the family's armorial or financial circumstances. On the walls, tall portraits of grim men with beards stared down with hauteur mixed with malice. What a house! thought James uncomfortably, without recognizing in his own reaction the likely echo of Susie faced with Hepburnstoun.

'Here we are,' she said, hobbling up a final step and opening one of a pair of massive double doors. 'Wake up, darling one! Look who's come to see you.'

Sir Cuthbert lay dwarfed in a truly imperial four-poster, the sheets muddied and disordered by five or six little spaniels who leapt up at the intrusion and ran barking shrilly towards their mistress.

'Down, Togo! Down Boofuls!' shouted Lady Maud from the door. 'Don't bite the nice gentleman!' This to the largest of the pack who had nipped James's ankle and was now busily worrying his trousers. 'Poor you, she doesn't mean it, you know.'

That's no consolation, thought James, while smilingly disclaiming any pain.

'My dear boy!' Sir Cuthbert was gesticulating with one hand. 'This is so very good of you.'

'Come and sit here,' said his wife, pulling up a little chair. 'He mustn't speak for long, you know,' she whispered. 'It's his chest.'

'Nonsense!' said the invalid in a loud voice, and was immediately shaken by a curious dry coughing fit. A lurid scarlet invaded his cheeks, and sweat ran through his eyebrows and trickled down his nose. 'I shall be there for the vote on steel tomorrow.'

'It was last week,' said James. 'We were very grateful for your support.' The dogs were all assembled on the bed again.

'I only let him go for your sake,' said Lady Maud with a sniff. 'He adored your father. Did you know they were at Monte Cassino together? That's where Cuthbert got his MC.'

'I know.' James smiled down at the invalid. 'My father said he was the best-organized officer in the battalion.'

The old man winked up at him. 'Now, you run along, my dear,' he said, his voice now slow and weak. 'I must talk to Hepburn here without interruption.'

A lifetime of inbred obedience sent his wife hobbling back across the parquet floor, calling the dogs after her. 'Walkies!' she cried. 'Come on, sweethearts!' They flew off the bed, and scampered after her, filling the room with shrill whining and barking.

'Bloody tarts!' muttered Sir Cuthbert. 'Not an ounce of fidelity amongst them when there's a better offer.' He reached out for a glass of colourless medicine. James handed it to him, and he took a sip. 'Filthy muck!' he said, his mouth twisted in disgust. 'What I do to please the quacks! Come and sit down, my boy. I have two things I particularly want to say to you.' James perched himself, not without some anxiety, on the spindly little chair. 'Contrary to what you may think, I do expect to be back for the next vote, and I shall, as always, vote with my party.'

'I think you have the best record in the House for that.'

Sir Cuthbert smiled. 'Never mind that,' he said.

'Obey your commanding officer, not a bad rule in life. Much ridiculed nowadays, of course. But then the ones who do the ridiculing don't seem so outstandingly successful, do they?' He grinned up wolfishly. 'I don't mean to be malicious,' he said, his eyes suddenly alive with something remarkably close to malice, 'but in old age, there is something peculiarly satisfactory in observing the groaners and grumblers ending their days with no more to show for it than faces etched with discontent!' His own face was a picture of impish delight.

'But,' he raised a single wavering finger. 'As your father's son, I want you to be aware of something in case I don't get a chance to speak in the debate.' Sir Cuthbert to speak in a debate! James must have betrayed his surprise because the old man fairly shook with laughter. 'Oh, I know my reputation,' he wheezed. 'Cuthbert the Silent!' His face had turned scarlet again, the skin blotched with blood fighting its way through the old arteries just beneath the faded surface. 'But what I say is: what's the point of churning out platitudes and stating the obvious, just to get one's name into *Hansard*? My constituents send me to Westminster to represent them in the Tory interest. There's been no-one in trouble, Left or Right, who's ever had owt to complain of down here, and plenty of ministers who know I talk loud enough behind the scenes. I spoke up for Anthony and Jakie over Suez, you know, and several times for Enoch, not that it did any good in the end. In my day, the scandals were for whispering in Whites', not for shouting out from the treetops. I mean, of course we knew about Mountbatten, and the Duke . . . and everybody knew old Lady Dorothy was being up-ended by Bob Boothby, and good luck to them, I used to say. It never affected the way you voted, because it wasn't relevant unless it did get into the papers, like poor old Jack. One can only keep the dream alive,' he sighed, 'if one hides the facts . . . even from oneself.'

He lay back and wiped his forehead. 'In fact . . . particularly from oneself. The dream! How silly that all seems now, everything that once seemed the bedrock on which we depended, rested . . . "th'immortal rock", that hymn.' He sighed. 'But what I wanted to say to you is this . . . this . . . *No. 4* business is very bad.'

'Very bad?'

'I'm afraid so. Old Anstruther didn't like it, he told me so in Whites' the night before he died. It's the civil servants who want it. Fancy putting a mealy-mouthed idiot like Dutton in charge.'

'But what precisely does it enact?' said James.

'Ha, ha! Your father would be proud of you. A Government Whip who doesn't understand his own legislation! Quite right too! It's my belief no-one understands it. But Anstruther did, and he was against it. He told me,' the old voice sank almost to a whisper, 'it was the beginning of the end!'

'This one little Bill?' James was astounded at the old politician's suddenly serious tone.

'This one little Bill. He was going to stop it, you know. I always wondered . . .' A violent paroxysm shook him.

'That's enough!' Lady Maud had hobbled back into the room. 'No more talking! Come on, James. Time to go!' Faced with such diminutive determination, he had no choice but to rise. 'Out! Out! Out!' She was smiling but firm.

'Wait, please.' The voice from the bed was very faint. 'I'll be there for you. You know that.'

Part Two

June

Chapter Thirteen

The inaugural meeting of James's new committee on government confidentiality was held on Thursday the second of June, on the third floor of the Home Office's tower block in Queen Anne's Gate. It was a very select group: himself, John Pope (chosen to placate his doubts on the *No. 4* Bill by signs of approaching promotion) and Gerry Paine, with a Mrs Robson from the Home Office, Miss Whisby-Royland from Special Branch, and, as a last minute sop to the Opposition, Iain Mackenzie, the Scottish Labour member.

'Shall I act as minute-taker?' Mrs Robson was a comfortable-looking woman, with fine grey hair and a rather parched complexion.

'Thank you, Mrs Robson.' James was practising not looking at their name badges. He felt he should be able to remember this many without too many mishaps. There was a scuffling sound from the door, which vibrated and then bulged alarmingly.

'That'll be Commander Trent,' said Miss Whisby-Royland, jumping up to open the door. The thickset policeman, holding a cup of steaming tea with one hand while balancing his papers in the other, stumbled to a vacant chair. 'Commander Trent is just observing,' said Mrs Robson after a short silence.

'Good,' said James. 'Now, you've all got agendas?' He cocked one eye at the faces round the table. 'Item one, apologies.'

'Point of order, Mr Chairman!' It was Mackenzie, of course.

'We haven't reached any substantive item, Iain,' said

James with a friendly smile. 'We just want to hear if there are any apologies for absence.'

'Point of order!' snapped Mackenzie belligerently.

'Look,' said James. 'We're all here. There *aren't* going to be any apologies. Do you think we might just get as far as item two before we start wrangling?'

Mackenzie stood up. 'I have a point of order, Mr Chairman, and I demand to be heard.' He reached inside his jacket and pulled out a small green booklet. 'Treadgold's *Rules of Procedure*. And it's the new edition.' Commander Trent made a growling noise in the back of his throat.

'Oh, very well,' said James with a sigh. 'Let's hear your point of order.'

'Excuse me.' It was Mrs Robson, who had gone rather pink in the face. 'This meeting is not covered under Treadgold. This is an ad hoc committee set up by the Cabinet Secretary under an executive order in council. There are no strict rules of procedure, other than those the committee may, in their absolute discretion, choose to adopt for the purposes of their own deliberations. Any such rules would not of course be taken as creating any precedent for any similar committee.'

'You mean, we can set our own rules?' asked Pope with a smirk. 'I move we exclude points of order.'

'I second,' muttered Paine, who was quite angry enough already that he was wasting time on a committee of nonentities.

'And I,' said Mackenzie, 'move an amendment, proposing that we adopt standard House of Commons committee rules.'

There was a long silence. 'I'm sorry,' said James, keeping a very straight face. 'It seems you don't have a seconder.'

'And who says I need one,' demanded Mackenzie triumphantly, 'since we can set our own rules, so we're told?'

'Would you mind if I opened the window?' said Paine. 'It's very stuffy in here.'

'Do,' said James, glad of the respite.

'I'm afraid,' said Mrs Robson gently, 'that these windows are sealed. Security prevention. I'm sure you understand.'

'Do you mean to say,' asked Paine in outrage, 'that we've got to stifle to death on a boiling June day without any fresh air?'

'I can turn on the fan. Mr Chairman?'

'Please.'

She crossed to the door and pressed a switch whereupon the fan above their heads began to revolve with such speed that it swept James's agenda in a whirling arc across the room. Commander Trent, showing his first sign of life, leapt out of his chair, chased it across the room and snatched it up from the floor. He brought it back to James.

'Thank you, Commander.' The big policeman grunted. 'Now. Iain. Couldn't we just hear the apologies, or rather the absence of them, and move on to the agenda proper where you can raise all the points you want?'

'Thank you, Chairman,' said Mackenzie. 'I've proposed an amendment to Mr Pilkington's motion. I'm rather hoping you're going to put that to the vote, and . . .'

'And?' snapped James, conscious of everyone's eyes upon him.

'And that I'll be allowed the chance to speak in its favour.' Two hours later, they broke up without having made any progress at all.

Chapter Fourteen

'Our panel tonight includes two politicians from the unseasonably frozen North.' The television chairman paused to acknowledge sycophantic laughter from the regular Thursday night studio audience, mugging at them with a flash from his large moon spectacles. 'James Hepburn is standing in at the last minute for Ralph Dutton who has flu. Mr Hepburn is a junior Government Whip representing the rural constituency Glenbuchat in Duffshire, and Iain Mackenzie comes from that centre of Scots industry and bastion of Labour Party support, Newtown Strathurquhart just across the river. Aileen Hope is Deputy-Chair of the Liberal Democrat Women's Section,' the earnest young woman with dyed red hair smiled modestly, 'and Brigadier General Rupert Timpson is the prospective British National candidate for Southend.' The general, a tubby man with slightly protruding eyes, nodded vigorously. 'My name is John Hardy, that's your panel. May I have the first question?'

The chairman sat back in his seat, unable to resist an anxious finger straying to check that his new wig was still in place. The last one had come perilously adrift during the preceding week's broadcast, prompting anguished and conflicting advice through his concealed headphone.

'Good evening, John.' The camera had turned by preordained arrangement on to a grizzled man in the second row.

'Good evening to you. Your name, please.'

'Gregory Wiggetts.'

'And your question, please.'

The grizzled man consulted a card. 'Can the panel advise us why the Government attaches such importance to the *Miscellaneous Provisions No. 4* Bill currently approaching its third reading?'

Hardy stared at him. 'That's not the question I was expecting,' he said. 'You're down to ask about council houses.'

'Nevertheless,' pursued his dogged guest. 'That is the question I should like answered.'

'Cut him off!' the producer was screaming in Hardy's ear. 'Tell the fucker to go screw himself!'

'Um,' Hardy was trying to preserve an orderly front. 'I'm afraid . . .'

But the general, perhaps of those present the one most used to dealing with the unexpected, suddenly said, 'I agree. It's a good question. He deserves an answer.'

'Yes,' said Miss Hope. 'And I'd particularly like to hear Mr Hepburn's answer!'

'And you shall,' said Hardy, capitulating while trying to ignore the increasingly foul-mouthed voice in his ear. 'You shall. But first, Iain Mackenzie.' He swivelled in his chair to confront the Labour Member.

'Well,' said Mackenzie, fighting for time. 'It's the last keystone in a veritable gearbox of clashing legislation. We on the Labour side have fought it tooth and nail. My front bench have pinned their colours to the mast of sinking this Government and all their works with them. You ask about *No. 4*?'

The grizzled man nodded. 'I do.'

'But what about *No. 1*, hey, or *Nos. 2* and *3*? We fought those too, and precious little help we got from these other so-called opposition parties. When the chips are down, it's Labour as has to rake the gravel . . . every time.'

'I see,' said Hardy after a pause. 'General Timpson?'

The retired soldier shifted in his seat. 'It's a big issue,' he said. 'A very big issue. This latest act seems quite innocuous in its own way, but people I know, people I trust, people who count, are dead set against it. Mark my words,' he leant towards the camera he believed to be recording him only to see its red winking light promptly extinguished, 'this one has to be stopped.'

'Thank you. Aileen Hope?'

The young woman squared her shoulders. 'I don't know,' she said after a pause. 'I just don't know.'

'Well, that's honest,' said Hardy with a desperate little smile up at the producer's box. 'Mr Hepburn. It's your Government who are pushing through this legislation. What have you to tell us?'

Eleven million watched this programme weekly, drawn as much by Hardy's much-trumpeted charisma as by the prospect of politicians defending their corners. Recordings were invariably scrutinized by each party's central office as both a guide and a warning to aspiring national figures. Some reputations had been made, but many more lost through these critical analyses. James was only there by chance. Dutton, the Chancellor of the Duchy, had dropped out an hour before the show. James had actually been with Walter Meyrick when the call came through. With no time to waste, he had been given the job, and now was facing a question for which Dutton would have been the ideal recipient, but about which he knew next to nothing. At least he appeared to be in good company!

'The original act,' he began, dropping his voice an octave in the search for gravitas, 'provided for variations in purely national legislation to be temporarily enforceable by orders in council, though subject to retrospective scrutiny by the relevant Cabinet committee.' At least he had partly memorized a factsheet circulated by Dutton's office, and regurgitated it now, praying inwardly that no-one knew better. 'These subsequent enabling Bills simply extend this principle to financial and hybrid legislation where not affecting other sovereign governments, except in so far as allowed for by the Treaty of Glasgow.'

'Stuff and nonsense!' shouted Mackenzie. 'You wouldn't get that past the citizens of Newtown Strathurquhart!'

'Not if they're used to your standard of debate,' said James with a grateful smile. At least he could handle invective; it always showed your opponent had nothing better in his armoury. 'But personally I always find them eager to learn the truth.'

'The truth?' Aileen Hope's face was distorted by an expression of puzzled nervousness. 'Where's the truth in what you say when the terms of the Treaty of Glasgow have never been made fully public?' She was even biting her nails now.

A good point, thought James, while continuing to beam at her in a consciously irritating way. Luckily for him, the general suddenly weighed in with a diatribe against mindless opposition. 'We, in my great party,' he concluded, 'would willingly support Her Majesty's Government, if only we knew what they were proposing!'

'Let's hear from our questioner,' said Hardy, adopting an air of matey familiarity. 'Er, Gregory?'

'Greg.'

'Well, Greg then.'

'I don't think any of them have the foggiest idea of what they're talking about.' For the first time, the audience came to life and applauded him with enthusiasm. 'We're being taken down on a mystery tour whose destination nobody knows, least of all our Government. If it's so important, why not have a referendum?' He was still reading from his card.

'Hear! Hear!' The general, responding to his tone, was thumping the table vigorously. 'Well said, young man!'

'Young Hepburn's not doing a bad job, Walter!' said the Prime Minister, using his remote control to turn off the sound. 'Is he as honest as he looks? Or do I mean simple? Perhaps he really does understand it all. That was a wise decision of yours to pull our friend here out at the last minute.' He turned to Dutton, who was busily refilling his glass, the dark rings under his eyes darker than ever. It didn't look as if he had shaved very thoroughly, and his suit was crumpled. 'Aren't you glad now you didn't go?' Dutton shrugged gloomily. So long as he kept his job, and with it the dwindling respect of his mother, he didn't much care what he was called upon to do. 'Did you think there might be a question on *No. 4*?'

'The Director-General assured me there wouldn't be. But I didn't think we could take the risk.'

Dutton shook his head with unexpected vigour. 'No!' he said. 'I really couldn't take any more of that. Not on live television.'

His two senior colleagues stared at him and then, surreptitiously, at each other. The Prime Minister switched off the television altogether. 'So, how are we doing on the vote?' he said.

Meyrick shrugged. 'We're working on it,' he said.

'Optimistic?'

Again Meyrick shrugged. 'There'll be a price, of course.'

'Yes, but what? A few medals in the constituencies, a special trip somewhere?'

Dutton sniffed. 'What price democracy!'

Meyrick stared at him. It wasn't so very long ago that this man had demanded a seat in the Cabinet as the price of his support, and had got it!

'No knighthoods, mind,' said the Prime Minister. 'I had a dreadful time at the Palace before Christmas. I was asked if the sole criterion for the accolade now was just getting elected at all!'

Meyrick slammed down his glass. 'Prime Minister!' he said. 'Do you want this Bill to go through or don't you? Have you forgotten what is at stake?'

His leader quailed before his irritable factotum. 'Yes, yes,' he said. 'I know it all. Less reliance on Commons' votes, peace in our time, stuff the voters, bugger the civil service. All very splendid. But please, not too many knighthoods this time, there's a good chap.' He sought a smile from Dutton, but the latter was too deep in his own thoughts, wondering what his missing wife was up to and regretting that he hadn't struck a harder bargain for his own vote. *Sir Ralph Dutton Bt* would have looked good on his correspondence. Or even *The Rt Hon. the Lord Dutton of Westminster*, only that would have meant a by-election, the last thing this Government needed! Still, it was interesting to see a Prime Minister at work. Who knew . . . in time . . . ? If only his wife had been able to keep her hands to herself, or rather to himself!

They chatted on, discussing the day's problems and their temporary solutions pending the new legislation until a tap on the door announced the next appointment.

'Goodbye, Ralph,' said the Prime Minister cheerily. 'Time for you to recover your flu. You'd better do some coughing at your departmental press conference tomorrow, just to reassure the reptiles. We don't want anyone thinking you funked it!'

'No, indeed,' said Meyrick, handing the confused minister out through the double doors and into the capable grasp of a private secretary. 'See you tomorrow then. Goodbye, Ralph.' He closed the door. 'What a frightful mess he looks!' he said walking back to the sofa. 'No wonder she preferred the chauffeur!'

'You can't say that,' laughed the Prime Minister, secretly rather shocked by Meyrick's remark. And yet, how might his own life be changed if *his* wife . . . ?

Chapter Fifteen

'You're back!'

Another week had passed. Susie had stayed up at Tring for four days and had then gone on to stay with an aunt for several days. 'Yes,' she said, leaving her suitcase in the doorway and going over to the mirror to examine her face. 'My poor darling! You look very tired.'

'We had an all-night sitting,' James said. 'Such a waste of time.'

'Can we talk?'

His heart sank. 'Yes,' he said, turning back to the desk, where he had been answering more correspondence. 'What about?'

'Us . . . well, me.' She smiled directly at him. 'I'm afraid I made a dreadful mistake.'

'Going to Tring?'

She shook her head, still smiling brightly. 'Will you mix me a martini?'

He stared. It was only half past ten in the morning! 'OK.' He went through the connecting door to the kitchen, bringing back some ice and the bottle of gin from the fridge. The rest of the ingredients lived on a tray beside the fireplace. 'How's that?'

She took a sip. 'Perfect!' she sighed. 'What a genius you are.'

'So?'

'I should never have married you,' she said. 'Mummy told me it was a mistake.'

'Did she indeed? A mistake you have managed to prolong for some little time,' he said drily, trying to conceal his sense of stinging shock. Apart from anything else, he had liked and admired his mother-in-law.

'I know!' she said impulsively. 'You're an angel to have put up with me. But meeting Fred again . . . he's done really well, you know.'

'Good.' James sat down heavily. There was some comfort to be found in the lumpen solidity of the old chair.

'He and I . . .' she seemed lost for words. 'It's sort of meant. Do you know what I mean, darling?'

'You want to have an affair with him?' He could feel a troublesome tic in his right eye. She giggled. 'Or rather you've both been hard at it for the last ten days.'

'Well . . .' There was no hiding the triumph in her eyes. She was actually *enjoying* the conversation.

'I don't give a damn what you and he do, so long as you don't involve the children.'

'The children?' Her eyes blurred over with confusion. 'The . . . ?'

'Your children. Our children. Sandy and Jennie. Remember them?'

Her expression cleared. 'But it's nothing whatever to do with them,' she said.

James wiped his forehead, which was damp with sweat. That, at least, was a relief. No divorce, no heartbreak. 'So we just carry on? You fucking Fred, me turning a blind eye? Quite like old times.'

'Oh no! He proposed on Sunday!'

'*What?*' He stood up, quivering with agitation.

'On his knees. By an old stone water trough.'

'How very romantic. Did you accept?' He only just had himself under control. How could she *joke*?

She sighed again. 'Now you're making fun. Of course he knows I'm still married to you.'

'And have been for eight years.' He was having difficulty again keeping his temper. 'I can't believe this conversation. Have you for one moment considered what divorce would mean for Sandy, for Jennie?'

'I know. It's very embarrassing.'

'*Embarrassing?* They're young children, for God's sake!' Suddenly, he realized how very much he minded, for their sakes. 'Have you considered them at all?'

'But they'll *love* Fred. He's wonderful with children. He's bought Gumby-in-the-Vale, you know. It's an amazing house. Fifty-seven bedrooms. Just south of Tring too.'

'What more could one ask? But I thought Hepburnstoun was supposed to be too big.'

'Oh darling, don't be *silly*! Gumby's a proper house. And it's less than an hour from London. It means they can go to proper schools, and have friends to stay. It's only poor you I'm worried about.'

It was quite a dilemma. Should he smash her pretty face against the wall, or simply suffocate her silently in the broom cupboard? 'The two of you seem to have it all worked out very neatly,' he said.

'There!' she said triumphantly. 'I knew you'd be sensible. You're SUCH a *politician*.' It was indisputably a sneer. 'So, if you can take the diamonds back to Coutts, I've got to meet Fred for lunch. He's longing to hear how you reacted. I think he was afraid you'd challenge him to pistols at dawn!' She laughed rather loudly.

'Another drink?'

'Thank you, darling. Just a teeny one.'

'How are we going to tell the children?'

'Will you do it, darling? It's not *quite* my sort of thing, not really.'

'Naturally I'll pay everything for them.'

'Oh, there's no need for that. Fred is just longing for responsibility. He says you must have quite enough on your plate at home. Of course they should be with their mother.'

He gaped at her. 'With their mother? The woman who's smashing up their home on a sexual whim?'

'But darling.' She peered mistily at him over the rim of her glass. 'They wouldn't want me to be unhappy.'

'UNHAPPY! When have you ever considered anyone but yourself?'

'Of course you can have access. After all, you're so busy.' She giggled. 'Fred says . . .' Her voice tailed away.

'I don't give a stuff what Fred says. I will agree to shared custody, nothing less.'

'We'll see,' she said quietly. 'But you're not to get in a state about money.'

'I should think not, in view of what I settled on you when we married.'

'Fred's so generous,' she said, slopping her drink and pausing to wipe away the drops. 'He insists I take nothing from you, apart from my own things of course.'

'Of course.'

'And one or two mementoes, perhaps. It would be nice for the children to have some familiar objects about their new home.'

'Such as?'

'Oh, I don't know,' she said vaguely. 'One or two pictures, perhaps. I've always loved that tall lady in white on the stairs.'

'I dare say you have,' he said heavily. 'But since it now belongs to the trustees, I can't see them sending it out of the house. Not even to so eminently desirable a spot as just south of Tring.'

'What a shame,' she said, draining her glass with a gurgle. 'Fred just dotes on Gainsborough.'

'But I don't understand.' The same evening James rang Hepburnstoun, only to find Mrs Granville at her most mulish. 'Mrs Hepburn said it was only for a month, and then she'd be back. I have my husband to consider too, you know.'

'But *I* understand, Mrs Granville. I understand everything you've been saying. But unfortunately she's had to go to New York.'

'New York? In America?'

'Yes. Very urgently.' He could hardly say she was going to meet Fred's parents, an elderly couple who lived on Long Island. 'I'm coming up tomorrow for a change. I just thought I ought to warn you.'

'Yes,' she said forthrightly. 'So you ought. It's very inconvenient.'

'I know,' he said soothingly. 'She would never have gone if it could have been avoided.'

'Indeed?' Mrs Granville clearly had her own ideas about this, and they were probably nearer the truth than James's version.

'May I speak to Sandy now?'

'Here you are,' she said. 'Jennie's asleep.' And then in the background, 'Your father wants a word.'

'Sandy?' He tried to keep his emotions out of his voice.

'Dad? When's Mummy coming back?'

'Very soon, I hope. She's got to go to America.'

'Bottoms!' A pause. 'Will she bring me back one of those new power-waterguns?'

'I'm sure she will. How's your work?'

'The END! Our teacher's had chicken pox, and her replacement is horrible.'

'But you're well?' James was desperate to think of something positive to say, something interesting.

'When are you coming back?'

'Tomorrow. I've got a day off early.'

'Why can't Mummy come too?'

'I told you. She's going to America.'

'Can I speak to her?'

'I'm sorry, Sandy. She's gone out.'

'All right then.' The little voice sounded quite defeated. 'Bye, Dad.'

'I love you.'

'I love you too.' The line went dead, leaving James staring at the telephone in his hand. But as soon as he put it down, he was overcome with a sense of helplessness, of his own futility and failure. The thought of his children, hopefully longing for their parents to return home to complete the family group, and instead . . . he laid his head on the desk, closing his eyes. On a sudden impulse, he decided to speak to Nick, to seek advice, or maybe just a consoling or invigorating word. He dialled the switchboard.

'House of Commons.'

'Nick Boynton, please.'

'One moment. His line's on answering service. Would you like to leave a message?'

'Could you try Annie's Bar, please?'

'One moment, sir. It's ringing.'

'Yes?'

'Is Mr Boynton there, please?'

'Yes, sir. I'll get him.'

'James!' It was Nick, and he sounded truculent. 'Now look! I've been rereading this *No. 4* Bill. It isn't on, you know. I really can't support it. I thought you'd better be the first to know.'

'But Nick! You've got to.'

'Why?'

'Well, for a start, you're a minister!'

'So?'

'You'd have to resign.'

'That can be arranged.'

'You've only just got the job. It's what you always wanted.'

'I know.' His voice sounded calmer, sadder. In truth, it had taken a lot of will-power and even more whisky to nerve himself to speak as he had. Now he was beyond rational thought.

'But the party . . .'

'SOD THE PARTY!'

James raised his eyes in despair, all thought of his own predicament brusquely swept aside. 'Well, then . . . think how cross you were when old Brotherton resigned!'

'I've already apologized. He's a giant among men!'

'It'll be a dreadful black mark.'

'I know. I'm sorry if it gets you into trouble.'

'Black mark for you, you idiot, not me.'

'Not as black as voting for the permanent emasculation of parliamentary democracy!'

'Voting for the what?'

Nick laughed loudly. 'Don't ask me to repeat it,' he said. 'I thought I did rather well to get it out the first time.'

'Have you been drinking?'

'I certainly have, and I intend to drink a lot more before the night is out.'

'I'll be there in ten minutes.' Flinging on his jacket, James ran down the stairs, and out into the street. The main point was to prevent Nick doing something silly. This legislation could hardly be any more important than any of the other piffling measures they were promoting. It surely wasn't worth Nick blighting his chances of further promotion. Life on the backbenches was for the likes of Paine, not for Nick, nor indeed for himself.

He found his friend slumped feverishly over a round table in the blue and gold bar behind the Star Chamber courtyard. An impressive number of glasses bore witness both to Nick's thirst and to the barman's idleness.

'I've ordered you a fine malt from Islay,' said Nick with a big smile. 'I started on the east coast, and I've got as far as the Moray Firth. But I'll catch you up shortly.' He downed his own glass. 'Hi! What's next?'

The barman limped over carrying a little map. 'Well, sir,' he said, studying the map. 'You could head north and try the Inverbeauly or make a slight detour south to Glenflichity.'

'I'll have them both,' said Nick loudly. 'And in the same glass!'

'Nick!'

'What?'

'Is this sensible?'

'No. But nor is this Bill you're pushing through. It's a shameful measure.'

'Tell me why.' A cool logical approach might work, thought James despairingly.

'I'll tell you why.' Nick's eyes suddenly cleared. 'I've only just read it. My civil servants were so enthusiastic about it I thought I'd better have a closer look. Not just the preamble, but the whole thing. Fifty pages of dangerous and incomprehensible rubbish, most of which we've nodded through like a bunch of donkeys, me included. And you.' His eyes had clouded again. He took a swig at his glass, slopping some of it down his chin. 'We all thought Toady was a simpleton, a safe pair of hands. And Anstruther, God rest his soul, was incorruptible, wasn't he? We couldn't imagine him presenting something off colour.' James nodded. The late Sir Godfrey Anstruther had been the conscience of the party, a massive man with scruples to match his frame. 'Well, we were wrong, all of us.' Nick shook his head violently. 'Dead wrong. Maybe he had us all fooled, or maybe he didn't understand it himself. At least I do. A bit late in the day, but there it is.'

'And you'd throw everything up for this?'

'Why', he said, leaning forward and nearly asphyxiating James with his breath, 'do you suppose I'm drinking this muck? Do you think I want to go back to the sodding back benches, mouldering away on that stinking compost heap with a lot of discarded old vegetables like Gerry Paine, for Christ's sake? The wrecking of everything I've worked for. Do you think that's what I WANT?'

'No,' said James quietly. 'Certainly not for such a little thing as this.'

'Little thing? LITTLE THING?'

'But what', asked James impatiently, 'actually is wrong with the Bill?'

'It's a dirty, snooping, lying, cheating piece of political chicanery that you and I would massacre if the other side tried it on!' Nick's voice had slurred to a standstill, and then, abruptly, he leant forward and whispered, 'So I can't, I mean I won't vote for it.' Then, placing his head on the table, he began to snore.

Leaving him there, James made his way gloomily to the Chamber where a debate on heating tax was being listened to by about thirty bored Members. Soon tiring of this, he climbed the east stairs to the Whips' office, presided over by the bulky figure of Mrs Davies.

'Hello, dear.' James was already a firm favourite of hers, since he didn't look away from the squinting stare with which she invariably challenged newcomers. 'You look all in.'

He shrugged. 'Life!'

'Tell me about it. Like a coffee?'

'I can make myself one.'

'Any of your lot still holding out on *No. 4*?' Despite her apparent kindliness, Mrs Davies kept a firm grasp on her office's work.

'Just one,' he said, switching on the kettle.

'That Mr Boynton?' He nodded miserably. 'I knew he'd be trouble,' she said. 'Terribly conceited and not very bright, just like his grandfather. You'd best have a word with his constituency chairman. Stay there, I'll get you the file.' She bustled out and came back with a thin green folder. 'There you are, a Brigadier Gooch. He's a right tartar! He'll do your job for you.' She cackled loudly. 'Ring him from here.'

'Shouldn't I warn Nick first?'

'Oh no,' she said firmly. 'Take him by surprise. That's the way to get results.'

'He doesn't seem very clear why he's objecting.'

'He wouldn't vote against us, would he?' she asked sharply. 'I only ask because the muddled ones are always the worst.'

James laughed uneasily. 'No, I'm sure he wouldn't do that.'

'Hang on,' she said. 'Hasn't he just been made a minister?'

'Yes, but he says he'll resign if necessary.'

'Easier said than done for most of them,' she remarked. 'You just ring the brigadier, and that'll be the end of it, you'll see.' She actually picked up a receiver and handed it to him, while punching in the figures from the file.

'Yes! Who's that?' barked a voice in James's ear.

'Brigadier Gooch?'

'Yes, yes! Who are you?'

'James Hepburn. I'm Nick Boynton's Whip.'

'And?'

'We are rather worried that he's considering not supporting the Government over a forthcoming Bill.'

'Which one?'

'The *Miscellaneous Provisions No. 4 Enabling* Bill.'

'And what's that when it's at home?'

'Well . . . ' James cast a desperate look at Mrs Davies, but she was back at her computer screen, typing busily. 'It's hard to give you a précis,' he said, 'but it is very important.'

'And he's kicking over the traces, eh?'

'Yes,' said James, relieved. 'That's exactly it.'

'And you want me to bring him into line?'

'If that's not too much to ask?'

'It is.'

'I'm sorry?' Startled, James held the receiver closer to his ear.

'I said,' reiterated the brigadier in a forceful tone, 'that it's a damn sight too much to ask. An outrageous intrusion, in fact. Nicholas Boynton is elected by this constituency to act as our representative, not as some robot. He's not a delegate, you know. He's a good Member. And now he's a minister too, so your people must think highly of him. We like him and trust him. Hepburn, did you say?'

'Yes, James Hepburn.'

'I thought you were supposed to be a friend of his?'

'I am,' said James unhappily.

'Well, you shouldn't come sneaking to me,' said the gruff voice in his ear. 'I don't call that friendly. Not one bit. Good evening to you.' There was a click and the dialling tone resumed its penetrating hum.

'No good?' Mrs Davies had stopped typing and was watching him sympathetically.

'No.'

'You get some like that,' she said. 'I'll talk to the agent. He's an old friend of mine. We'll see what he can do.'

Chapter Sixteen

'That's terrible!' Lucy was staring at him from under her long dark lashes. Her eyes were a deep blue, almost violet, with specks of green. 'The children, they'll be devastated.'

'It happens,' said James wearily, though grateful for her implied support. He usually looked forward to his Saturday evenings at Hepburnstoun, but not this one. 'I don't expect they're altogether unfamiliar with the process of divorce. There must be other children at their school . . . ?'

Lucy shook her head. 'Not up here,' she said seriously. 'Maybe among your friends down south. Mrs Brodie left home, but that was because Mr Brodie beat her every Thursday.'

'Why Thursday?' asked James, glad to be diverted.

'Because he got paid on a Friday,' she said. Seeing him still mystified, she explained, 'He was too drunk on the other nights. But by Thursday, he'd run out of money. He had to stay home. That's when they fought. Or rather he did.'

'There you are then.'

'But they haven't divorced,' she said. 'It's not right, is it? Not when you've got kiddies.'

'There's not a lot I can do about it,' he said, trying not to pay any attention to her figure. She was wearing tight green jeans and a loose shirt. 'She's gone to meet her new in-laws in America.'

'I've made you a nice lamb casserole, and Mr Ogilvie brought in some fresh asparagus from the garden.'

'How's Mrs Ogilvie?'

'Still recuperating in that nursing home in Aberdeen. He says she's coming along fine. She'll be home in a fortnight.'

'And you?'

'Well,' she leant against the kitchen table and folded her arms across her breasts. 'If Mrs Granville won't stay on, I could stay for the children until October. I don't start at college till then.'

Immediately he felt guilty that he knew nothing about her except that her mother lived beyond Inchnabo. 'What college?'

'St Andrews,' she said. 'I'm going to study Biology.'

'The university?'

She nodded, amused by his tone of surprise. Did he imagine she was illiterate?

'But that's marvellous!'

'Yes, I'm looking forward to it.'

'But . . . ?' How old was she then?

She grinned, reading his thoughts. 'I'm twenty-one. I know it's old, but I had to study to retake my exams and then I took a year off to put some money in the bank. You wouldn't believe my first results. Shall I get you a drink?' As she brushed past him, he had to swallow an urgent impulse to touch her. Just a friendly embrace it would have been, but entirely out of order, he told himself. Married Members of Parliament in their thirties did not stroke virginal young maidens, he reminded himself, not if they wanted to avoid a sharp slap across the chops and three days on the front page of the *Sun*! Biology, was it? His own biology was giving him serious trouble. He retreated to the library, and sunk himself into the deepest armchair.

'Here.' She had brought him a reassuringly tall tumbler of whisky, the pale liquid washing round the firm translucent lumps of ice. 'How's that?'

'Perfect.' He didn't stand up, but stretched out a hand to receive the misted glass.

'When will you tell them?'

'Tomorrow,' he said, gazing up at her. 'Tomorrow will do.'

'I've put your dinner on the hotplate.'

'Thank you, Lucy,' he said, and watched her retreating figure with an aching desire that the whisky did nothing to dispel. Thank God she slept at home, safe from his atavistic instincts!

He went down to the cellar, and retrieved a dusty bottle from what remained of his father's store of favourite Burgundies. Pulling the cork, he decanted the wine carefully through a piece of muslin he found behind the pantry table. The stew was rich and meaty, and he drank the wine slowly, staring out into the twilight and remembering past days out on the hill when his father had begun to introduce him to the geography of their home. He remembered the time they had stalked an old stag the whole way up to the Blairgowan march, and the day his father had pushed him into the loch . . .

'What are you laughing about, all by yourself?' Lucy was standing in the doorway, her face in shadow.

'I thought you'd gone home.' He didn't mean it to sound rude, and she didn't take it as such.

'I'm staying here with Jennie and Sandy tonight,' she said. 'Mrs Granville's got trouble with her mother-in-law, and I said I'd take her place.'

'That's kind of you,' he said vaguely.

'And what have you done to these?' Was she laughing at him?

'I'm sorry, I can't quite see . . .'

'These!' She was waving the 'muslin' at him. 'My knickers!'

'Oh?' He could feel himself blushing, the unmistakable frisson of blood churning through his face.

'I'm dreadfully sorry. It didn't occur to me . . .'

'I wondered where they'd got to,' she said. 'How was the wine?'

'Here.' He held up his glass. 'It's really nice.'

She walked over to him, took the glass and sipped it doubtfully, while he watched her lips against the rim. 'Yum!' she said, giving it back. 'What is it?'

'Burgundy,' he said. 'One of my father's favourites.'

'I remember your father well.' She sat down beside him, looking rather shy. 'He used to bring my mother a haunch of venison every autumn.'

'And your father?'

'He died abroad,' she said softly. 'He worked in the Middle East.'

'I'm so sorry.'

'Back to work,' she said suddenly, swallowing hard as if assailed by some unexpected emotion. 'What time would you like breakfast?'

He stared up at her, trying to concentrate. He had drunk far too much. 'Won't you have some more wine? I could get you a glass.'

She shook her head, hair flying everywhere. 'No, thanks. I never drink. But that was rather delicious.' And hurried from the room.

Deciding to clear his head, and subdue his desire, he walked unsteadily across the hall, and out into the chilly evening air. The heavy clouds were almost low enough to touch the hills around him, and the mountains were completely obscured by the swirling vapour. A shrill cry announced the first oyster-catcher. Within a few days, there would be twenty, maybe thirty pairs, filling the air with their mournful music.

He strolled down through the rushes to the river bank. On an impulse, he lay down on the damp moss and, leaning over, plunged his head into the brimming river, gasping at the icy shock of the mountain water. The night was closing in, and with it came the almost imperceptible sounds of his nearest neighbours, the rabbits and frogs among the marshy grass, the duck and even an occasional cock pheasant along the river bank. Was that splash a trout rising, or even an otter? Someone had seen mink a few miles down river, a new threat to the indigenous life of the River Buchat, a pure unsullied stretch of water that was in every way the antithesis of that other great river, the many-faceted Thames. 'To hell with Susie!' he heard himself saying. 'Fred deserves her.' And, to his intense surprise, he realized he was smiling in the darkness. Then he remembered the children. Tomorrow he would have to tell them. Suddenly it began to rain.

Chapter Seventeen

The next morning it was still raining and cold. Lucy brought them to him in the big library, their small faces smiling and unsuspecting.

'Here's your father,' she said, and hurried out of the room, closing the door behind her.

'Come here.' He was sitting in a battered old tartan armchair beside the fire, and they rushed to join him. The room smelt of woodsmoke, and damp leather, and dust.

'Can I put a log on the fire, Dad?' Sandy's hair was sticking up on end, as if he was auditioning as a red Indian.

'Of course you can.'

'And me! And me!' shrieked Jennie, scenting an advantage gained by her brother.

'Go on then,' he said wearily, for he had hardly slept, 'but *please* be careful.' They both collected the largest logs they could find, and staggered in convoy towards the intense heat of the fire, teetering dangerously just out of reach of the flames.

'Happy now?' They both nodded. 'Come here then. I want to have a very serious talk with you both.'

Panic filled their eyes. What had they done? Was it the bath running over? Or had someone finally found Mrs Granville's kettle? Jennie screwed up her eyes ready to cry.

'It's nothing you've done,' he said soothingly. 'You've both been very good while Mummy and I have been away, and I'm very proud of you both.'

The smiles returned. 'Are you worried about

Muggy's coat?' asked Jennie, shyly. 'Jock says it will get better soon.'

'No.' James shook his head. 'I hadn't realized anything was wrong with her.'

'Only a bit of mange,' said Sandy dismissively. 'Nothing for anyone to worry about.'

'Well, *I* worry about her,' said Jennie stoutly. 'She needs someone to worry about her. Poor Muggy.'

'Look,' said James desperately. 'I've got to tell you something about Mummy and me.'

'At last he had their full and undivided attention. 'There you are!' said Sandy gloomily. 'I told you. They're getting divorced.'

James stared at him. 'How do you know about divorce?' he asked.

'I can read, Dad. Newspapers? You know, bits of paper with writing on. Appear at breakfast?'

'You're being cheeky!' hissed Jennie. She came over and put both her arms around James's neck, and looked him firmly in the eyes. 'Are you and Mummy really going to get divorced?'

He swallowed hard. 'I'm very sorry. But it won't affect either of you as much as you think.'

'Is Mummy sorry too?' asked Sandy, in a new hard voice.

'Of course she is,' said James. 'Very sorry. We both are.'

'So why isn't she here?'

Because she's screwing around with her stinking lover was what he wanted to say, but restricted himself with a simple: 'Because she's in America. She wanted you to know she loves you both very much.'

'Will Hepburnstoun be sold?' asked Jennie, her eyes watering again. 'Can I take Muggy with me?'

'No, no.' James felt on firmer ground now. 'There'll be no changes. Hepburnstoun will stay exactly the same.'

'I won't have to change bedrooms?'

'No, Jennie.'

'So where will Mummy live?' asked Sandy in the same hard voice.

'She's got a nice friend called Mr Tevis, who lives in ... er ... I think it's in Buckinghamshire. He's got a very beautiful house with lots of bedrooms. And you'll spend some of your time there.'

'Will you come too?' said Jennie, still clinging to him.

'No, Jennie. I won't be coming there. But you'll still spend lots of time with me here.'

Sandy had been standing apart all this time, kicking at the carpet with one foot, while balancing unsteadily on the other. Now he turned and stared hard at his father. 'Dad,' he said and stopped.

'Sandy? Come here.' James put out his arms, and the little boy ran sobbing to him.

'I love you,' he was saying, between gulps and tears, 'I love you.'

'It's all right.' James hugged them both to him, as close as he could. 'I love you too.' It was only when Lucy came back to say that lunch was on the table, that he realized that he was crying too.

Chapter Eighteen

'What do you mean, he won't support us?'

Back in London on the Monday morning, Walter Meyrick, puffing furiously on his pipe, was staring angrily at James, while Mrs Davies bustled round with cups of coffee for the assembled Whips. Since their last meeting, most of the recalcitrant Members had been brought into line. Only five remained. Three, having resisted the stick, were now being assessed for the appropriate carrot, a committee chair for one, one of the much prized offices in the Commons building itself for another, and, very reluctantly, an early knighthood for the third. This left Nick. Meyrick's desk was littered with scraps of paper covered in his neat calculations.

'Does it matter?' Meyrick's deputy was bored and wanted his lunch. 'We've got enough now, even if he voted against.'

'*Matter?* A junior minister voting against his own Government? Even if he resigned, which would almost be worse. Can you imagine the press? And there's never enough when it's this close,' said Meyrick, privately despairing of such insouciance. 'We can't be sure of Moore-Talbot making it, for example.'

James had decided against revealing the old man's unexpected apostasy. 'I'm quite certain,' he said now, 'having seen the state of Sir Cuthbert's health, that he won't be able to get to the Commons for the vote.' He was thinking of Sandy's white strained little face, and Jennie's cheerful incomprehension of the word *divorce*.

'Not even in an ambulance?'

'What? No, not even on a magic carpet. He's very frail, and he has difficulty breathing.'

'Good heavens!' shouted Meyrick, his frustration getting the better of him for once. 'All he's got to do is raise a *finger*! That takes it down to five, even if Boynton does do his duty, but only three if he went stark staring mad and voted against us. That is definitely the danger area. The Foreign Secretary is supposed to be going to some Common Market jamboree in Berlin. We'll have to tell him that's right out of the window. Buck up, James. You're going to have to earn your keep with young Boynton. Think of something and make it stick!'

'What if we sacked him and threatened to withdraw the party Whip altogether?' enquired his deputy.

'Brilliant!' snarled Meyrick. 'A brainwave. Reduce our working majority permanently by nearly twenty per cent. I wish I'd thought of that.'

'But that way he'd know he'd be out at the next election.'

'At the next election,' said Meyrick, speaking very, very slowly, 'we'll all be out unless things improve. Any other potential rebels?'

'Brotherton's against it,' said his deputy. 'But behind the scenes, as usual. Pure pique.'

Meyrick waved a languid hand. 'You needn't worry about David,' he said. 'He may grumble and intrigue, but he wants to get back to the honey-pot too much to rock the boat. You mark my words, he'll vote like a lamb when the time comes.'

The meeting broke up gradually and as James left the inner office, Mrs Davies laid one finger on his arm.

'I think I can help,' she said. 'Give me a few days. Don't do anything until you hear from me.'

'Thank you.' James was sincerely grateful. The last thing he wanted to do was to put more pressure on Nick himself. He already seemed to be becoming unusually unpredictable. 'That's very kind of you.' She smiled.

Back at his flat, he found two messages on his answer-machine. *'Hi! James, it's me. Fred Tevis. Can you meet me for a drink at Blunts' Club at six this evening? My secretary is on 071 931 8555 . . . that's 071 931 8555. Bye!'* The second message was from the Prime Minister's private office, asking him to ring Downing Street.

His heart pounding, he dialled the government number.

'Prime Minister's Office.'

'This is James Hepburn. I had a message to ring in.'

'Hold on, please.' A pause. 'I have the Principal Private Secretary for you.' James held his breath.

'Mr Hepburn?'

'Yes.'

'The Prime Minister wondered if you and your wife would like to spend the next weekend but one at Chequers. He's having a party on the twenty-fifth, the Saturday night.'

'How very kind. My wife will actually be away in America, but . . .'

'I see,' said the voice impersonally. 'I'm fairly sure the invitation would still be extended to you on your own, but I will have to check. Would you care to come on your own?'

'Certainly,' said James fervently. 'I'm very flattered to be asked.'

'Quite. I will come back to you shortly. Goodbye.'

Next James rang Fred's office.

'This is James Hepburn.' He distinctly heard muffled laughter at the other end of the line.

'Can you manage to meet with Mr Tevis?' asked the woman politely.

'I'll be there,' he said grimly, and was not encouraged to hear a further outburst of giggling as she put the telephone down.

Punctually at six, he climbed the steps of Blunts' Club and pushed through the swing-doors into the tall hall hung with massed Piranesi prints.

The hall porter, half-hidden within a mahogany and glass booth, was a stolid grey-haired man with thick spectacles who recognized him from previous visits, and raised a friendly hand in salutation.

'I've come to see Mr Tevis,' James said.

'It's Mr Hepburn, isn't it?' The porter prided himself on his memory. 'Friend of Mr Boynton's?' James nodded. 'You'll find Mr Tevis in the coffee room. Straight through, sir, and left by the staircase.'

James followed these directions, and found himself face to face with his wife's prospective second husband. The hair seemed even more waved and crinkled than usual, and shone with some aromatic preparation of unguessable provenance. Even the outstretched hand was soft and palpable, smooth as an odalisque's.

'James! This is so good of you.' Fred waved his guest towards a secluded sofa. The room was in any case entirely empty of other members. 'What'll you have? Cinzano, or is it a whisky?'

'Nothing, thank you.' He felt unwilling, even unable to accept anything from this man, and yet, perhaps Fred was doing him a considerable favour. If Susie no longer loved him, what was the point? Did he, for that matter, still love Susie? Love, after all, depends on some breath of reciprocity to keep the embers alive. Perhaps he hated her? He was too interested to hear what Fred had to say to bother to think about it.

'As you please.' Fred broadened his smile, not without some little effort, and sat down in a chair beside the sofa. 'Now, I understand from Susie that your marriage has really been over for some time.' As it was a statement rather than a question, James felt no need to respond. 'So perhaps we can dispense with unnecessary apologies and all that sort of thing.'

James gazed into the other man's eyes. They were grey, mottled with brown, and rather small. He had tiny pupils. 'You'll have heard I've bought Gumby-in-the-Vale. It's in a shocking state, of course. But I think Susie will have fun doing it up.'

'I thought you had both gone to America?'

Fred laughed delightedly. 'Susie went first, to meet my folks. I haven't seen much of them in recent years, and I'm hoping she'll smooth my path there when I join her next weekend.'

'I see.'

'Now let's talk business,' said Fred. 'This family trust of yours.'

James raised his eyebrows. 'The children's trust?'

'Yeah. Whatever.'

'What about it?'

'Susie's rather worried about it.'

'Really? Why?'

'She says it's very large, and we need to know how it affects any children we may have.'

'That's easy,' said James with a tight smile. 'It doesn't affect them at all.'

'Now come on,' said Fred, losing some of his relentless bonhomie. 'I've said I'll welcome Susie's children to Gumby and pay all the bills she wants. That's what husbands are for.' James said nothing. 'But I need to know that our own kids won't be adversely affected. I've had to take out a massive mortgage to buy that old heap of masonry.'

'I'm afraid I can't assist you,' said James. 'Trusts are administered by law, not by expediency.'

'But Susie says if you remarry and have more children . . .'

'Naturally they will share,' said James, 'since they will be Hepburns and it is Hepburn money. Not hers, and certainly not yours. I wish you a very pleasant flight.' He walked quickly out.

'Very entertaining gentleman, Mr Tevis,' commented the hall porter on seeing James's grim smile as he came through the hall.

'No doubt,' said James, who had actually been contemplating the agreeable thought of Fred and Susie squabbling over money already. 'Good afternoon.' No more of Susie's Pharisaic triumphs over other people's misfortune, no more exaggerated treacly compliments, no more complaints about Hepburnstoun. The June sunshine was still warming the stones of St James's Street, and casting splendid shadows across the dusty pavement. Really, if it weren't for distressing the children, he would have to admit that the whole idea of divorce had a great deal to offer.

He met Nick coming up the street carrying a sheaf of papers. 'Hi!'

'Not a word about politics,' warned Nick, stopping. 'I'm lecturing at the V and A this Friday and I need all my wits about me.'

'Not on the subject of *Miscellaneous No. 4* by any chance?' laughed James.

'Well, I'm glad you think it's funny. I've just had Walter Meyrick asking me if I have ambitions to join the Lords, at my age! No, it's on Hardman, the Victorian craftsman who made all the metalwork for both Houses of Parliament. I'm researching his unpublished drawings.'

'Good luck!'

'Sorry I can't wish you the same.'

'What did you say to Walter?'

'I said it was a scurrilous question, and only served further to decide me in favour of voting with the Opposition.'

'Nick!'

'What was it you used to say to me? "It's only politics", wasn't that it? "Do try to keep a sense of proportion." You ought to be able to identify when you're on a loser. The day for this sort of measure has long gone. Nothing we do matters any more. We're just clinging on to the wreck, pretending it's still afloat. Brussels decides these matters now. You and I are like Berington steel-workers, pulling faces in our own very decorative museum. I've never propounded the Boynton doctrine on wrecks to you, have I?' James shook his head impatiently. 'The more permanent and valuable an institution looks, the more closely you have to examine it to see if it's become a wreck. Doesn't matter how busy the crew look, or how gaudy the figurehead, if the captain's lost heart and the compass is kaput, they're heading straight towards the rocks. But the problems with wrecks is,' he tapped his nose, 'one never quite knows when to leave go, as anyone connected with Lloyds' would agree. You ought to cultivate a hobby, like me. Don't forget we've got an "Unmentionables" dinner on Thursday so that poor old Dutton can address us on your favourite topic.'

'Susie and I are getting divorced, Nick.' He blurted it out, without quite knowing why.

'There you are then,' said Nick. 'I'd have thought you two would make it. But seriously,' he moved forward and took James's arm. 'I'm very sorry.'

'Thanks.'

'Let me know how I can help. I'd love to have Sandy to stay for a weekend, Jennie too.'

'That's a kind thought,' said James, who had no intention of losing a moment of his children's time, and the two friends pursued their separate paths, Nick to the London Library, James back to the Commons. A wreck? He looked around him, at the busy crowds hurrying this way and that, their arms full of papers, their faces set in expressions of dedicated zeal. Nick's change of heart was so sudden, and yet there was, when he considered his own commitments, among this towering architecture, perhaps just a tiny measure of doubt. Was it all for decoration? Or was that decoration to be defended as balm for the reassurance that freedom could be maintained? How else to check the faceless power of civil servants if not by the pomp of representative Parliament? Perhaps the appearance of control, however deceptive, was the essential oil of peace.

The next morning, just as James was being reassured by Downing Street that he would indeed be welcome at Chequers the following Friday night, Lucy was experiencing a difficult three-way conversation at Hepburnstoun. Jock had cycled along the opposite bank, pausing only to wave up at the kitchen window as he manhandled his official red bicycle over the little grey footbridge, and presented himself eager and ready for his reception by Lucy at 11.15 as usual.

'Here's Postie!' Sandy had shouted, his parents' incomprehensible problems quite forgotten.

'Hello, young Sandy. When are we going up to the loch again?'

'Today?' cried the boy, his eyes shining.

Jock gave a comical shrug. 'We'll have to let the ladies decide,' he said. 'What do you say, Lucy?'

But she, heaving a sack of onions across from the larder, had given him no answering smile. Lately indeed she had seemed withdrawn, even lacking her usual joyousness. Now there was a new resolute air about her, and when Sandy said, 'Don't forget to give Jock his drink in the stables,' the young man was not altogether surprised when for the first time, she shook her head.

'There's no more,' she said, meeting his eyes across Sandy's head. 'The well is dry.'

'I bet I know how to get it running,' he replied, trying to adopt an attractively roguish air.

'I very much doubt it,' she said coldly.

'But you must give Postie his drink,' said Sandy, his eyes filling with sudden tears. Were all grown-ups bent on making each other unhappy? 'You always give him a drink.'

Jock knelt down beside the boy. 'Now then, Sandy,' he said gently. 'We all have to accept change. It's part of life.'

'But I want Lucy to give you your drink,' wailed Sandy, burying his head in the postman's thick uniform that smelt of dust and tobacco, and pouring out all his own repressed private sorrows into his lament for Jock's disappointment.

'So do I,' said Jock, winking up at Lucy, and stroking Sandy's heaving shoulders with unusual tenderness. 'But "I want doesn't get". Surely your Lucy hasn't neglected to teach you that!'

And when, twenty minutes later, half-blinded by a searing shaft of sunlight, he sank his grateful sweating head between her breasts, gasping at the strength of his paroxysm, it was in the certain knowledge that it was for the last time. Even as she had led him over to their hallowed den, even as she had tenderly undressed him, pausing expressionless to allow him his invariable routine with her body, not deigning now even to counterfeit a passion she no longer felt, he had known that he was possessing this wild creature through her kindness, not her desire. Surely this should have cancelled his feelings, made him angry or dismissive? So it must have been love that gave him the matching generosity to accept, without reproach, this last gift of sexual encounter.

Mrs Granville, watching through her husband's telescope from the attic window, wiped a drop of perspiration from her chin. It all depended on the light. Some days she could see nothing through the dingy stables' window. Today, thanks to that same brilliant shaft of sunlight, she had charted every change of position, even imagined she could hear Jock's final groan as he rendered up to Lucy the final tribute of his body. The slut! The filthy little trollop with her bulging body and silly lisping lips! Mrs Granville was as thin as a reed, persuading herself that this was the key to multiplying her husband's increasingly rare indulgences. Surely men couldn't want all that flapping flesh? Men! She pursed her lips and went downstairs to shout at Jennie for scribbling on the nursery wallpaper again.

Chapter Nineteen

Thursday the sixteenth of June and there they were again, the 'Unmentionables', nine plump young men, Nick the eldest at thirty-four, Rupert Pilkington the youngest at twenty-nine, seated around the dazzling table with its exuberant silver centre-piece piled high with crystallized fruits.

Between Nick and James, in the place of honour, sat the relatively modest figure of Ralph Dutton, Chancellor of the Duchy of Lancaster and, as such, responsible for initiating and carrying through the *Miscellaneous Provisions No. 4 Enabling* Bill, the cornerstone of a massively baroque pile of legislation destined to trumpet his renown down the centuries. Pitt, Canning, Peel, Gladstone and now Dutton! He helped himself to a little more of the Louis Latour Le Montrachet. A prince among wines, and no less than he deserved.

But if there was a drawback, a barrier almost to his complete enjoyment, as a perfect *consommé* was followed by the lightest of *quenelles*, in their turn pursued by a robust though meltingly tender baron of beef, it was the awkward remembrance, tugging painfully at the back of his brain, that shortly he was going to have to address these awesome gluttons on the subject of his dreaded Bill. And not just that. That alone could not have spoiled his digestion. *Questions!* That was what stuck in his throat and threatened to redistribute those delicate *profiteroles Charlus* all over the embroidered damask cloth. Questions! How on earth was he going to cope with their questions, when he hadn't the first idea of the answers?

'A nice glass of port, dearie?' Really these waitresses were the end! This one looked a bit like his mother-in-law, with her loose chins and vacant rheumy eye. She also looked distinctly drunk. Whereas Stubbings had been as great a paragon at the table as behind the wheel, serving with white gloves while retaining an irreproachably aloof expression. Poor Stubbings! What must the poor fellow be going through now with the errant Mrs Dutton?

'I said, would you like to start now?' Someone was jogging his elbow.

'Eh?'

'Would you like to speak now, Chancellor?'

'Oh? Yes, yes . . . of course.' He rose to his feet. Was it Churchill who had told his father that the secret of public-speaking was to look round your audience and say to yourself, 'I've never seen such a load of bloody fools in my life'? Preferably under your breath. Well, no problem about that tonight!

'Gentlemen.' He smiled down at their congested faces. 'Thank you for a truly remarkable dinner. It is my pleasure, and indeed my privilege, to talk to you, just a little,' he risked a smile, 'about this great Bill we are jointly going to enrich our country's legislative roll of honour . . . er . . . with. Yes.' He pulled out his clerk's notes. 'Ever since our late friend and colleague Sir Godfrey Anstruther of happy memory . . .' And so it went on. His audience, suffused with a superabundance of fine food and wines, settled down to their ordeal, assisted by a regular merry-go-round with the port and a humidor full of good cigars. 'And . . . and . . .' Dear God, he'd lost his place!

'Well said, sir!' Nick, who'd had quite enough wine, and more than enough of Ralph Dutton, clapped vigorously, immediately and gratefully echoed by the others. 'And now, after that masterly résumé, let me invite my colleagues to question the Chancellor.'

'I'm still not entirely sure,' this from Rupert Pilkington, 'exactly what effect the Bill will have on the passage of, for example, a simple finance Bill?'

Dutton beamed at him. 'A simple finance Bill. A SIMPLE finance Bill? That's a mammoth of a question, my dear fellow. Let's start with the basic history of finance Bills *per se* . . .' He kept that one going for nearly forty minutes. His face, so pale with apprehension during dinner, grew ruddy with his growing awareness of the steady progress of the clock. Surely there would be a vote tonight? It was almost ten o'clock. Didn't the damned division bell work in this part of the building? Once out of this room, no power on earth would persuade him to re-enter it.

'I'd like a straight answer,' said James abruptly. 'Does this Bill or doesn't it reduce the House's powers of scrutiny?'

'I don't quite follow your reasoning . . .'

'I should have thought it was clear enough.' James was tired, and fed up with all the monotonous persiflage. 'Does this Bill reduce the House's powers of scrutiny, or doesn't it? Could I have a plain answer?'

'Does it . . . er . . .' The bell outside the door began to ring. Never had a bell so fully earned the most generous lashings of sumptuous oil, the most lavish supply of invigorating electrical current! 'Gentlemen, forgive me. We must leave the pleasures of your hospitality and return to our duties. To the lobby!' One thing was quite certain, he'd stop that blasted smart alec James Hepburn from receiving so much as a smidgeon of further promotion, or die in the attempt.

Chapter Twenty

The following evening, James and Nick left the House together, James to catch his plane to Edinburgh, Nick to present his lecture. Having left James at the gate, Nick headed for the Tube. Coming down the steps of the Westminster Underground, he cannoned into a young man who dropped all his parcels, spilling tins of food across the crowded floor.

'I'm so sorry,' said Nick, groping to collect the elusive cans.

'That's all right,' said the young man. He had soft fair hair, worn long, and a wide luscious smile. Nick's heart undeniably missed a beat. How else could one explain that stifling hiatus in the ordered progress of his brain? The young man stared back, his pale eyes flickered, and then he had collected his belongings and was gone.

Only momentarily distressed, Nick went on to the lecture. 'And so,' he was saying in his peroration, staring out at his audience in the limited light shed by the slide-projector, 'I have tried to show you some of the rich variety of Hardman's work. No wonder Birmingham was looked upon as the Florence of its day, not for architectural richness, but for the wealth of entrepreneurial and innovatory energy that its citizens unleashed upon an Empire rich and confident enough to employ and harness this energy to the tasks which we can admire today. I leave you with one unsolved problem. This last slide shows a massive bracket,' he pressed the button in his hand and the machine at the back of the room whirred briefly before projecting over his head the likeness of a giant scroll of decorated metal onto the whitewashed wall of the lecture hall, 'apparently connected in some way with Hardman's work at Westminster. Hardman describes it in his diary as the "Wondrous Bracket". I am not familiar with it. Nor is anyone else. It only goes to show that there are always new frontiers to be pushed back, new mysteries to be unravelled.' He sat down to the polite applause of the two dozen-odd students, aged between twenty and seventy, who had enrolled in his course.

Walking out of the building, he was astonished to see the young man waiting for him. 'Hello.'

'I followed you.'

'Where's your shopping?'

'I threw it away.' The young man had strong shoulders, like an athlete.

'Do you like lifting weights?'

'When they taste nice.'

Nick could hardly breathe. How long had it been since . . . ? 'Where do you live?'

'Just round the corner. In Ennismore Gardens.'

'Well . . .'

'Come on,' said the young man. 'I'm thirsty.'

As soon as James reached Hepburnstoun, Mrs Granville demanded 'a word'. He could see she was bursting to say something, and something disagreeable at that.

He sighed. 'Come into the library, Mrs Granville. Can I get you something to drink?'

'No thank you.' She had folded her arms and looked sufficiently formidable for all her slight stature. 'It may not be my place . . .' she began.

'Mrs Granville,' said James, managing a smile, 'you pushed me up and down the drive in my pram. We've been friends, you and I, for more than thirty years. I can't think there's anything that's not your place here.'

'Well,' she said. 'It's that Lucy upstairs.'

'Yes?' He tried not to harden his tone, or betray any partiality for the supple young woman who was increasingly playing an involuntary and thrilling role in his thoughts.

'You see!' she said angrily. 'You men are all alike.'

'Mrs Granville,' said James, resisting the urge to counter-attack on the subject of women, 'I truly don't know what the problem is.'

'She's been doing dirty things with the postman in the stables,' she blurted. 'Shameful things. It's not right for the children.'

'Oh dear,' said James, torn between amusement and irrational jealousy. 'But perhaps they're secretly engaged?'

'That they are not!' she said indignantly. 'John Stewart is supposed to be engaged to Margaret McPherson, the minister's daughter.'

'Is her mother called Helen, the secretary of the Glenbuchat Ladies' Luncheon Guild?'

Mrs Granville nodded. 'But she's a decent girl,' she said. 'She'd no be riding him like a trollop.'

James had to struggle to keep a straight face. How on earth did Mrs Granville know such things? He could hardly accuse her of spying on the young couple. But to think of Lucy . . .

'I see,' he managed to say. 'And you want me to have a word . . . ?'

'I'm not staying in the same household as a slut like that,' grumbled the conscience of the glen. 'She's no right to be behaving like that in front of children.'

'You really think they've seen?'

Mrs Granville tossed her head. 'There's no telling what they have or haven't seen. But I thought you ought to know.'

'Quite right,' said James soothingly. 'Now I'd better go up and see the children. I hope they've been good?'

'As good as you can expect with no mother in the house.'

There was nothing to say to this, so he ran up the flights of stairs, and immersed himself in the particular pleasures of baths and bedtime.

When the children were finally, and reluctantly, asleep, he found that Lucy had again left him an excellent dinner on the hotplate and had gone home. Mrs Granville had also taken advantage of his return to spend two nights with her sorely-tried husband, so he was alone in the house apart from the sleepers above. Having eaten his dinner, he pulled out a folder of parliamentary papers from the heap on his desk and, having lit the library fire, he settled down to read. He must have dozed, because when he woke suddenly, his first impression was that the fire had gone out. Lucy was standing in the doorway, silently watching him, her long hair partly masking her face.

'You've come back?' he said, startled.

'Yes.'

'Why?'

'I was worried about you.'

He struggled to his feet. How pale she looked, and strangely fragile, despite the opulence of her figure.

'Are you all right?' he asked.

'What's she been saying?' She looked as if she was going to cry.

'Oh, that!' He grinned at her. 'I didn't pay any attention, not a bit.'

'Sodding old cow!' she said.

He laughed out loud. 'Poor Mrs Granville. She probably wishes it was her.'

'It was only to say goodbye,' she said miserably. 'Because he was so sweet to the children. Can you understand?'

The strange thing was that he did understand.

Without knowing her, some invisible empathy eased their path, smoothing away the creases of misunderstanding, that fatal and regular impediment to love. For what man means what he says? And what woman says what she means?

'I know.' He was beside her, stroking her hair, and felt her hand at his thigh.

'Look!' she murmured, her lips parting in a smile. Then, more confidently, 'I knew you wanted me.'

'And you?' he scarcely dared to whisper.

She moved his hand. 'See?'

'But . . .'

'Come on,' she said, encouraging him down onto the carpet, and drawing up her legs. She was wearing nothing under her skirt. 'Come on. There. *There*.'

And when, much later, having brought two cups of hot chocolate to where she lay, naked and half-asleep, in front of a rekindled fire of spitting and crackling pine logs, he said, 'I hope that wasn't "goodbye"', she curled her arm round his neck and drew him down to her, replying with a long fierce kiss.

Jennie, creeping downstairs through the darkened house in search of a fatherly hug, gazed fascinated at the two bodies blissfully entwined on the hearthrug. After a bit she got bored and went back upstairs.

'Where have you been?' demanded Sandy sleepily.

'Just went down to find Daddy,' said his sister.

'Is he all right?'

'Yes,' she said. 'Lucy's been giving him a drink.'

Chapter Twenty-one

Never had a weekend at Hepburnstoun seemed so frustrating to James. Saturday and Sunday turned out to be days unusually packed with constituency business. No less than ten supplicants at his Saturday 'surgery' had combined to keep him away from Lucy, followed by Doddie Gordon who had brought a friend, and a whole bottle of Vat 69, having heard something of James's troubles. Then there was to be a Games that afternoon at Castle Buchat in aid of the Young Conservatives, to be followed by two fund-raising dinners in outlying areas of his patch, to help fund their levy to Central Office in London. Away from witnesses, of whatever age, he and Lucy clung to each other whenever they could, smothering each other with hungry kisses.

'I love you.'

'I love you.' What more could they say? They seemed to live for the next embrace.

After a rather fraught lunch, during which both Jennie and Sandy became impossibly prone to giggling, James climbed into his car and very reluctantly drove down the valley to Castle Buchat. Ancient seat of the long defunct Earls of Buchat, this was a massive castellated lump of granite which lurked behind a tall stone wall ten miles downstream from the little town of Glenbuchat. Bought in the nineteenth century by a successful arms manufacturer, whose noisy products laid waste the tribes of four continents to the great advantage of his purse, it was now lived in by his great nephew, Major Harold Godman, a round bald little man with only four teeth and a heavy moustache dyed yellow with nicotine.

'Hepburn! Well done! Pity about the rain.'

It was pouring down, or rather across, since the strong westerly wind was sweeping it in swathes across the castle's pitted lawns. Here and there, sodden locals were sheltering under the little flapping tents of brown canvas, and one disconsolate soul was crouching under the platform erected for the dancing competition, apparently trying to read a newspaper.

'I'm sure it will clear,' announced the major, with imperturbable optimism. 'Look! If you look beyond the hills, there's *just* a patch of blue sky.' James couldn't even see the hills. 'Come in for a dram. We're all inside for the moment.'

The hall of the castle was a low dark space bisected by a titanic staircase of glittering white marble up which the major led him at a trot. 'Here we are, here we are!' A doorway crowned by a stuffed moose-head opened into a tall chamber with an oval ceiling, hung with tattered banners and full of people talking at the tops of their voices. 'You know Macadam, here, and Mrs King. Here's my old friend Potter. Now do you know Sir Ewan Grant?'

'He should do,' said the stooping old man indicated, 'since I'm his constituency chairman.'

'Sorry, sorry, sorry.' The major rushed on. 'Now, here's Dr Veitch. Do you know each other?'

James shook hands with the doctor, a short man with carefully groomed silver hair and a pink complexion, with some interest. He was wearing a short jacket of pale green twill, over a green and red tartan kilt embellished with a splendid white fur sporran. It was not too much to say that he was something of a legend in his own lifetime. The daughter of a local laird, christened Roberta, had studied to become a surgeon before changing course and becoming the first female general practitioner in the glen, and, as such, the welcome confidante of many intimate feminine secrets. Imagine, therefore, the consternation among the women of Glenbuchat, when their female confessor took a prolonged holiday and suddenly re-emerged as a man, and took to staying with their husbands over the after-dinner port, instead of joining them in the cosy sanctuary of the withdrawing-room. Bobbie Veitch had had to surmount a decade of innuendo and ridicule, but this, James could see, had left him with a huge supply of humane understanding for the problems of others.

'I was so fond of your dear father,' said the doctor. 'I hope you won't find contemporary political morals as distressing as he did.'

'He did?' James had never heard his father express any negative opinion of his colleagues.

'Dear me, yes!' The little doctor shook his head. 'He found them sadly wanting sometimes. I used to be on his management committee in those days. We often used to talk about their shortcomings. Do pop in one evening if you're passing. You'd always be most welcome. Most welcome.'

'COME ON! COME ON!' The major had jumped onto a table, and was whirling his arms in the air. 'It's stopped raining and we're going to start with the dancing.'

Amazingly, the rain had stopped, although the ground was completely waterlogged. A number of stalls were being set out, a coconut shy, a ring-the-bell competition, a table laden with heather honey, and an old woman in a purple beret came hobbling past him, weighed down by a bucket full of bemused goldfish. There was even the bitter-sweet tang of toffee apples wafting across from a smoking brazier. James was just longing for his fireside, and Lucy, when he heard, with a tingling at the back of his head, the first notes of the pipe band, that magical and romantic sound with which, in the Highlands, no other music can compete.

From somewhere behind the lumpen stable block, a growing hum, the occasional screech, an angry shout, and then the swelling heart-piercing volume of forty pipers filled the damp air with mystic drama. The tingle grew, and his whole spine seemed to be vibrating in time with their playing. A bellowed command, and round they swung, emerging through the trees, with the grandeur of the mountains revealed behind them, forty men in the fiery tartan of the Red Forbes of Buchat, kilts and sporrans swinging, with Major Godman, *jure heredii*, at their head, his moustache held high, brandishing his claymore and twinkling away at his acquiescent neighbours, not all of whom had any better right than he to lead a Highland march. 'The bluidy brides o' Buchat' was followed by 'Scotland the brave' and 'Tam i' the kirk' before the men, largely gathered from the Castle Buchat and Blairfeshie estates' staffs, were thoroughly blown out, and in need of their whisky, the sole and irreplaceable fuel of such events.

Immediately, four young girls, in tartans of red, green, blue and garish yellow, scampered onto the dais, which had been scrupulously scrubbed down after the rain and re-anointed with sawdust. They were followed by more sets, of seemingly identical girls, all accompanied by a dour piper of great age, dwarfed by a massive fur busby beneath which only his thick red lips could be seen, dripping with spittle.

'Will you toss the caber now, James?'

'What?' It was Hamish Reid, the chairman of the Young Conservatives, an eager young man with buck teeth and sticking out ears.

'You've been entered first with the caber. They want to start. It's over by the bothy.'

'It must be a joke.'

'No. You've got special sponsorship from old Mrs Field. We had the Young Conservatives' whist drive at Blairfeshie House last week. It was my idea. She's promised to give a hundred pounds for every yard you throw it.'

Masking his true feelings, James slashed a wide smile across the front of his face, and took off his jacket. 'Well done, Hamish,' he said. 'Let's get started.'

It was a bloody tree trunk! James stared at it. 'You can't mean that?'

'No, no. That's a tree trunk. It's over here.'

It was still bad enough. Quite a crowd had gathered round, despite the arrival of the twelfth dancing group. 'Here we go.' He managed to limber it onto his shoulder, just kept his footing, and locked his fingers painfully under the base.

'Ready?'

'I'm ready,' he gasped.

'One tip,' whispered a bearded veteran, edging forward.

'Make it a quick one.'

'Think of it as your enemy. You're throwing him right over a precipice. Imagine . . .'

'I've got it,' said James, in a croak, and then threw Fred Tevis so high and far that the whole of the Glenbuchat Young Conservatives' overdraft was paid off in one deliriously applauded swoop.

Chapter Twenty-two

By Sunday night, he was aching in every limb. But the time to part from Lucy, and his children, grew inexorably nearer. In a panic, James had cancelled his late Sunday night seat, booking himself onto the first flight on Monday morning so as to spend a third night wrapped in Lucy's soft white arms. He hardly slept at all, gazing at her face, its contours lit by the moonlight, her lips quivering sometimes as she breathed against his cheek. The curl of her lashes, that crease in her neck . . . he had never experienced anything like this frantic all-consuming passion. It was as if he wanted to blend with her, to be assimilated, two bodies turned to one. Once when, at dawn, she turned over with a heavy sigh, her cheeks flushed and pink, he cupped her left breast in his hand, feeling the outline fade as their body temperatures matched, their flesh becoming one. Was he crying? She turned over, kissing away a tear and drawing his body deep into hers, running her fingers lovingly over him until he seemed to burst within her.

'Two whole weeks apart?' His voice was husky with fatigue.

'Eleven days, and think what fun you'll have at Chequers,' she said, straightening his tie.

'No postal deliveries?' he asked, sternly.

She shook her head. 'And no slaving all day over hot secretaries either!' she replied, giving him a final lingering kiss before going upstairs to wake the children.

'When's Mummy coming back?' asked Sandy plaintively as James wound down the car window and prepared to drive away from the little group huddled on the front steps.

'I'm not certain,' said James. 'She'll probably telephone you from America.'

'By satellite?'

'Your father will miss his plane,' said Lucy firmly. 'Wave goodbye to him.'

In fact he made it with nearly a minute to spare.

'Typical Tory,' growled Iain Mackenzie, who had been up in his own constituency, from across the aisle. 'No consideration. Make everyone else wait! Seen the papers?' He thrust one of the tabloids across. 'You'll be out very soon, I reckon.'

'LORDY ME' screamed the headline. 'Prime Minister bribes Foreign Secretary with promise of hereditary earldom.' James read the story with increasing amazement. It purported to be a verbatim transcript of a conversation between the two titans of the Government, in which the Foreign Secretary confessed to reservations about the *No. 4 Enabling* Bill, but was persuaded to support it once the Prime Minister's offer of a future earldom was improved to the extent of making it hereditary.

'It's time your lot had a rest,' said Mackenzie. 'In an asylum! I think you've all gone soft in the head.' It was difficult for James to know how to reply. He was beginning to think the same thing himself.

As soon as he reached the Commons, he found his fellow Whips already assembling for a crisis meeting. Walter Meyrick, stinking of his pipe, was glowering at each new arrival, his head throbbing with the dull ache of approaching failure.

'There you are,' he snapped at James. 'That's the worst about you Scottish Members, always travelling up and down when you're wanted! Now this week has got to see Boynton falling into line and that old cretin Moore-Talbot up and about. I expect you to see to it.'

'He'll have his work cut out with the last part,' murmured his deputy, scanning the first Press Association tapes which Mrs Davies had just brought in. 'See for yourself. Sir Cuthbert died last night.'

The passing of Sir Cuthbert stimulated a wave of nostalgia for the England that he had seemed to represent, the England of village cricket, Sunday matins and furled umbrellas. Under an unexpectedly aggressive photograph of a young Lieutenant Cuthbert Moore-Talbot in khaki battledress, the *Telegraph* devoted a whole page to his obituary, beginning, *'A kinsman to the Earls of Shrewsbury and Drogheda, Charles Cuthbert St Aubyn Moore-Talbot was the only son of Major-General Sir Wrekin Moore-Talbot KCVO, and scion of a squirearchical family long settled at Great Fitchingham Hall in Norfolk and Groby Place, Bedfordshire,'* and ending *'He married, in 1943, Lady Maud Thorold, only child of the 9th and last Earl Thorold. There were no children.'*

At Westminster, however, the talk was more of majorities and choosing candidates in the forthcoming by-election. The late representative having been a Conservative, it rested with the present Government to initiate the by-election by moving the appropriate writ in the House of Commons. A fierce internal debate raged as to whether it was better to proceed with the *No. 4* Bill with a maximum majority of four (assuming Nick came into line) or to risk an immediate by-election which would restore their majority to five if they won, but decrease it to three if the electors of Bedfordshire (Woburn) should be so thoughtless as to return an Opposition candidate of whatever hue. Naturally all three Opposition parties accompanied this private quarrel with loud displays of public outrage, constantly calling for an immediate end to the temporary disenfranchisement of the wise and loyal inhabitants of the late Sir Cuthbert's constituency, each party proclaiming their total certainty that they would sweep the poll. The British Nationals even went so far as to leaflet every single voter on the subject, giving rise to some careful arithmetic by Walter Meyrick in case they should forget to include the cost of this in their subsequent electoral expenses.

By Friday, just as James was leaving the House to pack before driving down to Chequers, it was finally announced from on high that they would delay calling the by-election at least until after the crucial vote on the eleventh of July.

'So now it's up to you, Nick,' said James, passing his friend in the central lobby.

'I've told you all a dozen times,' smiled Nick equably. 'I'm voting against it. I think that's clear enough?'

'Then we'll both be in the soup,' said James.

'I know,' was the sorrowful reply. 'I'm really sorry that it affects your new career. But I'm sure you understand. I cannot support something I believe to be wrong.'

'You are the only Tory to say so.'

'Maybe. But I'm not the only one to think it if the papers are anything to go by. There's the Foreign Secretary for one, and one or two others lurking in the woodwork.'

'If so, the Government will fall.'

'Why? There'd be a vote of confidence, and of course I'd support that.'

'Toady's saying he can't proceed without this Bill. That would be a genuine wreck with no survivors.'

Nick laughed. 'Personally I could do with a spell on a desert island. But you watch out! Wrecks come in all disguises. This month's shiny new launch can easily become next month's rusting hulk. To change the subject, is it true you're in the Chequers crowd this weekend?' James nodded. 'Quite the coming man, and all at once,' said Nick, with a broad grin. 'Good luck to you. I'm very pleased.'

'Why this sudden cheeriness? Don't tell me you've got another promotion!'

Nick laughed. 'Oh no!' he said. 'Just a late spring! Have a nice weekend.' With a cheerful wave, he walked on down the corridor chuckling. David Brotherton, pausing to watch them from a bend in the massive staircase, more than matched their cheerful mood. 'Let them laugh,' he told himself, 'so long as Toady falls.' It was becoming something of an obsession.

Punctually at seven, James turned his car down the side drive of Chequers and halted at the barrier.

'Name?' The metallic enquiry presumably came via a microphone from behind the shaded glass of the police booth.

'Hepburn.'

'Be with you in a minute, sir.'

He waited patiently. After a while, two armed policemen wearing flak jackets sauntered out of the booth, one wheeling a mounted mirror-jack for checking the underside of his car.

'Would you mind opening the bonnet, sir?' said the second man, going round to open the car-boot while James fiddled with the catch.

'All clear. Do you know the way?' James shook his head. 'Go straight down to the second cross-roads. Turn right and then left into the front courtyard. You'll find someone there to receive you.' He waved James on. It was like going back to school, the same dry mouth and beating heart, the same empty tarmac road, the same empty green paddocks, the same (or nearly the same) grim red-brick Jacobean pile. Except now by the door, in place of 'Dr Death', his headmaster, with his ambiguous smile, was the much less oppressive figure of a sturdy policeman carrying a sawn-off shotgun in one hand, and a mobile phone in the other.

'Mr Hepburn? Welcome aboard!' He had long trailing moustaches and inquisitive eyes. 'Go straight in, will you, sir? Someone will deal with your bags and the car.'

'Thank you.'

A short smiling woman with grey hair swept back in a bun appeared in the doorway and put out her hand. 'Hello,' she said. 'I'm Elizabeth. Anything you need, just ask me. I'll take you to your room.' She led him up some dark stairs, across a landing overlooking a tall room plastered with portraits, and up another flight ending in a small lobby with several doors. 'You're in here,' she said kindly, opening the nearest. It was a bright room, with a flowered wallpaper and the heavy oak bed had a counterpane in matching material. 'You're sharing the Disraeli bathroom with Mr and Mrs Meyrick,' she said. 'It's the fourth door on the left. This is a hanging cupboard, and there's a wash-basin behind there.'

'It looks very comfortable,' he said. 'Who else is staying?'

She paused in the doorway and pulled out a list. 'There's the Meyricks, of course, and Mr Dutton, on his own this time, poor man.'

James nodded. 'I recognized his car in the drive.'

'Then there's Lord and Lady Berington, she's chairman of the Prime Minister's constituency, and Mrs Durham, Lord Berington's sister. She's an artist. The others arrive tomorrow.' Her pocket phone began to buzz. 'I'm wanted,' she said. 'There'll be cocktails in the long gallery at seven-thirty prompt. Someone will fetch you. Don't forget, now. If you need anything, just ask for Elizabeth, that's me.' And she hurried off down the corridor, brushing past a policeman on patrol, his stubby machine-pistol dangling on a leather strap round his neck. James shut his bedroom door and sat down to wait for his suitcase to arrive. He had telephoned Lucy and the children every evening and every morning since he had left, but still he was longing to return to her. The fruits of political success were very unappetizing indeed. And yet wasn't this the acme of his ambition: to be the personal guest of the Prime Minister, a member of his Government, with his feet firmly placed upon the ladder of power, which led seductively upwards towards the Cabinet table? Wasn't this why he had left his job at the bank, trudged up and down those dreary rows of cottages, soliciting votes in that biting February rain, mouthing platitudes as a small price to pay for delights such as this? Surely it wouldn't always seem so pointless and inconvenient?

Chapter Twenty-three

'So you're James Hepburn.' He was seated well down the table at dinner, with the Prime Minister's Private Secretary on one side, and Mrs Durham on the other. It was she who started the conversation.

'I am,' he agreed uncertainly. 'I don't think we've met?' She was a slight, slim woman, perhaps in her middle thirties, with pale golden hair cut short at the back.

'Oh, but I feel we have,' she said, 'because Nick Boynton used to go out with my youngest sister, Ruth, and she often talked about you.'

'I'm very fond of Nick,' he said, reflecting that this was a minority view in his present environment.

'Yes, he's a darling, isn't he, but so sad.'

'Sad?'

'Yes,' she said. 'I would say so. Perhaps because he bottles everything up. Such an English fault, wouldn't you say?'

James shrugged. 'Perhaps he doesn't choose to burden the rest of us with his private thoughts.'

'There!' she said. 'I can see you're another one. But Nick's such good company. And such a wonderful head. I drew him for his mother. His bone structure is perfect. It's the complexion which presents something of a challenge.'

'Ah.'

'And of course, I was at art school with your wife.' This was indeed news. He had no idea that Susie had ever shown the least inclination towards the arts. 'She didn't stay long.'

'This was . . . ?'

'The Byam Shaw. Tell me, do you draw?'

'No.' He shook his head regretfully. Lucy would be tucking the children up now, putting out the light.

'But you can speak . . . I mean, being a politician and all?' She was positively laughing at him. He made a conscious effort to concentrate and turned more towards her. Her own bone structure was pretty perfect, encompassing high cheekbones, a long straight nose and a small but determined chin. 'That's better!' she said. 'I'm Victoria Durham, since you didn't seem to be paying much attention during the introductions.'

He mimed a bow. 'I tried to draw once,' he said. 'It was not a success.'

'So you turned to politics instead?'

'Only by chance. I had no burning desire to preach at Westminster. I'm really a banker.'

'I'm sure that's the best qualification,' she said. 'Like being Pope. They shouldn't choose you unless you say you don't want it.'

'It's hard to imagine anyone wanting to be an MP nowadays,' he said. 'All the real decisions are taken in Brussels. We just get the blame.'

'And yet so many people do seem to want it!' she murmured with an ironical tilt to her eyebrows. 'Our distinguished host always says it's an excellent club!'

'So where do you paint?'

She looked him up and down. 'You'd make a good model,' she said. 'You have the three essential ingredients.'

'Namely?'

She ran her tongue round her lips. 'Profile, patience and danger.'

'Danger?' he laughed incredulously. 'I must be the least dangerous person in the world.'

'Not to me,' she said lightly, and turned to talk to

the mournful Ralph Dutton who was on her other side, leaving James staring at the soft curve of her bare shoulders, and the delicate line of her backbone before the stiff organza dress hid the rest of her body from view.

'Some of these votes are getting totally out of hand.' The Prime Minister's Private Secretary, on his left, had a long gloomy face and dreadful breath. 'We're going to lose one soon at this rate. You're one of the Whips, aren't you? What news on that front?'

'Who knows?' said James truthfully. 'Human beings are less predictable than computers.'

'But just as bloody complicated, eh?' said his neighbour, leaning close.

'Turbot, sir?' A nautical-looking waiter was grappling with a massive silver platter piled with gleaming lumps of glazed fish swimming in a red sea of sauce. James helped himself.

'So where is Susie?' demanded Victoria, turning back to him. 'It's not like her to miss a grand party.'

'She's in New York.'

'Oh yes,' she drawled. 'I think I did hear that. Are you sad?' James needed a moment to come to terms with this directness. He had three glasses of untouched wine beside him, the sherry for the soup, the Hock for the fish, and now some claret for the lamb cutlets which were making steady progress down the table towards him. He chose the claret and sipped it thoughtfully. 'No-one would call you a drinker, would they?' she said, looking at the full glasses. 'So, come on. Is your heart lying in bleeding fragments or are you having a whale of a time with a dusky bimbette?'

He tried a light smile. 'I'd much rather talk about Mr Durham. Where is he, for example?'

'I'm afraid he's dead,' she said. 'No . . .' She was

decisive in brushing away his embarrassed apologies. 'We had a glorious five years together and then, quite suddenly, he had a heart attack playing tennis. Just one of those things. He was a lovely man.'

'Do you have any children?' He was desperate to find something palatable to make amends and wash away the desolate look in her pale blue eyes.

'No.' She shook her head. 'Wasn't that bad luck? We'd just got round to thinking about it. And then he was gone.'

'And you live . . . ?'

She looked hard at him. 'Certainly I live! But if you mean where, I have a little house with a studio off the Vale, in Chelsea. I hope you'll come and see it if your bimbette can spare you!' She was laughing at him again. 'Men are so transparent. I could see you were daydreaming about her when you were *supposed* to be making polite conversation to me!'

'Of course not,' he said weakly, and was profoundly grateful when their hostess tapped a fork on her plate and demanded that they should all go out into the garden where strawberries and cream awaited them, accompanied by a string quartet, who had set up their music stands in a leafy rose-bower under the watchful eyes of the police marksmen on the roof.

The next morning dawned as bright on the peaceful meadows of Buckinghamshire as elsewhere in the country. The woods above Chequers were lit with shafting rays of rosy light, as the morning sun breasted the eastern hill and bleary-eyed policemen handed over their weapons to the freshly shaved colleagues who came to replace them. In the office beside the kitchen, Elizabeth, fresh from her morning shower, and cradling the first of many cups of scalding tea, reviewed the day's plans with the naval chef and the duty superintendent. Behind them, two ratings were preparing the Prime Ministerial breakfast tray, while another bustled in and out bearing plates and cutlery for the dining-room across the passage. All over the great house, curtains were being drawn and ashtrays emptied.

James, still half-asleep, dozily watched the stray beams of light that had penetrated the combined efforts of shutters and curtains. A butterfly, celebrating its brief existence, was dancing in and out of the warm light, and somewhere a bee was angrily demanding release to continue its search for the pollen awaiting its attention among the roses. What would Sandy be thinking now?

A sharp tap on his door was followed by a stealthy entry and then the scalding blast of light as the curtains and shutters were flung open by a round little Wren dressed in a starched white apron over her uniform.

'Good morning, Mr Hepburn,' she said crisply, placing a cup of tea with two shortbread biscuits balanced on its saucer beside him. 'A lovely morning for the Prime Minister's birthday.'

'Is it his birthday?' mumbled James, shielding his eyes beneath the sheet, ashamed of his stubbled untidiness.

'Oh yes!' she said with all the gaiety of one yet to reach twenty. 'Fifty-seven today. Chef's made a ginormous cake. It's a surprise.'

He peeped out at her. 'But I haven't got him a present.'

She smiled down at the tousled red hair. 'You could nip into Thame. That's got nice shops.'

'Thank you for the tea.'

'Breakfast's in forty minutes,' she said over her shoulder as she whisked up the dinner suit he had abandoned on the floor. 'I'll get these pressed for you. If you want a bath, you'd better look sharp. I'm about to call Mr and Mrs Meyrick and he always spends *hours* in the bathroom!' With an expert double-wiggle of her bottom, she was gone.

When he reached the dining-room, a glum panelled room facing north and enlivened only by some Victorian seascapes, Lady Berington was tucking into a plateful of fried eggs and kidneys.

'Morning!' she cried, waving a friendly fork at him. 'You look as if you've slept well.'

'Thank you,' he said, resolving to have a quick look in a mirror at the earliest opportunity. 'And you?'

'I did my best,' she said. 'My husband snores like a steam engine.'

He took some bacon and a grilled tomato from the dishes presided over by a sterner and less nubile colleague of his morning visitor. 'I believe one can tell them loudly to shut up and they do.'

'I've tried that,' said Lady Berington. 'He never pays the slightest attention. Story of my life.' It seemed highly unlikely. They munched in silence.

'More coffee, sir?' It was the girl from upstairs, now wielding a large silver jug.

'Yes, please.'

She filled his cup and marched smartly out of the room. 'Only wearing an effing wedding ring, isn't he!' she remarked morosely to her friend who was washing plates in the pantry.

'Shouldn't think that'd stop him,' replied her friend, adding another dish to the pile. 'Seeing as he's a *politician*. GOOD MORNING, MRS STONE,' she added loudly as Elizabeth hurried past them, her ear fixed to her little black telephone.

Elizabeth nodded vaguely. The first of the day's new guests was stuck at the checkpoint, having given the wrong registration number for his car. Her own office was down a side corridor beyond the great hall. There she found her secretary had already opened the post, and was busily typing out a fresh seating plan, the tenth, for the birthday dinner.

'There's a bishop down at the gate with the wrong car number. Can you check with his office?'

'Will they be open on a Saturday?'

'Just try, dear. To please me?' She hurried out again to check the flowers. One of the policemen was watering the vase in the Baldwin parlour. 'Careful,' she said, watching him slop water onto the marquetry table top. 'You'll have to wipe that.'

'Don't worry.' He held up a tea towel. 'I've come prepared. Hello . . . here's someone wants you.'

It was James, hovering uncertainly in her wake.

'Yes, Mr Hepburn?'

'Is it really the Prime Minister's birthday today?'

'It certainly is, though he doesn't like to make too much of it.'

'I really ought to go and get him a present.'

'Don't worry about that,' said Elizabeth cheerfully. 'I keep a store of useful bits and pieces in my cupboard. I can sell you boxes of chocolates, or a nice bottle of his favourite kirsch, a choice of paisley ties or even a pen set!' She laughed delightedly. 'I like to be prepared.'

He grinned. 'And if there was a change of government?'

'Aha!' She tapped her nose. 'Mine is a capacious cupboard. I still even have some of Lord Wilson's favourite cigars.'

'There you are.' It was Victoria, looking svelte and fresh with her short blond hair held down by a blue Alice band. 'I'm going over to see the horses. Want to come?'

'Fine.' He slipped into step beside her, nodding at the armed guard who saluted them as they crossed the terrace and walked slowly across the lawn to where two dappled mares were grazing beside the fence.

'Hello.' She took an apple out of her bag and offered it in her palm to the nearest. The large flapping lips parted to reveal a set of ravenous yellow teeth dripping with saliva. 'I'm serious about drawing you,' she said, stroking the horse's cheek, and then running one finger softly up and down its muzzle.

'I take it as a great compliment,' he said politely. 'I've never seen an artist's studio. Does it have a north window?'

'Certainly,' she said. 'It is well equipped in every way. Number two, Mulberry Mews. I'm there painting most evenings. Just drop in, do.'

The second horse came over, rolling its eyes and nudging its companion. 'I've even got something for you,' she said, producing the shortbread biscuits from her tea tray. The horse snatched them, scattering crumbs everywhere. 'Do you ride?'

'Not really. Horses give me hay fever.'

'Poor you.' She touched him lightly on the sleeve. 'Let's go back in. I need to find someone to explain all this fuss in the newspapers about this Bill they're all rabbiting on about.'

'Come and tell me when you have,' he said, 'because I don't understand the first thing about it.'

'I shall,' she said, and led the way back to the terrace where they found a bearded man in a purple shirt and crumpled dog-collar glowering into space, being solicitously but unsuccessfully plied with coffee and conversation by the Prime Minister's Private Secretary.

The birthday dinner was not a success. It was soon evident, even before lunch, that the Prime Minister and his wife were locked in some private quarrel of their own. Neither spoke much to their guests, and when James shyly presented his box of chocolate truffles, expertly wrapped in blue tissue by Elizabeth, it was scarcely acknowledged. They all spent the afternoon watching tennis on the television, huddled together in a small dark room on the first floor, anxious only to avoid precipitating further discord. James rang Lucy after tea, but having already warned her that the Chequers telephone would certainly be bugged, they could only exchange self-conscious platitudes on the weather and his children's immediate health. Deeply dissatisfied, he sank into a state of morose gloom not assisted by the news that the evening's entertainment was to consist of more music, in this case a series of scenes from modern English operas linked by a comic commentary devised by his hostess.

'So you're a junior Whip?' At dinner he had the new Home Secretary's wife on his right, a mousy woman with a broad face caked with make-up, wearing an orange flounced dress.

'Yes. It's very interesting.'

'You must feel very honoured to be here.'

'I do.'

'We don't know what to do now we've been offered Dorneywood. Our own place is in Gloucestershire, you know.'

'A beautiful county.'

'All our neighbours are Royals.'

'That must be nice.'

She turned away to her other neighbour, leaving James toying with his glass. The bishop, on his other side, flatly refused to address a word to anyone, so James spent his time trying to avoid Victoria's conspiratorial smiles from across the table. Why on earth had he accepted this invitation when he could be in Scotland, in Lucy's arms, and with his children? But could he actually have refused? Was it any worse than those interminable banking evenings, entertaining the foreign clients? After dinner, sitting through the musical entertainment, it didn't take more than the first operatic scene to decide him firmly in favour of bankers.

'I saw you!' whispered Victoria in the interval. 'Snoozing away.'

'Would that I had,' he said fervently. 'It would have been a compliment if I slept. This sort of music keeps me awake all night, with my hair standing on end.'

'You can always come and chat to me,' she said cosily. 'I'll find a way to calm you down.'

He smiled past her, lost for words. But when safely back in his room, he sought his own consolation by carefully packing his clothes ready for an early departure for London, and the privacy of his own telephone, so that he could chat peacefully to Lucy, free from official eavesdroppers.

Chapter Twenty-four

'So how was Chequers?' Nick was propping up the bar in Blunt's when James came in to join him for lunch after a long Monday morning in committee with assorted Scottish Office functionaries.

James pulled a face. 'So-so.'

'Gosh, very grand. Rupert was green with envy.'

'Good. He can go next time.'

'Good grub?'

'Yes, all of that was excellent.'

'I can see Toady might be a rather trying host. What about Mrs T?'

'Grisly.'

'I can imagine. Champagne?'

'Thanks.' They moved to the banquette.

This was an irregular tradition, a quiet lunch when working topics were tacitly ignored. James would no more have raised the *No. 4* Bill than Nick would have mentioned milk quotas. But it helped to maintain their friendship, providing the chance to put the rest of their lives on one side, and find a quiet pleasure in chatting inconsequentially about their shared interests.

Today, however, Nick looked uncomfortable, and deliberately steered James, who was his guest in this particular club, to the furthest table in the upstairs dining-room, the one in the bow window separated from the others by the long serving table that also carried the day's choice of hors d'oeuvres.

'What'll you have?'

James studied the menu, and said, 'Smoked salmon, please, and then the stew.

'Vegetables, sir?' The steward was a kindly rotund man with a slight lisp. 'We've got some lovely marrow. Or Chef's made a special ratatouille.' He licked his lips in anticipation.

'The marrow please, and new potatoes.'

'Very wise choice, sir. And Mr Boynton?'

'Vichyssoise, and the toad-in-the-hole.'

'And the ratatouille, sir?'

'No fear. I'll have mashed potatoes and lots of gravy please.' Whatever disappointment he may have felt, the steward bowed delightedly and hurried away to summon their food.

'James.' Nick sounded tentative, nervous even.

'Mmm?'

'There's a lot of talk about you and Susie.'

'Really?'

'It's nobody's business, of course. But if you did want to talk about it . . .'

'Is that why we're stuck in this corner?'

'Yes.'

James sighed. 'I did tell you that we were getting divorced.'

'That little turd Fred Tevis, I suppose?'

'Holed in one.'

'What a bastard.'

'He couldn't have done it on his own.'

'I like Susie,' said Nick. 'You mustn't fall out too severely. That'd only make it worse for Sandy, and Jennie.'

'I know.' Nick was Sandy's godfather, and, as such, James acknowledged to himself, he had a perfectly valid interest in the coming upheaval. 'I'll try not to. But it's not always as easy as people think. You wait till you get married.'

Nick flashed him a bright smile. 'Plenty of time for that,' he said. 'Maybe you were in too much of a hurry?'

'Maybe so.' A glistening plate of fish was slid dexterously in front of him. 'Thank you.' He picked up the half lemon and squeezed it hard.

'Black pepper?'

'After you.' There was silence for a space, while they ate.

'Can you believe he thought any children they might have could inherit from our family trust?'

Nick chuckled. 'Cheeky!'

'*Cheeky!* Halfwitted more like. It makes me worried to have a man who doesn't understand simple tax law as chief operating officer of an outfit like Schumann and Goldwater.'

'I wouldn't pursue that analogy too far,' murmured Nick. 'We wouldn't want to apply it to our own dear Chancellor of the Exchequer, would we?'

'No.' James smiled.

'You'll get joint custody?'

'I imagine so.'

'Now, James.' Nick leant forward seriously. 'Be careful. You're a good father, and I know you love them both. You may have to be firm on that point. Like her as I do, I can imagine Susie going all soppy with the lawyers and saying a child's place is with his mummy. Watch out. They need you as well as her, maybe more so.'

'Don't worry,' said James grimly. 'I'd fight for them, as for nothing else. Oh! This looks excellent.' Their main courses had arrived, discreetly unveiled by the beaming steward. James's stew was crammed with moist dumplings glistening with sheer well-being.

'At least it doesn't put you off your food,' said Nick approvingly. 'Another drop of claret?'

'So.' James at last leant back in his seat. 'You haven't told me what you're up to. Something's going right. You look really happy.'

Nick's eyelids flickered. 'I am,' he said. 'I'm loving

my work at the Ministry, and I'm planning another book on arts and crafts.'

'Was that Jane Whitehead you were with at the Ferrers do?'

'Certainly was. She likes you, by the way.'

'Are you bringing her to the dreaded Smith Square Ball?'

'I am *not*. I wouldn't take my worst enemy to that. Now, that's enough fishing. I want to hear all about Toad Hall. Who else was there?'

Chapter Twenty-five

They buried Sir Cuthbert on the following Wednesday. Having been nearly 17 per cent of the Government's majority, he might have rated a couple of junior Cabinet Ministers. But as the grand old man of British politics, and last emblem of the age of altruism, four ex-Prime Ministers, six dukes and half a regiment of Scots Guards accompanied the old man to his final resting-place, under the flagstones of the side aisle of St Anne's, the parish church of Groby. The front three pews had been kept empty for the royal stand-ins, James being unexpectedly asked to represent Prince Arthur. The Lord Lieutenant, a tall old soldier called Colonel Banbury, was there to welcome him at the door.

'You go in just before Sir Neil Bond here who is representing Her Majesty.' It was the first time James had seen the fabled courtier whose influence over politics was popularly supposed to border on the unconstitutional. They shook hands gravely.

'The best of old England,' murmured Sir Neil, looking over James's shoulder at the church whose walls, though venerable, were showing distinct signs of decay.

'Fifteenth century, isn't it?' enquired James politely.

'I was speaking of Sir Cuthbert,' said the courtier, shifting his gaze to James's tie.

'Come along,' said Colonel Banbury. 'You're on!'

James walked hesitantly into the long church, past the ranks of uniformed soldiers, his steps ringing in the grim silence as some heads in the congregation turned to see who was joining them. One or two faces smiled, but most were strangers, and elderly strangers at that. The overwhelming colours were black and white. Black clothes and white hair.

He had hardly taken his seat, followed by Sir Neil in the front pew, than a heavy rhythmic tread announced the arrival of the coffin. It seemed pitifully small, considering Sir Cuthbert's buoyant presence. Someone started sobbing somewhere behind James. And then the voice of the tall organ, whose gaily painted pipes dominated the chancel, thundered out the opening hymn and they all stood.

'O Valiant Hearts,

Who to your Glory came, . . .'

Even James, who prided himself on a healthy scepticism when it came to group emotion, found his throat constricting, as the whole church echoed with the sound of all these old people, their voices apparently undimmed by the passing of their age, their eyes shining in the celebration of their dead friend's promotion to the paradise that he, at least, believed to await him.

'In my Father's house are many mansions . . .' An impossibly ancient cleric, clutching grimly at the brass lectern, was reading the lesson with a thin firm voice. Sir Cuthbert should feel at home then! *'Were it not so, I would have told you . . .'* Not, thought James irreverently, if You were Cabinet Secretary, You wouldn't. But at least one may reasonably hope that the Ancient of Days has no need to resort to economy with His Truth.

More hymns, followed by a rousing address from the Prime Minister who, delivering his speech without notes, ended by declaring: 'And so we bid farewell to a great soldier and statesman, a politician whose wisdom and experience will be sorely missed from the corridors of power, where we, who have to struggle on without him, will all be the poorer without this fine countryman's sagacious advice. When shall we look upon his like again? Who will contradict me when I say that when the Almighty had made dear Cuthbert, surely He broke the mould.' Then the Last Post, and Sir Cuthbert's peers clustered awkwardly round the newly excavated hole into the vault below and watched his coffin lowered tenderly by eight gorgeously decorated soldiers until a dull thud announced it had reached the bottom. Someone no doubt would descend later to stack him neatly alongside his ancestors. But for the moment, it was enough. And, politely waiting for first Sir Neil and then James, still wrapped in their borrowed glory as royal representatives, to leave, the congregation tottered out, variously on sticks, walking frames and even on each others' arms, into the light summer rain.

'Thank God that's over,' said the Prime Minister, coming over to speak to his youngest Whip. 'Back to work.'

'I did enjoy the weekend,' said James untruthfully. 'Thank you so much for inviting me.'

'Not a bit, my boy.' The Prime Minister was wiping his glasses on a mottled silk handkerchief. 'It was a great pleasure to have you. Walter says you're doing a good job. We just need you to get young Boynton into line. I can't sack him now until this is all over. See to it, won't you?'

There was something in this that made James pause and stifle what might otherwise have been the automatic acquiescence of a junior politician to the country's elected leader. Instead he said, 'Well, he does feel very strongly about this. And so,' ploughing on despite his leader's reptilian frown, 'did Sir Cuthbert.'

'Sir Cuthbert!' The Prime Minister let out a loud and liquid snort of derision. 'What did he ever know of anything? Ah! Excuse me, young man. I must go and pay my respects to the widow.'

Staring after the Prime Minister's waddling form, James was amazed to find himself regretting his promotion. Not overly ambitious, he had accepted the change of ladder from banking to politics with complete equanimity, even fatalism. It was not only his wife who accused him of being unemotional to the point of coldness. But it was in his nature to want to do well, and perhaps also to be seen to do well, at whatever job claimed his time. His very public success, so soon, had therefore been a source of considerable though strictly private satisfaction. Unlike Dutton, he had not succumbed to the temptation of already naming his future Cabinet; he had just cast a covert eye over those junior ministerial posts that were likely to become available whether through the promotion or dismissal of their current incumbents. And now, having only just secured his first promotion, he was actually regretting it.

He regretted it a sight more when, on returning to the Whips' office, Mrs Davies wordlessly presented him with a large manila envelope. Slitting it open, his mouth dropped at what emerged: six glossy photographs of Nick and a young man, Nick kissing him, Nick astride him, Nick actually . . . There was also a single piece of A4 paper. It gave the young man's name and address, and his date of birth. He was just *fifteen*.

Hurriedly he thrust the photographs back into the envelope. Walter Meyrick bustled in, his arms full of the day's newspapers. He stopped and stared at James.

'You've seen them?'

'These?' James glared at him. He could feel his arms shaking.

'He's been a naughty boy.'

'You don't expect me to use these?'

Walter threw the newspapers onto a chair, and sat down. 'Look at it this way,' he said in the carefully controlled voice of reason. 'Of course we shouldn't condone a crime, especially one which could, would, command a custodial sentence. And a minister too! But perhaps Boynton's gratitude at our suppressing these might possibly lead him to want to show some matching generosity . . . perhaps *even* to the extent of supporting his own party, for example?'

'That's blackmail!'

Walter parted his thick lips in a smile. 'I thought it sounded more like closing ranks to protect a *fwiend*,' he lisped. 'We all like Nick. I don't want to see him pilloried in the dock. Do you?'

'And if I refuse?'

'Then I don't think I could risk being a party to hiding this. Too many people in the know . . . the classic recipe for a scandal. I must confess I thought you'd *want* to help him.'

'You wouldn't dare! A scandal would finish the Government.'

'On the contrary,' said Meyrick. 'It would have a very salutary effect on other potential dissidents. There's a couple in the Cabinet might like to reflect on what I've got in my files. And it would distract the tabloids. You know they love a really juicy titbit. And they don't come much juicier than this.' He all but suppressed a tiny giggle. 'And then, if we could prevail upon the court to deny him bail, perhaps to prevent him from corrupting other minors, why he couldn't vote against us, could he? That's the beauty of a criminal prosecution, there's no parliamentary immunity. In fact, I really think we might do better to let the law take its course.'

'It would kill his mother.'

Meyrick nodded. 'That's rather what I thought. That's why I'm so hoping you'll grab this chance of saving him.'

'I think it stinks. This comes via Special Branch anyway. What's to stop them using it later?'

'Do you know?' said Meyrick cheerfully. 'I do believe you're coming round to my way of thinking! Just show him the pictures. He'll understand all right. You can promise him complete protection on my authority. If he votes with us, that is. And he can stay in office.'

'Like your promise to Paine, I suppose? It stinks!' James was quivering with anger. It was all he could do not to strike out at the older man beside him, discussing such evil with so treacherously smooth a manner.

'The "black arts" of the Whips' office?' said the imperturbable Meyrick in a mocking voice. 'You'll come to enjoy it all in time.'

'Never!'

'Then you won't hold office for very long,' retorted Meyrick, losing patience and picking up his newspapers again. 'Heaven knows, I don't do this job for my own amusement. But it has to be done, and if I'm doing it, it will be done effectively. Now I'm going for a quiet smoke. Tell me later how you get on, there's a good chap.' He went into his inner office, and silently closed the door. James stalked out to the reception area.

'Mrs Davies?'

She looked curiously up at him. 'Yes, dear?'

'Did you set this up?'

She didn't reply at first, but continued to tap away at her computer. Then she said, 'It's so important to have one's priorities straight, isn't it? I can see you're a nice young man, and you've got determination too, underneath that quiet manner. You want to succeed, but sometimes you don't like the methods. We all start like that, I suppose.' She paused to stir the cup of tea beside her keyboard. 'But there comes a time when we have to choose between being amiable failures or finding the toughness needed for success. Mr Boynton is committing a messy little crime. The Government is trying to administer this country's affairs in an honourable way amid great difficulties. I know which side my priorities lie.'

'Is that a long way of saying "yes"?'

Again she met his gaze without flinching. 'My friend in Special Branch has his own methods. It's not my place to question them. But yes, I got the evidence for you. I want you to succeed. But if you don't, assuredly someone else will. And what will you have gained by that?'

'I'll have kept my self-respect.'

She laughed out loud. 'In *this* place? I've always thought that a very pompous word for pride. And you aren't pompous at all, Mr Hepburn. Whoever heard of a politician with *self-respect*?' She started to laugh again. 'Let me make you a nice cup of tea.'

'No thanks,' he said gloomily. 'I'll have to go and think about this.'

'You do that,' she said, and as he walked away, still clutching the envelope, he heard her chuckling away to herself and repeating the word *'self-respect'* as if he had made a memorable joke.

But what was he to do? He didn't doubt that Walter Meyrick would indeed allow, perhaps even encourage, a prosecution. There was a ghastly logic in what he had said. Sexual scandals were, if not the publicly accepted prerogative of the Conservative Party, then certainly not so unusual as to leave permanent mud on anyone other than the perpetrator. He himself held no strong views on the sexual mores of others. But Nick's mother was a different matter, an old lady who doted on her mercurial son. Ignoring the various other duties of the day, he left the Commons and walked back towards Tothill Street, deep in thought.

Priorities! There was no dilemma in accepting Susie's departure for all the pain it must cause his children. There was no dilemma in throwing himself wholeheartedly into Lucy's arms, whatever the cost to both of them. But this! This was the scalding truth behind the many clichéd insults about politicians, the shaming depth to which he had allowed himself to sink, thoughtlessly allowing himself to believe that he was safely incorruptible in a profession in which his father had surely remained honourable. For the sake of an inconclusive, perhaps irrelevant, piece of minor legislation, Nick, his closest friend, was now ensnared in a nightmarish dilemma of his own: to be forced to deny his conscience, whether right or wrong, or face savage disgrace. And he, James, he was the appointed executioner of his colleagues' machinations. He could resign, leaving Nick to the courts and the press, or he could do as they wanted, and see his friend humiliated by his own hand. And gradually, as he walked, his anger turned cold, and he began, very slowly, to plan beyond this nightmare, to consider how best to face the future.

Chapter Twenty-six

With Mrs Granville sulking in her lodge, Lucy was left alone in Hepburnstoun that Thursday with Sandy and Jennie. This suited her. She had greatly disliked the older woman's sour face and domineering ways, and was happy caring for the children. The house was big enough to look after itself. When alone, she sat happily musing about the sudden new interest in her life, this wholly unexpected love for James. Why had she gone back that night, knowing to what it would lead?

She had never lacked admirers, and long before her sixteenth birthday her high spirits had led her into a series of deliciously carefree and energetic liaisons. And why not? Mr Brodie the chemist in Glenbuchat was a man who believed in meeting his market in contraceptives halfway. Certainly no-one had ever been turned away on the grounds of age, and some girls muttered darkly of free supplies granted for unspecified favours in a dark little room smelling of carbolic at the back of his shop. Lucy had never been interested in this, being plentifully supplied with pocket money by her mother. Despite one or two anxious days, and the dreadful 'week of the unexplained rash', she had never received, or given, anything but pleasure through these magical mystery tours of the body. But this time was different.

'Isn't it always?' remarked her mother cynically, when Lucy confessed that a deep but unspecified love was the reason for her glowing cheeks and alternate highs and lows. 'Be careful, Lucy. Married men are trouble.'

'I never said he was married!' protested her anxious daughter, who had been secretly rather appalled by her mother's unexpected visit to the house.

'Lucy,' said Mrs Smith. 'There's no-one in the glen doesn't know you're going with James Hepburn. It doesn't matter to me. His wife's a stuck-up bitch and the minister's wife says she's run off with a millionaire. But when there's children, there's always trouble.' And then she refused to say another word on the subject, insisting instead on staying to help her daughter bath the children before cycling off home. As she turned out of the drive, she had to swerve to avoid being struck by a large black car which turned sharply in at the gates.

'Mummy! It's Mummy!' shouted Sandy boisterously running over from his bedroom window to where Lucy was quietly reading her book, prematurely believing her day to be drawing peacefully to a close.

'Your mother? Where?' Downstairs they could hear the front bell jangling furiously on its spring.

'There! At the door. She's come in a big black Rolls Royce!'

Lucy ran downstairs and hurriedly unbolted the heavy oak door.

'Where is Mrs Granville?' demanded Susie, pushing past her and hurrying up the staircase. 'And why is the house so filthy? Darlings! It's ME-EE!'

'Hell-o!' said a nervous-looking Fred, eyeing Lucy's figure. 'What do you do when you're off duty? Or needn't I ask?'

She ignored him and stalked away to the kitchen, banging the door behind her. Very reluctantly she lifted the big metal cover on the stove and, filling the largest kettle from the separate filter tap, she placed it on the hob. Next she took two ice trays from the giant refrigerator that stood grumbling and vibrating all year round and emptied them into a gilt ice-bucket shaped like a pineapple. Then, taking a deep breath, she marched out into the corridor, across the hall and dumped the ice on the drinks tray in the drawing-room. Mercifully the man had gone upstairs too. She could hear lots of excited sounds. She went back to the kitchen and sullenly watched the kettle until she heard her name being called.

'Yes?' She poked her head round the door.

'Yes, *Mrs Hepburn*,' corrected Susie in an acid tone. 'Go up and pack the children enough clothes for a month. I'm taking them south for a bit.'

'But their school . . .'

'And hurry up, will you? We've got a long drive ahead of us.'

'Does Mr Hepburn know?'

Susie glared at her. 'That's none of your business,' she snapped. 'Kindly do as I say this instant.'

Lucy shrugged. What could she do? With deliberately maddening slowness, she climbed the stairs and began to pack two cases, taking care to include everything that would comfort her two charges during what she suspected would be a less than uproarious excursion.

'Haven't you finished yet, young woman?' Fred was smiling at her roguishly from the doorway. 'Shall I give you a hand?' He moved forward and thrust his fingers under her bottom. Turning slowly round, she smiled at him and then struck him across the face with one hand while kneeing him hard in the groin.

'Thank you,' she said to the writhing figure on the floor. 'I really enjoyed that. You can give me a hand any time.'

'For heaven's sake!' They could hear Susie's infuriated voice from the first-floor landing. 'Are you going to be all day? Fred? Where are you?'

'Coming,' he called weakly, getting to his feet.

'Don't bank on it,' said Lucy with a thin smile. 'Now take these cases and get out, unless you want to explain this last episode to that stick-insect downstairs.' He stared at her, his mouth slack. 'Here!' She flung the cases at him. 'Piss OFF.' Finally satisfied, she picked up her book and started to read where she had left off.

But after she had heard the car's heavy wheels leaving the gravel, and then the sound of the horn by the lodge, she laid down the book and began to sob.

'She said WHAT?' James's tired voice had turned hoarse with shock and anger.

'She said it was none of my business.' An hour later, Lucy was still in tears.

'Poor darling. Of course there was nothing you could do. I had no idea they were back from America. She's perfectly within her rights, at this stage.' He was striving to decelerate his whirling thoughts, to defuse the sickening mixture of anger and fear that threatened to spill over into his precious contact with Lucy. What could she have done? Even if he had foreseen this move, Susie was undoubtedly entitled to claim at least half their children's time. What a day!

'What's that noise?' she said.

'Me grinding my teeth.' He banged the table with his fist, then said, more calmly, 'There's been no formal separation or anything like that. But it must have been a horrible shock for you. You'd think she'd have warned us.' After a short pause, 'Was she on her own?' She related the incident in the nursery, uncertain whether to be pleased or angry at his delighted laughter.

'You are a star! Poor Fred, I bet that's a first for him.'

'It wasn't too pleasant for me,' she said, remembering the intrusive violence of those thrusting fingers.

'I know, darling. I'm sorry,' he said hastily. 'But you handled it brilliantly.'

'The benefits of a Comprehensive education,' she said drily. 'Jennie won't learn *that* at boarding school.'

'Quite.' He was lost for words.

'When will I see you?'

'I'll try to come up Saturday evening, on the seven o'clock, I hope. I should be with you by midnight or before.'

'Should I go back to my mother's?'

'Of course not. You stay put.' When she didn't reply, he added, 'I love you very much. You know that, don't you?'

She smiled. 'I love you,' she whispered, and they continued to talk for another twenty minutes, much to the amazed delight of Susie's private detective, parked half a mile along the Glenbuchat road, whose radio bug they had had time to insert in the kitchen telephone while Lucy was doing the packing upstairs.

Part Three

July

Chapter Twenty-seven

Friday the first of July, and James woke early, his head still aching from the whisky he had needed to sleep at all. Angrily, he threw back the sheet and, crossing to the bathroom, he plunged his face into a basinful of Thames water, a poor substitute indeed for the Buchat's peaty fragrance.

Was it only six weeks ago that his life had seemed so bewitchingly secure and successful? And now? His marriage over, his children gone and his job so vile that immediate resignation seemed the only possible course open to him.

He collected the newspapers and the day's post, spending a desultory hour staring sightlessly at both. Then, with a conscious effort, he had a quick bath, dressed and rang Blake, his solicitor, to get one chore out of the way.

'What should I do?'

'It's quite simple. I can recommend a couple of divorce specialists for you to choose between. I'm sure you realize we don't handle that sort of thing here.'

'Right.' Why not?

'They will deal with custody, but it is extremely rare nowadays for it not to be shared.'

'What if they were taken abroad?'

'Is that really likely?'

James could sense the other man's distaste. He had always had a soft spot for Susie. 'No,' he said. 'To be fair, I don't think it is.' He could hardly imagine Fred giving up his new job simply for the dubious pleasure of securing the permanent presence of two step-children.

'No doubt you will want to make generous provision for Susie?'

Nothing was further from his mind. 'No doubt.'

'We can handle that for you, with pleasure.'

'Thank you.' Whose side was the bloody man on? And yet it wouldn't do to fall out with the architect of his family trust structure. James was beginning to regret not staying with his father's Edinburgh solicitors. They would have had a much more robust approach to errant wives. It was not too late, he reflected savagely, now that his domicile was back in Scotland.

'As it happens,' said Blake cautiously, 'I had already heard indirectly.'

'Really?'

'Mmm. I've had a letter from Susie, addressed to the trustees. She's suggesting they might like to invest some of the trust funds in this new house she's moving to.'

'WHAT?' The pulse in James's head had acquired a sudden new lease of life. 'She can't be serious?'

'Actually,' Blake's voice was especially silken, 'it is a well-argued case. The idea is that the children would feel they had a stake in their new home.'

'And does this letter,' said James heavily, 'envisage moving some of the contents of Hepburnstoun?'

'Oh, one or two things, to make them feel at home.'

'The Gainsborough, perhaps?'

'Exactly.' The solicitor sounded relieved. 'That's just the sort of thing.'

'But there are no trust funds as such. All you've got is the estate and contents. There wasn't much left of the Alma-Tadema money after you'd paid those advance school fees.'

'Quite.' A long silence followed.

'So how could you invest in Gumby or wherever?'

'Well . . .' another pause, 'I suppose we *could* sell some of the outlying land at Hepburnstoun.'

'To take a minority interest in someone else's collapsed mansion? This is trust property you're responsible for, not Susie's private fiefdom.'

'Nor yours,' said Blake shortly. 'You've put it in the trust for the children. It's up to the trustees to decide how best to use the fund, to their advantage.'

'Regardless of my views as settlor?'

'Naturally we would consult you. Oh dear, James I've got someone on the other line. Could we . . . ?'

'Goodbye.' James slammed the receiver down and sat staring at it for what seemed like an hour. His hands were shaking, and, to his consternation, he suddenly realized that for the first time he was wishing somebody dead. Not as a mere idle joke, but ice-cold, frozen-corpsed, finished-and-buried, disembowelled-dead. Susie! Simpering so sweetly as she poured her poison wherever it might do most harm. The two other trustees were his cousin Hew and Mr Trenchard, his Edinburgh accountant. Which way would they vote? Hew would surely support family piety, the continuity of Hepburns at Hepburnstoun, but Mr Trenchard had droned on many times about 'a wasting asset'. There was much to be done.

But these were his own battles. More importantly, who could he turn to about poor Nick? What would his father have done? More particularly, how could his father, so gentle and uncomplicated, have ever involved himself with people like Meyrick and the Prime Minister? There was no help for it, he decided. He was just going to have to face up to it by himself.

Chapter Twenty-eight

'Don't forget,' murmured Lucy in his ear on Sunday morning as they lay blissfully entwined in the worm-eaten old four-poster which Susie had banished to a far bedroom. 'You've got to make that speech to the Ladies' Guild in two hours' time.'

'I don't want to leave you.' They had spent twelve hours together, twelve hours in which he had half, but only half, managed to forget Susie's machinations and Nick's dreadful predicament.

'If you don't talk for too long, you can be back by three.'

'Will you be safe on your own?'

She stared at him. 'Why shouldn't I be?'

'Well . . .' The image of the postman, and others, hovered over him. 'You're a very beautiful young woman.'

'Oh, I see! Temptation might come *my* way while you are entertaining the assembled Ladies of Glenbuchat?'

'Do you mind that I'm jealous?'

'You've no cause.'

'I can't help it.'

'Why would I want to be unfaithful when I have you?'

'Because,' he said sadly, 'you might find something more valuable than my love for you, or than your love for me. Lots and lots of men will proposition you, that's what men are like.' She raised her eyebrows and smiled. 'They *are*,' he insisted. 'It's ridiculous but true. Some men make passes as a matter of course, just in case . . .'

'Oh thanks!'

They both laughed. 'But I'm serious,' he said. 'And that first moment of physical infidelity is the last moment of real togetherness. The comedy is over. What follows is just the finale: lies, discoveries, apologies, forgiveness, attempts at complaisance, growing desolation and finally contempt.'

'Is this how people talk in Parliament?' she demanded.

'A fair point,' he conceded with a wry smile. 'It's harder than you'd think not to be pompous.'

She leant over and stroked his neck. 'And if women should proposition you?' she said with a smile.

'Women are too wise to try to sell their wares like door-to-door salesmen,' he replied. 'They know the value men place on appearing to take the initiative. Why would I risk our happiness for a few seconds of sordid adventure?' And if while he was speaking his thoughts strayed treacherously towards the lissom Mrs Durham, he managed to conceal this if not from himself, then at least from Lucy.

After a quick shower, he drove further down the valley to the little town of Glenbuchat. The hills he loved so much were shrouded in low cloud, but never had he gazed out at the sodden countryside with more emotion. 'No-one possesses a landscape,' he told himself, 'but this is our home.'

A dense driving rain drenched him as soon as he climbed out of the car, having parked it beside the long-closed railway station, a low shuttered building with elaborately carved cornices of painted pine.

The Inverdhuiver Hotel, originally a temperance establishment for travelling salesmen, had never attracted much trade. Re-opened in the Sixties as a tourist trap with a strong emphasis on local distillations, it was now a thriving business, so thriving indeed that the proprietor had tacked on a long ugly extension in glass and timber which served both as sun lounge and function room. The Ladies' Luncheon Guild was a serious affair, for which people dressed in their best even if they did not patronize the kirk where the minister, Mrs McPherson's husband, held sway. As their local Member, it was a tradition that James addressed them on the first Sunday in July. Whatever other calls on his time might arise, this, in the shifting sands of the British political scene, was a fixed point from which no excuse might release him.

'It is a great pleasure for me to be given the chance of addressing you today, after enjoying such a delicious and substantial lunch.' The Guild were strangers to the cult of vegetarianism. Whole poached salmon, fresh from the lower reaches of the Buchat, had been followed by steaming barons of Angus beef and the strawberries had been submerged in enough cholesterol, masquerading as cream, to clog the clearest of arteries. He smiled down at Mrs McPherson, presiding beside him. She appeared to be asleep, her massive jaw supported quietly on the foothills of her neck.

'Is it true you're voting for the Government's selling away of our milk quotas?' The raucous voice came from a farmer's wife, one of his staunchest and most affectionate local canvassers.

'The deal arranged in Brussels by the Agriculture Minister is not one that any of us here would have chosen. But I do believe he did his best, and the increase in the hill beef subsidy should balance the books, I think?'

'We elect you to fight in our corner, not act as London's yes-man!' There was little enough affection in her voice today. 'You ought to be fighting it tooth and nail!'

'No,' he said. 'I can't agree with that. Let me quote you Edmund Burke on the subject, if I can remember it. He said, "It is an MP's duty to sacrifice his repose, his pleasures, his satisfactions to his constituents."' One or two of the lunching ladies exchanged significant looks. '"And above all, ever, and in all cases, to prefer their interests to his own. But his unbiased opinion, his mature judgement, his enlightened conscience, he ought not to sacrifice. Your representative owes you, not his industry only, but his judgement; and he betrays, instead of serving you, if he sacrifices it to your opinion."' James paused and looked round the room, meeting those eyes which were fixed on him. 'Now most of you know me well enough to accept that I do not boast that my judgement is mature, or that my conscience is exceptionally enlightened.' A few murmurs of assent. 'But I do boast that such judgement and conscience that I can deploy, I do so for Glenbuchat. To the best of my ability, I consider what I hear on your behalf at Westminster, and I hear what you tell me here at home. Then I have to come to a conclusion. That is how I represent you, and nobody born in Glenbuchat needs reminding that we none of us place too great a respect on deliberations in London or Edinburgh!' This time he was rewarded with some friendly laughter. 'I think it may not be too long before you will have another chance to pass judgement on me as your Member. When Burke made that speech I quoted just now, his electors threw him straight out at the next election.' This confession got a loud appreciative response. 'Even if the Government scrapes through this next vote, a General Election cannot be far away. I was very flattered to be asked to represent you all at Westminster, and I have enormously enjoyed the work, not least for the opportunity it has given me, through canvassing and through my correspondence,' he cast a quick smile at Mrs McPherson (it went unacknowledged), 'to meet many more of my neighbours than I should otherwise have done. Your hall clock tells me that I have far outstayed my welcome, so may I end by again thanking you for your generous hospitality this afternoon, and to remind you that all are welcome at my constituency surgery, whenever you think I may be able to advise or help.'

'How did it go?' Lucy took his sopping coat and spread it over the clothes-horse before hauling it up on its pulley so that it swayed suspended beneath the kitchen ceiling.

'Not too bad.'

'Come and sit down,' she said, leaning for comfort against the warmth of the stove.

He obeyed. 'Well?'

'I've been thinking about us.'

'Yes?' He gazed cautiously at her, disturbed by her tenseness. Her eyes veered away from his. More problems? And in so short a time?

'I don't want to be hurt,' she said. 'And I don't want to hurt you.'

'Sounds fair.'

She shook her head at his flippancy. 'I'll stay with you, if you want me to . . .' He nodded his head vigorously. 'Until the end of this month. I don't know how much time that will give us. Then I'm leaving. I won't say goodbye. I shall just go.'

'You're not serious?' It was so obvious that she was. A numbing sense of total despair enveloped him.

'It's not that I don't love you.' She crossed the room and settled on his lap, stroking his damp hair with one finger. 'It's because I do. But I can't see a future for us. And I'd rather take the responsibility of stopping it too soon, than see it die out too late.' She stared into his eyes. 'Can you understand that?'

'You do know how much I love you?' He was trying not to cry, not to expose his weakness to her.

'Yes,' she said tenderly. 'But you have children. You have to think of them too. And I have to think about my studies. And about the job I want when I graduate. Now hurry and pack. I'll have tea ready in ten minutes, and then you must go or you'll miss your plane.'

'Why not the end of August?'

Her eyes flashed at him. By negotiating, he was tacitly accepting a deadline. 'No!'

He thought hard for a moment. 'Let's compromise,' he said, misunderstanding her shifting mood. 'I'll let you go when the "Pride of Hepburnstoun" produces its berries. Then they will always remind me of my one great love.'

'When's that? The beginning of autumn?'

'They appeared mid-August last year,' he said gloomily.

'I agree.' She turned away, stung by his manner, leaning over the stove and making herself seem busy. 'You go up and pack,' she said again, without looking round. 'Tea will be ready when you come down.'

Chapter Twenty-nine

'Are we all here?' The following Tuesday Houston Blake peered over his spectacles at the hastily assembled trustees and the original source of the funds now under their personal control: the settlor, James Hepburn. Mr Trenchard had caught an afternoon flight down from Edinburgh, and Major Hew Hepburn-Kerr had driven up from Aldershot. 'I should like to catch the seven nineteen,' added Blake. 'Otherwise I shall miss my supper.'

Trenchard, the accountant, pursed his thin lips and ran a pencil down a column of figures, muttering under his breath. 'It's a sorry picture,' he said, shaking his head mournfully at James, who was trying to control his impatience. 'A sorry sorry picture.'

'In that?' For all James's efforts, when he spoke, his voice sounded very sharp.

'These figures show,' Trenchard sniffed and seemed to draw his narrow shoulders closer together, 'that you have been subsidizing the estate to the tune of an average of nearly forty-five thousand pounds per annum over the last four years.' The major, a bulky figure with fine moustaches, drew his breath in with an audible hiss.

'Why shouldn't that be called an investment? It's little enough seen in that light,' said James.

Trenchard shrugged. 'Because,' he said, turning to Blake as if to a more rational audience, 'there has been no "improvement" in the balance sheet. This money has gone to meet an excess of running costs over income. It's hardly an "investment" to employ more men than the income warrants.'

'I pay my rent, don't I?' snapped James, stung by their apparent hostility. 'How I spend my own money is surely my affair. And if it is to the benefit of the upkeep of trust property, I should have thought you'd all be pleased?' He looked round at them angrily.

Blake took off his glasses. 'We have to consider the beneficiaries' interests here. That is what we are paid for.' The major looked up sharply. 'I mean,' added Blake hastily, 'those of us who act in our professional capacity. Of course there is no suggestion but that James is a model tenant, as well as the donor of the trust's assets. But . . .'

'What would the estate fetch?' said Trenchard suddenly. 'On the open market?'

Blake turned over a sheet of paper. 'I've got a note here from Strutt and Parker,' he said. 'With vacant possession, they would recommend an asking price of three point seven five million pounds, with the fishing rights and contents being sold off separately.'

James leant back in his chair and stared at him, open-mouthed. 'Are you telling me that you have been seriously canvassing the sale of my home?'

Blake put his glasses back on. 'I had Susie and an American adviser of hers all yesterday afternoon. They had some very persuasive points. Rents at Hepburnstoun average . . .'

'Thirty-two pounds per acre on the low ground, fourteen pounds overall when you include the hill,' said Trenchard drearily.

'Exactly! A return on capital of less than three per cent gross. Land round Tring is averaging a net return of over five per cent. We do have to consider our duty to Sandy and Jennie, you know.'

'And what', said James coldly, 'did Strutt and Parker

suggest if the estate is sold subject to my continuing tenancy?'

'You wouldn't want to hang on, surely?' asked the major. 'Not if it damaged your own children's inheritance.'

James bared his teeth at him. 'The damage to my children's inheritance is in this room,' he said, 'not in what I'm doing. They love Hepburnstoun. That's more important than the difference of 2 per cent in yield before income tax, for God's sake! If Susie wants to leave me for her American lover, that's one thing. Selling Hepburnstoun to keep them in land is quite another.'

There was a communal sound of throats clearing.

'Susie did say,' murmured the major, 'that she was leaving because you had formed an attachment with your . . . um . . . *cook*.' Trenchard and Blake nodded at each other, with solemn faces devoid of expression.

Unexpectedly, James burst out laughing. 'If you could all see yourselves!' he said, wiping away a tear. 'You're all so wrong about this. You've got the whole thing back to front, you idiots.' There were loud murmurs of protest.

'This is really none of our business,' said the major, with a touch of acid in his tone.

'Then why mention it?' snapped James. 'But you're right. It *is* none of your business. What is your business is to administer my family trust in a responsible way.'

'That,' said Trenchard, 'is what I have been trying to tell these two gentlemen for the last two hours.' He nodded his head several times. 'On the figures.'

'Without emotion,' added Blake. 'It doesn't pay any bills.'

'Look,' said James, more calmly, 'I can see you've made your minds up for the moment, and if I can't make you see sense, that is my, and my children's, misfortune. But I can assure you of one thing: I shall

not surrender my tenancy. Make of that what you will.'
He stood up. 'And if you persist in this crazy scheme
to invest their money in anything as hare-brained as
Gumby-in-the-Vale, you'd better be damned sure it
makes a lot of money for them, because I wouldn't
bank on them seeing it in retrospect as having been
a prudent move. The first thing they asked me was
if they'd have to leave Hepburnstoun. Like a fool, I
assumed I knew how you'd all react. I was wrong.' He
could feel himself becoming incoherent. It was time to
leave before he made matters even worse. 'It's all right,
Houston. I know my way out.'

Once out in the fresh air, he took a cab to St James's
Park, and sat there for an hour, still simmering. Yet
for all his anger at Susie's success in threatening to
undermine so much that he believed in, the greatest menace to his equilibrium remained Nick. Walter
Meyrick had already rung him twice to ask whether
he had spoken to Nick, and those damned photographs
were still sitting locked in the bottom drawer of his
desk. This was the fifth of July, and the crucial vote
was now only six days away.

It was growing dark when he let himself into the
depressing little flat in Tothill Street. There was a
message from Blake's secretary to say that Susie had
finally agreed to his seeing Sandy and Jennie for
precisely two hours at two o'clock on Thursday. On
an impulse, he rang Nick. The answering-machine
was on. He announced he would call the following
morning. His Opposition pairing-partner being abroad,
he was free for the evening, and amused himself by
going to a film in Curzon Street, before retiring to
bed with a fresh heap of Education Department papers
dealing with some proposed new legislation.

Chapter Thirty

'Why here?' Nick had a smart low-built house off Eaton Square, differentiated from its neighbours by the gilded tips of its black railings. Once this had been a source of complaint with his landlords, but since they had been forced to sell him the freehold by legislation which he had enthusiastically promoted, a psychedelic kaleidoscope of colours had blossomed in the street, a garish development which the local council had found itself altogether too poor to prevent. He had kept his gold, but now grumbled instead about his neighbours' pink, mauve and green stripes and their imaginative taste in window frames.

'I wanted to chat to you in private.'

'Oh God!' groaned Nick. 'Not bloody *No. 4* again? I have a not insubstantial mass of work from my Home Office people. *And* I'm on the track of something potentially revolutionary in the art world. I believe I've discovered a new golden mean, and you want to bore the pants off me with Miscellaneous Provisions Number Sodding 4! You're so wrong, you know.'

'Nick,' said James, not willing to be diverted now that he had set himself to accomplish his dreadful task, 'I'm afraid this is serious.'

Something in his voice, or in his face, made Nick stop. He stood completely still, just as he was turning to reach for a packet of cigarettes from the mantelpiece. He blinked a couple of times, and then passed a hand over his eyes. 'How serious? Perhaps I ought to tell you that I know a lot more about this Bill than you seem to.'

James passed him the envelope. Nick stared at it, seemingly afraid to find what lay within. Then, with a grimace, he opened the flap, and pulled out the photographs. He studied each one intently, as if searching for some hidden message. Then he put them carefully back and handed the envelope back to James. The silence was intense. Nick took hold of the packet of cigarettes, shook one out and placed it in his mouth.

'Do you know how long I'd been celibate?' he muttered out of the corner of his mouth, sitting down and lighting the cigarette with the green onyx lighter on the table beside him. James shook his head. 'Eleven years. There were a couple of flingettes at Oxford, but once I started in this job, I knew I had to be squeaky clean if I was to get to the top. And I managed it. Until now.'

'I hadn't realized . . .'

'There's a lot you don't realize,' snapped Nick suddenly. 'It's a dirty job you've chosen to do.' James looked at the floor. He had nothing to say. 'And I really thought he loved me. I really honestly did.' He leant forward and pressed his face onto his clenched fists. 'I suppose I was set up?'

'I'm afraid so.'

'By you?'

'Of course not.'

'The stinking little bitch!' Nick stood up and flung the smouldering cigarette into the empty fireplace. 'Knowing we were being photographed! The BITCH!' There were tears running down his nose.

'Walter wants me to talk you into supporting the vote.'

Nick stared at him blankly. 'He knew we were being photographed,' he repeated, 'and still . . .'

'Walter says this can all be suppressed.'

'I love him. That's the worst of it.' He brushed his tears away angrily, shaking his head as if to clear it. 'I love the little tart.'

'Perhaps he was under pressure,' said James. 'Perhaps he had no choice.'

'Everyone has a choice,' said Nick, with a dangerous edge to his voice. He was staring sightlessly at the floor. 'Even you.'

'Nick, I'm very sorry about this. I know how you must feel.'

'GOD!' shouted Nick. 'Spare me your sanctimonious pity. What do you and people like you know about what it's like to have to hide every feeling in your body? To have to pretend? To have to agree with your infantile crushes on stinking women with bumpy fronts just because YOU think it's normal? NORMAL!' He started to laugh. 'You wouldn't know a real orgasm if it hit you smack in the face!'

'Nick,' said James calmly. 'That boy is only *fifteen*.'

'So?' Yet it was obviously a shock. 'So I'm to be done for corrupting a minor? Is that it? Government Minister screws CHILD!' He laughed again, a terrible sound. 'If there was any corrupting . . . and what about whoever set this up? Conspiracy, blackmail, accessory after the fact, not a pretty portrait of our ultra respectable Chief Whip. Oh *God*!'

'I totally agree, for what it's worth.' James stared at him, shattered by the depth of Nick's grief. This wasn't political manoeuvring; it was the destruction of a human heart.

'Nothing. It's worth fuck all. They must want this Bill pretty damn badly to do this.'

'Nick.' James pulled in his feet and leant forward towards his friend. 'Couldn't you just push all of this to one side, and look at the issue very simply? Surely you can't doubt that our party is the right one to govern the country? We don't rely on backhanders to pay our household bills, we can recognize the need for income before expenditure, we're grown-up enough to be able to say no to the bleeding-heart industries. So what if this Bill is imperfect? It can always be repealed. It can't be worth throwing away your career for, and risking a Socialist Armageddon into the bargain, undoing everything that's been achieved in the last eighteen years.'

Nick shook his head. 'I wish you could hear yourself, James. You sound like some copybook Central Office bovver-boy, trimming with the best of them. I'm actually ashamed of you. Do you know that? I came into Parliament to try to improve things. No, I won't support spending without full funding; no, I don't believe problems are readily solved by throwing money at them; but above all, NO, I don't believe in letting a dangerous Bill through simply to let the gravy train flow smoother. No-one wanted a Ministry more than me, but no-one will let it go easier than I will, if the cost is voting against my conscience.'

'I'm only trying to help you see sense,' said James desperately.

'It's you who needs the help.'

'You could go to prison.'

'That's the least of my worries.'

'You mean . . . ?'

'I mean,' said Nick slowly, lighting another cigarette and throwing it into the grate, 'my family.'

'I'm very sorry.'

Nick stared hard at him. 'I'm not sure you're not worse than the others. You're supposed to be my friend. YOU BASTARD!' His face had suddenly flooded with colour. 'You creeping fucking sanctimonious traitor.'

'Would you rather Walter had seen you? He was in two minds as to whether to let them prosecute you as an example to others.'

'*Pour encourager les autres?*' Nick was calm again, calm and resigned. James wasn't certain he didn't prefer the rage.

'Precisely.'

Nick chuckled. 'Funnily enough, I've always had a soft spot for old Walter,' he said. 'He knows what he wants, and goes for it. Do you know what I'd have done in your place?' Again he lit a cigarette, and sucked in a lungful of smoke.

'What?'

'I'd have resigned on the spot and threatened to whip up every available vote against the Bill if these charming pictures reached the press.'

James shrugged. 'I would have preferred that. Except you would have been prosecuted forthwith. What a *triumph*! The Government fallen, and you in the dock. Just what the country needs. Then I could have felt really proud of myself, I suppose.'

'Hoity-toity! What you don't understand,' said Nick fiercely, 'is that this Bill *is* betraying our country. It's the negation of parliamentary democracy, it's just that you're all too blind to see it. What a mess.'

'What shall I tell Walter?' James was suddenly tired, tired of Nick and very tired of politics.

'Tell him I shall give him an answer on Monday, when I've finished my research on my project. He can wait till then.' Nick stretched himself out on the sofa. 'You may leave me now,' he said. 'I'm bored with your silly sympathetic expression. It's giving me indigestion. Tell your lord and master I will speak to him Monday.' He picked up a magazine and pointedly gave it his full attention. James let himself out, feeling very far from content with his own role in the affair. Perhaps he should have resigned? And the law? Here was one fifteen-year-old who seemed more of a threat than a victim, or was there another side to that story too? What else in his life could go wrong? It gave him a grim sense of satisfaction to see that his car had been clamped.

Chapter Thirty-one

Thursday the seventh being the day agreed for him to visit Sandy and Jennie, he drove out of London on the Westway, forking north round the M25 and then up the old Aylesbury road towards Tring. The cornfields were full of poppies and blue cornflowers, symbols of the cyclical nature of agricultural policy. Now that farmers were penalized for overproduction, the frenetic dressings of fertilizer and weedkiller had been abandoned, allowing Nature to reassert her colourful presence among the monotonous crops of human cultivation. Yellow burdock and white hedge parsley added to the kaleidoscope.

Pulling onto the verge to consult his map, he saw the villages of Gumby St Leonard and Gumby Puerorum marked as lying somewhere to the north-west of where he had stopped. And sure enough, half a mile further on, he found a signpost announcing 'The Gumbys' and directing him down a narrow lane hedged in with tall trees overgrown with pink and white wild roses.

He was totally unprepared for the house which suddenly loomed above him, a fantastic creation of glowing yellow stone on a precipitous rock cliff which reared up through a forest of oaks and beeches. The centre was of the eighteenth century, in pale stone, with a tall portico flanked by arched windows with wrought iron balconies, while above them statues writhed in rococo abandon, women with tridents and spears, unicorns striving with centaurs. But on either side, evidence perhaps of an earlier structure, stout towers in red and blue diapered brick served to accentuate the glossy Italianate extravaganza of the central block.

As theatrically as it had appeared, the house abruptly vanished behind a curtain of foliage and the narrow road wound up a hill and into a low brownstone village with roofs of discoloured decaying thatch. A tall whitewashed three-storeyed inn, 'The Gumby Arms', stood like an exclamation mark among these gloomy dwellings. Some of the gardens were bright with bedding plants, but several had unkempt borders and one or two seemed completely abandoned.

At the turn of the village street, a stucco arch, its triumphal coat of arms badly decayed, showed the way to the big house. A newly painted sign read: 'POLITE NOTICE. KEEP OUT!' while another, beneath a skull and crossbones, announced the presence of guard dogs. Undeterred, James drove under the arch, and up the pitted drive, avoiding the worst of the potholes and admiring the radiating avenues, all the more romantic for being ragged and overgrown. On this side, the house was anchored firmly in its landscape by long straight single-storey wings with tattered green shutters and wisps of grass growing among the ruined chimneys. And this was to be the chosen alternative to keeping the mountains of Hepburnstoun. A fine investment indeed! Half a dozen large cars were parked beneath the curving entrance and there, running towards him, he saw Sandy, a solitary figure of animated life amid all this dead masonry.

'Dad!' Father and son seemed to join the frozen statues, locked together in a long loving embrace. 'Can we go home now?'

'There you are.' He looked up to see Susie, in a maroon trouser suit, standing at the top of the steps, holding Jennie firmly by the hand. They made a discordant pair, the daughter shouting and laughing, the mother grim and hostile. 'They've got friends coming to play with them at four,' she called down. 'Please make sure you don't make them late.'

'Where are we going?' With both children strapped into their seats in the back of the car, they bucketed back through the potholes.

'There's a small private zoo beyond Brill. Would you like to see the monkeys?'

'Great!'

'Don't forget to wave to Mummy.'

They turned round, but Susie had already disappeared back into the house.

They laughed at the monkeys, stared at the sea horses, craned their necks over to study the fruit-bats hanging upside down behind their barricades. They gorged themselves on walnut cake and chocolate ice-cream, and played the fruit machines until James had no more change.

'Time to go back,' he announced, consulting his watch.

'Can we go home? I mean, really home?' Both children had been very slow about getting in to the car, and now Sandy had a hesitant whine in his voice.

'I want to go up to the loch and see if the baby heron has come out of her egg,' said Jennie. 'I want to see Muggy.'

'Very soon,' said James. 'I want you both to say all this to the three men who look after your money. But you must spend some time with Mummy too. She loves you very much.'

'Why doesn't she love you any more?' asked Sandy.

James stared at the passing traffic. 'Things change,' he said at last. 'Mostly, we want them to stay as they are. But they don't. The secret of being happy is to work hard and make the best of what comes your way. People change too. Mummy and I just don't hit it off any more. That's all.'

'I don't like that Fred,' said Sandy. 'And I'm NOT going to call him "Dadda". Dadda! Pass the SICK bag!' He screwed his face up in comical disgust. 'You're my dad!'

'Certainly I am,' said James, meeting his son's puzzled eyes in the mirror. 'And I always will be.'

'He sleeps in a nightshirt,' said Jennie. 'And he's a show-off. He's always saying how rich he is.'

'I don't ever want to be rich,' said Sandy. 'Not like HIM.'

'You've got to remember he makes Mummy happy,' said James judiciously. 'That's important, isn't it?' Two pairs of mutinous eyes stared back at him. *'Isn't it?'* Overawed, they both nodded reluctantly.

'Does Lucy make *you* happy?' enquired Jennie, demurely. Sandy was grinning broadly.

James, speechless, drove on in silence. Then he said, 'Yes. Since you ask, yes. Yes, she does.'

'I'm glad,' said Jennie. 'I thought she did. I like Lucy.'

'Mummy and Fred were talking about it,' blurted Sandy. 'I was listening.'

'Well, you shouldn't have been, should you?' said James, shocked.

'Then they shouldn't listen in on your telephone,' said Sandy triumphantly. 'They've got a BUG!'

'Have they indeed?' That was useful information for him to store. He didn't imagine Fred Tevis's employers would relish the news that their managing director was breaking the law in a divorce case. He had reached the arch, and again they were bumping up the drive towards the old house. 'If I were you,' he added, seeing his wife in the distance, standing tautly, hands on hips, at the top of the steps, 'I wouldn't say anything about that.'

It was on the way back into London that, having tried to ring Lucy without success and overwhelmed by a sudden spasm of loneliness, he decided to take up Victoria Durham's casual invitation. Diverting impulsively down the Earl's Court Road, he drove through Chelsea until he found himself in Mulberry Walk. The mews was a jumble of little cottages, reached through a narrow lane, but number two was immediately identifiable by its disproportionately tall central window, spanning two storeys. He parked outside and rang the bell.

'I'm so glad you've come.' She was dressed in a loose cotton smock, covered in smears of oil-paint, reds clashing with oranges, blues with greens. 'Tea? Or something stronger? You look all in.'

'I am.' He sat down heavily on a *chaise longue*, draped with a zebra skin. 'Tea would be fine.' She hurried out of sight behind a painted screen, but the sounds of clattering crockery and whistling steam gave him the image of her preparations. The cottage appeared to have been gutted. Above him a conventional pitched roof displayed its bare timbers and felted slats. There was no sign of a staircase. Everywhere, canvasses lay stacked or scattered, and two plain deal tables were smothered with the impedimenta of an artist, bottles of turpentine, half-used tubes of paint and jamjars crammed with brushes.

'Milk, one sugar, isn't it?'

'Yes.' He was absurdly grateful that she should remember.

'Here. It's hot.' She handed him a heavy mug.

'Thank you.' They drank in silence. 'What are you painting?'

'Come and see.'

Her easel stood on a low dais beside the looming window. He walked round and studied the work she had started. It was very abstract, with the pattern coming from tonal shapes rather than from drawing, but the colours were startling and oddly beautiful.

'Do you like it?'

He turned and smiled. 'Very much.'

'I was going to make myself some pasta. Would you like some?'

He looked at his watch. It was after seven, and he was not likely to be needed at the House until ten. 'That would be nice.'

'Garlic OK?'

'Why not?'

They ate and chatted about their lives. He told her about his day with Sandy and Jennie, she told him about her elderly and very demanding mother, marooned in an expensive but forbidding old people's home near Regent's Park.

Suddenly she said, 'Don't be offended, but I really feel like a good fuck.'

He felt himself colouring. He stared into her face. She was grinning, and her eyes held an expression of delighted amusement. 'Are you cross with me? Perhaps it was rather blunt!'

'No, it's just that . . .' There was no denying her beauty.

'You're not in the mood?'

'No . . .'

'You've got a headache?' She slipped out of her smock, her body firm and lithe, her skin so pale as to be almost translucent. She arched herself over him, wriggling with excited anticipation. 'Oh! I want you in me now!'

'No . . .' The worst of it was, he could feel his body responding.

'You're worried about your bimbette!' She turned round and sat on his lap. 'Gracious!' She stroked his cheek. 'I promise you she shan't know. What a *lucky* girl she is.'

'It's wrong,' he heard himself saying. 'Of course we can give each other sexual pleasure. But it's the warmth of love that would be missing, and which we . . .'

'I can tell you're a politician,' she said, kneeling down and undoing his trousers, 'I've never heard so much *waffle*. Now then,' pursing her lips, 'let me just see what happens if I . . .'

'Was that fun, or was that fun?' She was wiping herself vigorously with what appeared to be a paint rag. He nodded, also naked and on his knees, too exhausted or too ashamed to speak. 'Come on. I'm going to get you up and under the shower and off to the House in plenty of time. When do you go back to Scotland?'

'*Tomorrow.*'

'So? *Plenty* of time to rebuild the reserves! I shan't write or ring. But you know where I am. I'd like to think you know you can drop in when you feel like it. I'm not one for serious relationships,' she said, standing up. 'But I really do enjoy a good bonk!'

After he had gone, she rang Walter Meyrick. 'The things I do for the party!' she said. 'I'll expect to be a Dame in due course.'

'But you're so good at it.' She heard him chuckling the other end. 'And you enjoy it.'

'You wouldn't know,' she riposted. 'But I'll tell you what. This time was not unrewarding. I hope you don't have to use it against him. I'd like him back!'

Chapter Thirty-two

When James woke on the Friday morning, his first thought was still of Nick's anguished expression. This weekend, he decided, he was going to read the full unexpurgated text of the *Miscellaneous Provisions No. 4* Bill, or die in the attempt.

Not that this still formed the main focus of his mind. Being able to excuse the frailties of others made it no easier to condone his own. How could he have put his love for Lucy at risk by submitting to Victoria's aggressive sexuality? And he was still married! How many of his colleagues, he thought wryly, were in as shaky a position as he? He shrugged. Surrounded by disaster, perhaps it was he himself who was to be, had always been, the principal wreck? But so long as he could be with Lucy, he was beginning to feel impervious to whatever else might arise.

Having dealt with the minutiæ of the Whips' Office by lunchtime, he spent the afternoon in a tall redbrick building off Seething Lane. This had for many years housed the headquarters of Hockmans', a law firm which specialized in major private clients to the exclusion of corporate work, an admirable self-denial made practical since there were only two partners, Hockman father and son, and between them they owned the freehold of their building, and of much else besides.

It took him over two hours to explain his position to the father, a short man with clear kindly eyes, who kept pressing him to accept more tea.

At last the old man leant back in his chair and sighed. 'I will think over all that you have told me.'

'Can I stop them?'

'You'd like me to be able to say "yes", I know.'

'I would.'

The old man shook his head. 'As far as the children's trust is concerned, the one that owns Hepburnstoun House and the majority of the land, you made them an irrevocable gift, by deed, to hold the property in trust for your children. If the trustees judge it prudent to sell and re-invest in land elsewhere with a higher rent, who could claim that a breach of trust? They are specifically empowered both to realize assets within the corpus of the trust fund, and to invest in, among other things, land.'

'And if they were to invest in a jointly owned old house with a tree growing out of its roof?'

'Then they might need a good lawyer of their own!' The old man cackled away for several minutes. 'I'll talk to my son. At least I *can* reassure you about the Gainsborough. Like the Raeburns, that remains the property of the separate chattels trust set up under your late father's will, which explains the confusion. Since the trustees of *that* settlement are you yourself and your late father's factor, a . . .' he paused to consult his spidery notes, 'Major Hamish Scott-Leith, I think you may expect to see it rest at Hepburnstoun for a good few years yet. If you want us to represent you, you will need to clarify your position with Stirling, Gadsby and Chown.'

'I certainly will,' said James grimly, and shortly afterwards he left the building.

But when he reached Hepburnstoun that evening, bearing a last-minute bunch of cold-storage roses he had picked up at Heathrow, he found himself subjected to a searching stare.

'Why are you looking so sheepish?'

'I'm not,' he protested.

'Yes, you are. There's something strange in your expression. Something furtive. It's horrid.'

'Anyone would look furtive subjected to this inquisition rather than a loving hug.'

'Most people look furtive when there's something to hide,' she retorted, stepping back a little and continuing to examine his face. She still hadn't accepted the antiseptic little bunch of flowers. 'There'll be enough time for hugs when you've explained yourself.'

'Explained what?' He could hear his voice ascending into an unconvincing and unattractive squeak.

'Oh God!' Her eyes suddenly filled with tears. 'You've gone back to *her*. She's been chucked by that American oaf and you've fallen for her drippy line in self-pity!'

He smiled.

'OH! SO IT'S NOT HER!' She ran at him and slapped his face. 'IT'S SOMEONE ELSE! YOU BASTARD!'

Luckily for him, he kept his head. 'I love you,' he said, blinking from the pain. 'There's no-one else. I hated being away from you. Perhaps I feel guilty at showing how much I depend on you. It's not a weakness, it's a strength. The weakness is in shrinking from admitting that I need you so much. I couldn't begin to look at another woman except you.'

She stared at him, softened by this barrage of disinformation. And yet it was all true. He knew now that he did love her. And his concentrated self-disgust at accepting Victoria's lubricious embrace served only to accentuate his internal sense of crisis, lending added emphasis to his words. 'Is that really true?' she said, uncertain now, and wanting to believe him.

He opened his arms to her, throwing the flowers to one side. 'You *know* it is.'

He knew he was asleep, and yet there was something hot on his eyelids. And a buzzing. Was the house on fire? He opened one eye. The sunshine was bright and very warm, and a bumblebee, so close that he could see its fur, hovered just above him. Lucy, her bare skin speckled with perspiration, lay beside him, her lips open, her breasts rising and falling as she breathed in her sleep. They were at the furthest point on the estate, up by the shore of Loch Rullig, with the peak of Ben Rullig rising steeply above them, capped with its massive monolithic 'Faerie Rocks', ancient sentinels posted in past millennia before the age of men. How could he ever choose to leave this place?

Across the still blue waters of the loch, he could see the ruined stone walls of Fort Rullig, a long abandoned outpost of George II's redcoats, sent into these inhospitable hills to subdue the sullen clansmen, still sulking from the brutalities of Culloden, barely a hundred miles to the north. So remote had been the garrison, and so incompetent the military administration, that they had been entirely forgotten. Twenty years later, an alert clerk in the War Department had queried the unchanging nature of the payments sent twice a year to Rullig, and a weary emissary had ridden north from Edinburgh to inspect this remarkably reticent outpost. Two men remained in the fort, sole survivors of a wintry raid by brigands who had fired the castle and butchered the emerging troops. When these two, saved by their absence on an excise patrol, returned to the scene of devastation, they had hidden themselves in the pine forest lower down for several weeks. Then came a boy with the news that the wages saddlebag had been delivered as usual at the notary's in Glenbuchat.

For twenty years, the two privates continued to draw the garrison's pay, methodically carrying out such duties as they agreed between them. When the astounded War Office learnt the full facts, the men were already well entrenched in the local culture, having taken wives from among their erstwhile enemies.

Surrounded now by their thriving families, they had built themselves new steadings on the more fertile land down by the River Buchat, as tenants of the Hepburns. It had hardly seemed worthwhile to the authorities to make a fuss. The money was spent, the region was peaceful, the relevant general was now very senior indeed. So the papers were removed, and the story suppressed. But in the countryside round Glenbuchat, the legend persisted that official administration in Edinburgh and London left much to be desired.

This place had not changed, not since the first syllable of recorded time, when rosy-fingered dawn had stretched out and prodded Odysseus to wake and wrestle with the wine-dark sea. Life here followed the brief bleak cycle of the seasons, and the mountains mocked the earnest attempts of man to impose dominion on their granite hills. Down beside the Buchat water, the slopes were scattered with the bleached and unremembered stones of former steadings, sheep-pens, byres and homesteads, the tombstones of long-dead communities. So now, thought James, perhaps Hepburnstoun too will join this congregation of ghosts, wrecks not of nature, but of man's paltry ambition and pride.

Lucy stirred in her sleep, stretching out her hand to reassure herself that he was beside her.

'Are you burning?' The skin along her flank was very pink.

She smiled up at him. 'What about you?' Reluctantly he pulled on his shirt, and covered her by laying her skirt and blouse across her. 'Isn't this lovely?' The bumblebee had been replaced by a pale-blue dragonfly, which ruffled the warm air with its frenetic wings. Muggy and one of the stalking ponies, tethered in the shade of a group of rowans, were watching them, eager no doubt for the cool of the stables.

'Another sandwich?'

'Yes please.' He bit into the coarse brown bread,

watching her hands smoothing her flesh, wiping away the sweat from her eyes.

'I can't believe you're taking her eavesdropping so lightly,' she said sleepily. 'Won't it affect custody of the children?'

He stared up at the sky. 'Not really. I don't think it matters much. Divorces nowadays concentrate more on the children than on blame. It's very rare not to share custody. I did speak to my new lawyer about it. If anything, he says it will work for us, or would do if you were going to stay with me, have our own children.' He risked a darting glance at her. She too was staring upwards.

She grabbed his hand. 'Let's swim!'

'It'll be freezing.'

'So much the better!' She leapt up and dragged him after her, scampering barefoot across the pebbles and into the sparkling water. The shock to their naked bodies was intense. Whatever effect the sun may have had on their skin, Loch Rullig, more than a hundred feet deep and fed by melting snow and mountain springs, remained impervious. Lucy struck out towards the middle, and he followed, flailing his arms and legs to counteract the icy effect of the loch. They swam in a long circle, splashing each other and laughing at the invigorating exertion.

'It's too cold,' he said at last. 'Come on. I'll race you to the shore.' She beat him easily, her body slicing through the water as he churned along in her wake.

'You need more exercise,' she panted, patting his dripping belly, and pulling him down onto the stubby mountain grass beside their rug. 'Starting now!'

Later that evening, while Lucy sat opposite him, working on some books she had already bought for her future degree course, he started to read the first of the parliamentary papers relating to the controversial Bill.

They paused only briefly for a quick supper, and then resumed their companionable silence, each immersed in their reading.

At some point, she must have fallen asleep, because when he finally laid aside the last report, it was nearly dawn, and she was slumped in her chair, her face flushed and tranquil. Very carefully, he picked her up in his arms. Not daring to risk the stairs, he laid her, murmuring something indistinct, on the wide library sofa, undressed and lay down beside her, pulling the tartan hearthrug over them. She wriggled briefly, and he moulded himself alongside her.

They were still there at ten the next morning when an outraged Mrs Granville, on her way to the church, and entering the house only for the pleasure of announcing her decision to take a job at the manse instead, looked into the room, stared at the peaceful sleepers and left, cycling angrily the whole way to Glenbuchat for the pleasure of announcing this latest affront to an enthralled audience gathered outside the kirk to recover from the minister's latest diatribe against the sinful souls committed to his care.

'You mean there's nothing wrong with the Bill?' They were sitting in the kitchen, sharing a cup of coffee.

'Nothing much.' He was almost laughing with relief. 'I can see why purists might be uneasy, because it's so obscurely worded. But no, it's relatively harmless, given what we've already conceded to Brussels. When I think of what happened in the Forties, I think almost any price is worth paying to keep war at bay. In any case, it doesn't even apply to Scotland.'

'Why not?'

'Because we have our own opt-out arrangements direct to the European Commission via the Scottish Office, thank God. At least the draughtsman got that right!'

'Are you sure you haven't missed something?'

'Thank you!' He laughed. 'It's reassuring you have such faith. No, I've read it all twice at least. I must tell Nick as soon as possible. He'd be mad to risk a scandal over a little parliamentary chicanery.'

'Shouldn't you ring him?' She had managed to listen to his gloomy description of all that had passed with Nick without giving him her private opinion, which was that he should never have let himself be a party to such pressure. If he asked, she would say so; if he didn't, she would preserve the same restraint she would expect from him if the positions were reversed. And he hadn't asked.

'Good idea.' He reached across the kitchen table and lifted the telephone towards him. There was no reply.

Earlier that Sunday morning, Nick had dressed, shaved and driven down to the little country town where he had been educated. What little remained of the medieval town lay immediately beside the river, huddled in low half-timbered streets around a sturdy Norman church. A double line of handsome Georgian shops and houses, the High Street, led to a wholly different encampment: the ancient college buildings and their spreading Victorian and modern boarding houses and classrooms, all in dignified Institutional Gothic or Queen Anne, rearing up like so many country mansions yet crowded together among the domes, turrets and pinnacles of the college's principal chapels and libraries. There was even, across the main courtyard, an authentic Tudor tower fronting a shaded classical quadrangle where he sat now, two steps up a side staircase, smoking the first cigarette of the day, where indeed he had smoked the first cigarette of his life.

'Good morning, Boynton.' An elderly schoolmaster in winged collar and flowing black robe had swept down the staircase. 'Still smoking, I see.'

'Good morning, sir.' It was all he could do to restrain the schoolboys' salute. 'I didn't hear you.'

'Let me see . . . you went into politics, I think?'

'Yes, sir.'

'Any progress? Minister? What-have-you?'

'I've just decided to resign.'

The old man gave a dry chuckle. 'Probably very sensible,' he said. 'Do you ever see Blunden(mi) these days?'

'No, sir.' Nick knew he was blushing, at his age!

'Pity,' said the schoolmaster drily. 'Well, I'm Vice-Provost these days, so I'd better set a good example by being on time, don't you think?'

'Yes, sir.'

'Goodbye, Boynton. Don't leave that butt lying around, or someone else might get the blame.'

'No, sir.'

The old man hurried on. The bell high in the tower was ringing now, a steady solemn tocsin that reverberated all over the town, summoning boys in their starched white collars and stained black tailcoats to chapel, until the cobbled courtyard was full of their scuffling hurrying feet. Nick drew on a second cigarette and watched them with a smile of fond reminiscence. Once they were all inside, he heard the great painted organ begin to thunder out its accelerated air, blowing clouds of dust up at the frescoed ceiling where bare frolicking cherubs blew imaginary trumpets down towards the over-dressed cherubs below.

Blunden(mi)! How prosaic a way to describe the nimble roseate body and greedy silken lips of his first and only true lover. It was up that staircase, in one of the many disused rooms of the old cloister, that Toby had first yielded to his desperate entreaties. Yielded? Perhaps it had been Toby's idea from the start, flapping those round blue eyes and pouting at him across the chapel aisle? What did it matter now? He glanced at his watch. Time to visit the cricket pavilion.

Walking out into the sunlit yard, he could hear six hundred young voices eagerly singing a psalm. A frantic boy rushed past him, his collar still adrift, one shoe half-off. No doubt he would be seeing the headmaster at a quarter past twelve.

After visiting the cricket pavilion, he made his way quietly into the old town, and settled down for coffee and a croissant in what had once been the coaching inn, rendezvous for parents in the distant past. Across the river, an ancient castle reared its angry grey walls, a golden flag flapping lazily from the central tower. Did anyone still live there? He ordered another cup of coffee and began to write some letters. After lunch in a wine bar across the road, he wandered aimlessly along the towpath. Several times he had to jump aside to make way for the careering bicycles of anxious coaches, as they pedalled furiously after their boys rowing in fours up and down the river. Always he acknowledged their grunted thanks with a cheery wave, watching as they sped precariously along the rutted track, their hoarse shouts competing with the splash of the oars in the warm summer air.

As the afternoon wore on, he took off his jacket and lay down in the long grass to doze, listening peacefully to the raucous cries of the coxes on the river, and the grasshoppers' mesmerizing music.

It was dark when he awoke. He must have been asleep for several hours. All that wine. He was just a few yards downstream from where a blue and yellow iron railway bridge crossed the river. The railway had been closed years ago, before even his time there, but the bridge was an important milestone for the bumping races, and so the school kept it painted and smart.

Carefully he folded his jacket, and laid it on the towpath. Picking up a brown paper bag he had brought from the wine bar, he scrambled up the railway embankment and walked across the bridge until he was midway above the swirling water below. Very gingerly, he manoeuvred himself under the guardrail, so that he was sitting astride one of the main cross-beams, balancing the paper bag on his lap. One arm crooked round an upright, he carefully extracted first a bottle of pills, which he placed beside him, and then a bottle of gin. Smiling, he began to swallow the gritty tablets, washing them down with swigs from the gin bottle. It made for a disgusting cocktail. Would they think he minded a scandal? Or recanting? He smiled bitterly. He had loved only twice, and each time . . .

Across the meadows, he could see lights shining in the boys' bedrooms. Could that really be the room where . . . ? He could hardly see for the tears pouring down his cheeks. Defiantly, he emptied first one bottle, and then the other into his mouth, choking on the contents. Defiantly, but defying whom? His head was swimming with nausea and the effects of the alcohol. He opened his mouth to sing, no, at all costs he mustn't vomit. He clamped his lips stubbornly tight. Without any warning, the bridge veered sharply over and struck him on the head; he reached out to protect himself, slipped and cried out at the shocking impact as he hit the churning waters below. A brief confused struggle, a sickening gulp of putrefying sewage and the waters closed over his head.

'There's still no reply.' It was the tenth time James had rung Nick's number.

'Are you worried?' Lucy lay beside him, stroking his neck.

'Not really. Except I would have expected him to leave his answer-machine on.'

'Come to sleep,' she murmured. 'You've got an early start.'

Chapter Thirty-three

'James?'

'Yes, who is it?' He was still half-asleep.

'It's Hew. Sorry to ring so early, but we've got a tank exercise.'

'Really?' It was 5 a.m.!

'I felt really bad about last week. I've been talking to Floss and she thinks I've paid far too much attention to Blake and Susie.'

'Oh?'

'It seems she's never thought Susie was entirely fair to you.'

'Hmm.'

'I just wanted to tell you. Oh, and James?'

'Yes.'

'If you do end up selling, we'd like to be considered for Castle Farm, and a bit of the fishing, perhaps. It would be a shame if there were no Hepburns to keep the flag flying, eh?'

'I'll bear that in mind,' said James. 'I hope the exercise goes well.'

'Yes. It's rather a humdinger. Six feints. And counter-feints, of course. And then a Guderian double scissor-drive!'

'Sounds great.'

'Glad to have a word, old boy. Remember what I said about Castle Farm. Take care.'

'And you, Hew.' James put the receiver back with a sigh. He had dreamt of Nick, his face obscured by seaweed and yet talking endlessly about fine wine.

Now he had to face reality, and his own face in the shaving mirror.

Lucy had just placed his plate of eggs and bacon in front of him, when the telephone went again. She answered it. 'It's for you,' she said. 'Walter Meyrick?'

'Yes?' He walked across to the wall.

'James? You must prepare yourself for some rather dreadful news, I'm afraid.'

'What?' His voice wasn't working properly and Lucy looked sharply at him. 'Tell me! Is it Sandy?'

'Oh God!' Lucy had run to his side.

'Who? No, it's about Boynton. They've picked his body out of the river near Fellows' Eyot. Quite dead, I'm afraid.'

'How awful,' he said, very slowly, as if hardly able to take it in. Lucy had brought him a chair, and he sank down on to it. 'How awful.'

'What is it?' she whispered, frantic to know. He put one hand over the receiver. 'It's my friend Nick,' he said. 'He's been drowned.' She put her arms round him, and laid her cheek against his.

'Are you there?' Meyrick's voice crackled in his ear.

'Yes,' said James drearily. 'I'm here.' His first reaction had been one of ecstatic relief that his children were safe. The second had been a searing sense of guilt and sorrow for his friend. He should have known! He should have stayed with him. Above all he should have telephoned earlier, flown back, anything rather than pursue his own pleasure while Nick was in such terrible trouble.

'They found some letters. One of them's addressed to you. Commander Trent's in charge, I'm glad to say. He'll keep the lid on.' James wanted to shout at him, insult him, blame him, yet his overwhelming feeling now was disgust with himself. There was nothing to say, so he let the receiver fall back into place.

* * *

After she had watched his car turn into the bend in the drive, and disappear behind the planting, Lucy walked up from the house, and settled herself down to lie beside the tall waterfall, listening to the water and to the wind in the trees behind her.

The morning sun had scarcely risen and, far below her, the 'Pride of Hepburnstoun' was swaying slightly, creaking within its metal straitjacket. Soon the new clusters of red berries would celebrate another year of Hepburns guarding their ancient if no longer profitable inheritance.

What was her future? The man she loved was married, and with children of his own. It was impossible to feel any enthusiasm for sharing any life with him in London, locked up in some fusty flat, wheeled out to smile dutifully at dreary gatherings of half-drunk politicians old enough to be her parents. And here? She felt refreshed by the cool glitter of the waterfall, and the deepest indigo of the pool beneath it, a blue so deep and yet so translucent as to seem almost magical, a blue so deep that Lucy longed for it to be indelibly impressed upon her heart's memory. There was something poignantly fragile about the waterfall, its individual droplets, the drifting spray where it plunged into the pool, lit occasionally by the silvery flash of a salmon jumping again and again in its relentless search for its roots, the anonymous little rivulet where, only a year ago, it had miraculously evolved from its parents' spawn among the smooth flat stones along the bottom of the burn.

A grouse called out on the hillside beyond; there was no answer. On the far hill, she could just make out the keepers' battered green Land Rover returning from some distant errand, perhaps checking the gin traps up by the loch. Trapping had been made illegal twenty years ago by the politicians, but, following the custom of the whole valley, no-one paid the slightest attention to edicts from Edinburgh or London. The foreigners who paid for the August shooting, and supported the only jobs in the glen, sent their money in the hopes of seeing grouse, not hen harriers and foxes.

And if James could turn his back on London, and settle here, what on earth would he do? The lowground was let to half a dozen farmers, all with their own families hoping to carry on their family business, scratching the meanest of livings from the thin soil and scrubby grass thanks only to grudging subsidies from the taxes levied in the cities. But most of the land was bare hillside, good only as a habitat for the grouse or stunted forestry, the whole of whose niggardly income must go towards the wages of the three keepers and four foresters who James continued to employ, no doubt subsidizing them as well as, she assumed, the whole of the upkeep of the house, cottages and steadings. Twelve families in all, where a century ago her great-grandfather, fresh from university, had come north from Berwick to run a school for over a hundred children! All up and down the valley, the stones of the long-abandoned steadings bore witness to that vanished civilization, a busy community thriving on their crofts. But there were no local villains, least of all the Hepburns. Cynical Highland clearances were a feature of the west coast; here, in the east, it was the agricultural depression coupled with cheaper produce from the great prairies of North America that had driven the children from their ancestral settlements to the dank backstreets of industrial Newtown Strathurquhart. No doubt the Hepburns would have gone too, had not a timely inheritance and prudent investment given them the means to continue to enjoy their idyll, supporting as many survivors on the land as their dividends would allow. But for how much longer? Her gaze strayed back to the massive rowan. It looked remarkably healthy.

James could immerse himself in rural affairs no doubt; there was the council, and the tourist board, and, if he was utterly desperate, the local health board. But he would take to the drink, like old Major Godman at Castle Buchat or the rich American widow who had bought Blairfeshie. This wasn't how she saw him, nor would it make an agreeable setting for her own life. She wanted a career, independence, a sense of personal achievement. What was more, she knew she would achieve it. Her mother talked of men as sustainers, essential props. She saw them as good friends, partners in sexual pleasures, companions at the table and, sometimes, as liabilities. But she sighed.

'I must love him,' she said to herself, 'because I can't imagine going back to being without him.' She stared round angrily at the paradise that could not support itself. Its sheer vastness, its cool air of total indifference to the human ants who came and went, who longed to stay but were unable to make a living from such rugged splendour. Unmelted snow still winked at her from the peaks of Ben Rullig and Ben Gierach. Life in an office? She stood up and tried to stifle her feelings by running hard all the way back to the house. It was still before 7 a.m.

Five hundred miles south, the day of the crucial vote dawned less bright and clear in Downing Street. The Prime Minister and his wife rose at eight, awkwardly sharing a bath out of dismal tradition while avoiding too careful a scrutiny of each other's bodies. One can take intimacy too far.

The very real threat that twenty-four hours might see them both ejected from this lavish building was at the forefront of his mind. Home was an indisputably charming old rectory set among Lord Berington's estate cottages in Plumby-sub-Wrawton, and there was also a neat little maisonette in Pimlico, currently sublet. Neither, however, boasted portraits by Sargent or desks by Caffieri, nor were they cared for by liveried servants with respectful smiles. The best he could hope for in that line was the Plumby sub-postmistress, Mrs Lazonby, with her crack-toothed scowl and the very audible sniff she deployed with insolent regularity. And all this at risk for *Miscellaneous Provisions No. 4*!

'Have you got the soap?' he enquired of his wife's bony back.

'You'll just have to wait,' she said, performing some unguessable ablution outside his line of vision.

'Walter thinks we'll win easily tonight,' he said, feeling a desperate need to defuse her backbone's grim reproach.

'Walter won't have to pack if you don't,' she replied. 'You can have the soap now if you can find it.'

The Chief Whip was also in his bath by nine, an elaborate sunken affair backed by murals of Mediterranean sunsets, but he was in a very different mood. While it would not be at all true to say that he hoped to lose the vote (he was far too professionally engaged for such unprincipled amateurism), nevertheless the prospect of loss was beginning to present him with a not unpleasant list of alternatives. Toady would resign, he was sure of that. But perhaps Soames could rally enough support for a majority, or even, stretching a point to its most elastic, dear old Webb-Carter. He himself would return to the back benches, that went without saying. Chief Whips who failed to deliver majorities were seldom reappointed, even one who had served as long and as successfully as he.

So! A drop in income, and a massive increase in leisure time. Time for his neglected water-colours, time for wine-tasting, above all, time for the Château de la Colinière, with its limpid overhung pools and rambling water meadows. As an ex-Chief Whip, he could count on innumerable overseas jaunts, and a peerage, too, when he got fed up with canvassing.

'What *are* you singing?' called his wife from their bedroom.

'A little song of the Languedoc.'

'Well, don't. It's perfectly frightful.'

He sank back luxuriously in the water's soothing embrace. How odd to think of Boynton drowning himself. Such a *fool*!

Just off the tip of Cap Estel, aboard his sixty-foot schooner, the *Elysium*, as she drifted lazily towards the morning sun a few kilometres west of Nice, David Brotherton, subject of many anxious and inconclusive telephone calls from the Whips' Office, lay stretched out naked on the pink and white striped sunbed. His mind delightfully at rest, he gazed peacefully back at a blue-sailed fishing boat that was skimming the silver surface of the sea in their wake. No committees, no papers, no *votes*! Just the sea and the sun. By his right hand, a small gilt table presented half a bottle of Krug, thoroughly iced, and a delicious little silver goblet.

'You look very comfortable.' The young steward came and sat beside him.

'Yes, I've had excellent news from London. Truly excellent.' With young Boynton unexpectedly dead, and thus unable to relate his own small part in events, and Toady heading for oblivion, the gentle Mediterranean breeze that just brushed his face with the lightest of caresses held infinite promise. He would continue to serve his constituency as assiduously as ever once this temporary exile ('*doctor's orders*, such a *bore*') was over. Toady would fall, and how could a new Prime Minister resist an experienced heavyweight like Brotherton? Brotherton the quintessential administrator, Brotherton the safe pair of hands.

'Anything else you'd like?'

Brotherton squinted up into the steward's pale eyes. 'Well, since you ask,' he said, holding one hand up as a shield against the sun, 'the answer is actually no. There aren't so many pleasures at my age, but one of the greatest is freedom from the imperative burdens of my youth. Be a good chap and bring me a cup of coffee, will you?'

Chapter Thirty-four

As soon as he reached his flat from Heathrow that morning, James spent the rest of the day drearily ringing round his crew of Members. None were pleased to hear him, and some were downright hostile, but all of them assured him that they would dutifully support the Government line. Paine reminded him that he had still heard nothing about the anticipated knighthood, and James heard himself cheerfully reassuring the anxious little man that it was surely only a matter of time.

On his way to the House late that afternoon, he called in at old Mrs Boynton's house in Victoria Square. The door was answered by a tiny old woman with bright orange hair in curlers.

'Hello, dearie,' she said.

'Hello.' He'd never set eyes on her in his life. 'My name is Hepburn. I wondered if Mrs Boynton would see me?'

She let out a disconcerting cackle. 'You go right up, dearie. She'll like a little company. First floor, it's the door on your left.'

Gloomily, he climbed the stairs, and knocked.

'Come in.'

He opened the door and peered cautiously in. Nick's mother was sitting very upright in a big old chair with carved wooden arms, looking out over the square.

'It's James Hepburn,' he said, since she didn't turn her head.

'How very nice,' she said. 'Come and sit near me.'

There was a battered sofa beside the window, and

he settled there, trying to match her gentle smile of welcome.

'I'm most dreadfully sorry,' he said after a pause. 'It's terrible news.'

She nodded. She was a large woman, with short grey hair and big vacant blue eyes. 'Quite a blow,' she said, in a strong quiet voice.

'I heard they found some letters.'

She made a vague gesture towards a single sheet of paper on the little table beside her, which stopped well short of inviting him to read it. 'I wish he'd told me what was troubling him.'

James looked at the floor. 'It seems such a waste,' he muttered.

'You were a good friend of his,' she said. 'I'm very grateful for that. He didn't make many friends. Actually, I wondered if it was something to do with his other life?'

James stared harder at the floor, which was close-carpeted with plain green Wilton. 'Other life?'

'Well, you know, his boys.'

This time he raised his eyes and stared at her. 'I don't think he thought you knew about all that,' he said.

'But of course I did,' she said. 'I'm not a complete fool. I always hoped he'd talk to me about it, but he never did.'

'You didn't mention it yourself?'

'Of course not!' She sounded shocked. 'Everyone's entitled to some privacy, don't you think? Especially from their parents.'

'Did you mind?'

'Why should I? It was nothing to me. His brother used to drop little barbed hints to me when he wanted to score, but I never paid the slightest attention.' A single tear ran down her cheek. She brushed it angrily aside.

James felt utterly inadequate in the presence of such stoical grief. 'Is there anything I can do?

Funeral arrangements or anything like that?'

'How kind.' Again she smiled. 'But no, I think we have that safely in hand. His brother rather enjoys that sort of thing.'

'I wish I'd done something to help him,' James said.

She shook her head vigorously. 'When people decide to go, it's best to let them get on with it. I do think that of all the most unpleasant of human emotions, self-pity is the very worst.' She fixed a direct stare upon him, and James, having nothing further to add, made his way back down the stairs and out into the street.

When he reached the House, he was summoned to Meyrick's office where he found Commander Trent standing beside the window. Seeing James, he held out a sheet of paper.

'Dear James, (ran Nick's last letter to his friend) *I know I was very wrong to reproach you last Wednesday. Messengers with bad news used to be shot, or so we were both taught by old K.P.St.G. Forgive me? By chance I saw the old bugger this morning – he hasn't changed one bit. James, I'm afraid I can't face the scandal. I couldn't support the Govt. on this one, and I couldn't bear my mother being shamed by all the row. This way no-one need make a great fuss. Pretend I lost a lot at Lloyds if that seems best. (Actually I got my best cheque yet, but only because I refused to join a syndicate which Windy wasn't in himself.) Two fingers to Walter and Toady, a kiss to Susie (if you're still speaking to her) and don't forget to send my brother back his very vulgar piece of silver which graces (if that is the word) the Unmentionables' table. If you should all feel inclined to drink a toast, let it be "Good luck on his new voyage!" You can see I'm getting maudlin. Too much vino for lunch, and a lousy vintage at that. Don't do anything I wouldn't.*

love etc'

Meticulously neat, it was signed with a straggling N, as if the writer had suddenly lost confidence. James read the letter twice and handed it silently back to Commander Trent whose office had been given the letters as soon as they were found in the jacket on the towpath. Nick's body had been caught in a weir downstream. Two drunken boatmen had risked their lives to pull him out, but he was already dead.

'"Toady" refers to the Prime Minister?' The policeman's eyes held no humour.

'Yes. Walter is, of course, Walter Meyrick here, and Susie is my wife.'

'And "Windy"?'

'That'll be his Lloyds agent, Captain Roper. I'm pretty sure he's known as "Windy".'

'I see.' Trent put the letter back into its envelope, and the envelope back into his pocket. 'And the problem he refers to?'

James risked a glance at Walter, who interrupted by saying, 'Just a minor matter. Mr Boynton was going to resign and vote against a government Bill. No-one in his family had ever done such a thing. Naturally, his mother would have been devastated.'

Trent raised his eyebrows. 'Whereas by committing suicide . . . ?'

Walter spread out his hands. 'These political families,' he said apologetically. 'Feelings do run very high. I know it seems odd to ordinary folk like you and me, Commander, but . . .' He shook his head sorrowfully. 'Poor old Nick. Not a high flier, though. If only he'd stuck to the *usual channels*, as we say in the House.'

The commander stood up. 'Goodbye, Mr Meyrick. I will be in touch.'

'Goodbye, Commander. Thank you for treating this sad affair with such delicacy. Naturally the poor young man's family will be hoping for a verdict of accidental death.'

'We'll see what we can do,' said Trent stolidly. 'But I'll need to keep these letters for a little while longer.'

'Of course. Mrs Davies! Will you show Commander Trent out? Thank you so much.'

Left alone together, Walter and James sat in glum silence. Eventually, Walter said, 'You mustn't blame yourself.'

James laughed harshly. 'I wasn't thinking of doing so,' he said.

'Or me,' snapped the sensitive Chief Whip. 'I came into politics to make things better, to build council houses, to keep the country safe. I didn't start this job because I liked bullying overweight *fairies*.'

'As a matter of fact, I was blaming Nick,' said James calmly. 'I saw his mother this evening. Suicide is a tolerable choice if you have no family, but with parents or children, it's the most brutal form of self-indulgence.'

'I note you exclude wives.'

'Certainly,' said James smiling. 'If the suicide is married, there probably lies the most likely cause.'

'What a cynic you have become,' sighed Walter. 'But aren't you being too hard on Nick? It would have been a messy scandal.'

'What I blame him most for is getting so worked up over this Bill. There's nothing really so crucial in it.'

'Nothing?' Walter stared at him. Perhaps the young Whip was even stupider than he looked.

'Nothing at all. I read it from cover to cover several times over the weekend. Yes, it dilutes parliamentary scrutiny, but so does the Treaty of Rome. Certainly it's better than letting the Opposition in. I tried to ring him on Sunday, but he'd already left.'

'You know,' said Walter slowly, 'I think you could

be in line for early promotion. I'm impressed with your way of thinking.'

The monitor above the door told them that the debate on the third reading had now begun. By their nature, third readings tend to be rather perfunctory, since they are restricted to the theory rather than the detail of the Bill, the precise wording having been exhaustively debated during the committee stage leading up to the second reading. This had been completed just after the Easter recess, and it was only the Government's uncertainty on other topics which had delayed this vote until now.

But as soon as James walked back into Mrs Davies's outer office, he found his fellow Whips in turmoil. Brotherton, the recently departed Home Secretary, had been bombarded with messages but was now supposed to be out of reach on his yacht in the Mediterranean, a Scottish Member had been taken to hospital with appendicitis and one of the Irish Members was nowhere to be found. With Nick and Sir Cuthbert both dead, this left the Government with a notional majority of two.

'That's all right then.'

'You mean you haven't heard?' said one of his colleagues.

'Heard what?'

'About Pilkington.'

James stared. 'Rupert?'

'He's thrown a queeny fit. He says he's heard we were hounding Nick, and he's going to vote with the Opposition just to show his disapproval.'

'I can't really blame him,' said James.

The other man narrowed his eyes. 'Is it true then?'

James met his stare and held it. 'He was in a bit of a dilemma.'

'Do *you* want to talk to Pilkington?'

James shook his head. 'I'm the last person who ought to do that.'

'That's what Dutton said. He went down to the Chamber to try to catch him himself before the debate started. He's in a panic in case we lose the "bachelor" vote! If they all come whinneying out of their closets at the same time, that'd be the end of this Bill at least . . .'

'Just Pilkington changing sides would make it a dead heat,' mused James. 'Surely the Speaker would give his casting vote to the Government?'

'Not likely! Toady vetoed redecorating his apartments. He'll say he's supporting the status quo by convention, and drop us all down the bloody plughole.'

The Deputy Chief Whip put his head round the door. 'It's started!' Picking up their papers, they all hurried down to the Chamber, where Ralph Dutton was laboriously introducing the Bill.

'May I remind Honourable Members that this comparatively minor measure . . .' (some shouts) 'has had its full share of parliamentary time. The House approved its second reading by a majority of eleven votes and it is purely a procedural measure to bring our various legislative procedures into line with the Treaties of Maastricht and Glasgow. Let me remind the House of its conceptual basis . . .' On and on he droned, his voice punctuated only by the excited baying of an Opposition united for once by the unmistakable scent of a government's lifeblood. '. . . no! I will not give way again. If the Honourable Member will bear with me, I have nearly done. Finally I would commend this Bill to the House as a model of good housekeeping and legislative honour.' He sat down, to muted encouragement from his own side, and strident barracking from those opposite.

'The Honourable Member for Newtown Strathurquhart.'

Iain Mackenzie, timing his intervention to coincide with the resumption of the television's live broadcast, rose to his feet just as the arc lights blazed into life, and dozens of Members scurried in from their dinners visibly to take their seats.

'This is a scandalous measure,' he began. 'It is the most degraded and dishonest piece of legislation to be brought before this House in living memory. Not since "Maastricht" has this House been so grossly misled as to the nature of what they are being asked to support. I have read the wording very carefully, and it is nothing less than a blatant attempt to by-pass this House and present the Executive with a carte blanche . . .' James rose to his feet. 'I shall not give way.'

James remained standing.

'Order.' The Speaker turned his bleary gaze upon James and stared at him with disfavour. 'The Honourable Member is not giving way.' James sat down.

'I repeat,' continued Mackenzie after a brief glare at James. 'I have read the wording with great care, and . . .' James stood up again. 'I've no idea why the Honourable Member for Glenbuchat is choosing to do aerobics in this House. I will not give way.' James sat down. 'I have read the wording very carefully . . .'

'Get on with it!' shouted Paine from behind James. 'We'll concede you can read. Just.'

'As I say . . .' Mackenzie was beginning to lose his thread. And the merciless eye of the camera was all the time beaming his discomfort to the dozing millions. James stood up a third time. 'Oh, very well!' Mackenzie sat back, anxious to recheck his notes.

'Mr Hepburn.'

'Thank you, Mr Speaker. I only wanted to say that I, like my Honourable, and neighbouring, opponent across the way, have also read the wording. It is far from clear, but if he has time to read it just once more, and I realize it's fifty pages long, particularly concentrating on page thirty-eight, he will find that his fears are groundless. I commend this to him not as an adversary, but as a fellow Scotsman.' James sat down, being rewarded by a searching stare from the Prime Minister, who had turned round in his seat now just two rows in front since James's promotion to the Whips' Office.

'May I thank my fellow countryman,' snarled Mackenzie, resuming his stance with one eye cocked at the cameras, 'for a typically unhelpful piece of Tory obfuscation. Now, to resume, I have read . . .'

The thin hands of the Commons clock edged their way remorselessly on, as more and more speakers rose to illustrate their existence for the benefits of Hansard and the nation's screens. None added much to the matter, except Rupert Pilkington, his youthful paunch adorned on this occasion with a waistcoat of funereal black velvet. He spoke briefly and to the point:

'I shall be voting against this Bill simply as a protest against what I believe to have been the disgraceful pressure put upon my late and Honourable friend the erstwhile Member for Spitalfields. Nor do I believe I shall be alone. If this Bill fails, it will be principally due to the heavy-handed methods of the Whips' Office.' He sat down to angry cries of 'Shame!', 'Give us the facts!', and repeated cries of 'Hear! Hear!' from both sides of the House. Nine o'clock and only an hour to go. James felt a hand on his shoulder. It was Walter Meyrick, his face impassive.

'Can you spare a moment?' he said. 'My office.'

Bowing to the Speaker, they hurried down the gangway and out through the crowded hall. At the far end of the corridor, he could see the squat figure of the Prime Minister preceding them, with Dutton scurrying after him in servile attendance. The four of them had difficulty climbing the broad staircase because of a throng of people hurrying downwards for the closing stages of the debate.

'Now then!' The Prime Minister rounded on James as

soon as the four of them were safely and privately ensconced in the Chief Whip's office. 'What's this about this Bill being a nonsense?'

'He didn't quite say that, Prime Minister,' interrupted Meyrick smoothly.

'Eh?'

'What he did say was that it was broadly neutral, and not therefore of any lasting significance.'

'Neutral?' The Prime Minister's large moist eyes swivelled between James and Meyrick. 'Neutral? Is that what you think, young man?'

'Well, what do you think it achieves?' asked James, greatly daring.

'What do *I* think?' The Prime Minister turned to Dutton and Meyrick. 'He wants to know what *I* think! My dear fellow, I'm only the *Prime Minister*. It never signifies at all what *I* think.' The other two began laughing sycophantically as the little round man shook with delight at his own wit. Slow at first, after working at it all three of them were throbbing with uncontrolled mirth.

James stared at them. Suddenly, he knew why he had had enough. 'I'm going to vote against it too,' he said, and made for the door.

'No, you're not!' snapped Meyrick.

'And why not?'

'Because . . .' But Walter Meyrick had not reached his eminence by indiscriminate violence. He had a fine sense of values, even if these were sometimes different to those of many other men. It occurred to him that his particular ammunition, the incident of the supple and insinuating Mrs Durham, was of limited value against a man already engaged in a divorce and might keep with advantage for another more crucial day, so he simply raised his arms, and halted his words, forcing his face into a beneficent smile. 'You must use your own judgement, dear boy,' he said. 'Of course.'

'Yes, yes. But are you sure about this Bill?' The Prime Minister thrust Meyrick aside.

'I am,' said James.

'Well then! I'll withdraw the silly thing. I don't mind being slaughtered for a lamb or even a sheep, but I'm buggered if I'll be slaughtered for an empty bloody fleece. Come on, Ralph. This'll give them something to chew on!' He bustled out of the room, chuckling mightily.

'You've done yourself some good there,' remarked Meyrick, applying a thoughtful match to his pipe.

'How so?'

There was a sucking sound, and then the older man disappeared behind a cloud of smoke. After a bit he said, 'You've just saved the Government.'

'Despite threatening to vote against them?' asked James with a dismissive shrug.

'Oh, I expect that will all be forgotten in the general relief,' said Meyrick airily, scrutinizing James carefully through his smokescreen. It wouldn't do to lose so candid a recruit from the corridors of power. They needed a few genuinely decent men nowadays, to lend tone to an increasingly murky business. Particularly the only one to understand this wretched Bill. 'No,' decided Meyrick inwardly, 'this young man shall be kept against a rainy day.' 'Come on,' he said aloud. 'We don't want to miss the show.' And then, quite unexpectedly, he added, almost involuntarily, 'Do you know? I believe my *father* would have approved of you.' It was, unconsciously, his very highest expression of praise, but sounded very odd coming from one so old and addressed to one so young. Outside, beyond the ramparts of that great parliamentary palace, Old Father Thames twinkled with deceptive charm, flowing ever seawards, intent upon its changeless task.

Far ahead of them, the Prime Minister bustled back towards the Chamber. No ignominious defeat!

No resignation! No packing up and leaving Number Ten! Toady the Magnificent reigns again. There should be unexampled cataracts of good things to celebrate: knighthoods, bishoprics, sashes and stars should cascade onto the heads of his friends and supporters. Perhaps it really was time to bring back an earldom or two? After all, he didn't want people to take it amiss when his own turn came.

'They're waiting for you.' The Chamber was positively pullulating with vociferous shouts and hullabaloo, as the time for taking the vote approached. He took his seat, and, just to tease his opponents, he huddled down in his seat, assuming an air of gloom.

'WAKE UP, TOADY!' shouted one man.

'BACK TO POND-LIFE, MY SON!' jeered another.

With a well-acted heavy sigh, the round little man rose wearily to his feet. 'Mr Speaker.' The House fell reluctantly silent as everyone's attention focused on the Prime Minister. 'The measure before us tonight has been the subject of impassioned debate, much of it remarkably ill informed . . .'

'GET ON WITH IT!' shouted a voice from the back.

'However, the primary purpose of this House is for debate, and having listened to the weighty arguments advanced by men of goodwill on both sides, Her Majesty's Government have decided to postpone . . .' There was a deafening outburst of shouting. 'To postpone indefinitely the promotion of this very minor measure. We shall therefore be withdrawing the motion.' He sat down, as the Commons second-hand reached its zenith, amid a thunderous outcry of cheers and counter-cheers, and shortly afterwards quit the Chamber, ignoring his opponents' repeated demands for further explanation. An hour or so's nap in his private room was what he needed. There was no way he would quit the House of Commons until he could be sure his wife was safely gone to bed.

Part Four

August

Chapter Thirty-five

With the dropping of the controversial legislation, the summer session came to an unexpectedly quiet end. The two by-elections, for Bedfordshire (Woburn) and Spitalfields, would be held in October, once the party conference season was over, and the Members departed for their summer recess safe in the knowledge that they had done their duty and could now holiday with whomsoever they chose without undue harassment from press or public. There was even some press speculation about a major reshuffle, with David Brotherton being authoritatively trailed as a likely candidate for the Treasury.

Having attended Nick Boynton's funeral, a very private ceremony in the country, James had decided to drive home, and having loaded the car with everything personal from the flat, he set off on the tenth of August on the long journey north up the A1.

The changing landscape seemed like a season in reverse. In Hertfordshire, the stubbles were already ploughed, the heavy machinery churning through the clay with its attendant flock of seagulls. But once into the Bedfordshire levels, big blocks of straw bales still punctuated the scenery, and twice the traffic slowed behind laden carts towed by tiny tractors. At the wheel, hunched farmers turned their faces grimly away from gesticulating motorists. In Lincolnshire and Yorkshire, golden cornfields were being greedily devoured by the combine harvesters, great red and yellow leviathans, giants' toys, occasionally halting to ejaculate thick streams of seed into patient lorries, waiting passively in the dust for their fill of corn.

Then, rising into the chillier air of the north, the fields began to lose their lustre. The wheat was still greenish-gold, the wheelmarks of earlier workings visible among the shorter growth. He half-expected to find them still sowing north of the Forth, but there the half-ripe crops were laid flat, battered by a recent storm, with clouds of pigeons eagerly settling to pick at the ears, rising automatically at the regular report of a farmer's gas-driven alarm-gun, only to return immediately to resume their unofficial tithe. 'No-one ever went bust on a flattened harvest,' James reminded himself cheerfully. 'If it's heavy enough to fall over, it's heavy enough to feed a few birds and keep the bank happy as well.'

By now the cornfields were giving way to grazing lands, steep pastures and boggy meadows, stocked with stately milking cows and their humbler beefier cousins, next year's butcher's meat, but now still animate, eking out a dry season's last vestiges of grass, one eye kept beadily focused on fresh growth beyond the electric fence. And then up into the hills; but hills transformed from the spring's dour greyness and the summer's muted green.

It was as if the whole force of the sun had been filtered through a purple gauze. While the far peaks still shimmered blue beyond his immediate horizon, the rearing hills of the glen were washed with mauve, almost overwhelming in its bright translucent sheen. James stopped the car in a lay-by, and got out, the better to enjoy the view. Each year it was the same: like a butterfly breaking from its chrysalis, these hills would suddenly emerge from dullness into startling splendour, as the heather bloomed. The heather! So humble a plant on its own, and so majestic in its millions.

James sighed. To have to turn his back on all this beauty. And the image of the fox returned to him, the fox who had chosen life on three legs to a slow death inviolate. Was that the choice? Grudgingly he listed those aspects of the last few months that Nick would have categorized as wrecks: first the Berington steel works, then his marriage, and then Nick's lonely death. And Westminster? Must Hepburnstoun also be added to the roll? Lucy, he recognized, was a future from which he was debarred by his excessive concentration on the past. But the essence of the battle is to choose the right ground. The fox had chosen life; he, James, would choose life with his children. Let Susie have her Gainsborough, and Hew his Castle Farm and mile of fishing! One last look at the landscape, and resolutely he returned to the car and started to make, and receive, a series of telephone calls.

By teatime, he was in Lucy's arms, in Lucy's bed. 'I do love you,' he said, rolling over and staring up at his grandfather's heavy ornate ceiling. '*How* long did you promise you'd stay with me?'

'Until that bloody tree produces its berries!' she laughed. 'Then I'm off!' She sat up.

'What! No more rows?' His voice sounded suddenly indistinct.

'Yes, and no more *politics*!'

'No more bonks by the loch?' There was a long silence.

'And no more jealousy either.' She gave a slight cough.

'I'll miss you.' He laid his head in her lap.

'Well,' she whispered, caressing him, utterly crushed by her own aching sadness, 'we'll make the most of what time is left, won't we?'

He opened one eye. 'You're not saying you'll miss me?'

She rolled over and seized him, wrapping her bare

arms round him. 'I love you!' she cried. 'Of course I'll bloody miss you.'

'Put your clothes on then. Let's go for a last walk up to the loch. It looks like there'll be another good sunset.'

They walked for hours, drinking in the mountain air, gazing at the soft purplish light on the hills as the heather was ruffled by gusts of a warm westerly wind. For a change, they took an independent sheep track across the moraine, through the hags, deep and black and springy, the black peat sliced here and there like cake, with little bogs and rivulets eating away at the spongy labyrinth. As they climbed, the wind began to tear at their faces and a rich red colour was stealing over the sky. Within a week, these hills would resonate with the crackle of gunfire, when his French shooting tenants would take their places in the stone butts, and the local farmers, appropriately furnished with white flags, would march warily towards them in line across the heather, driving the grouse towards their annual encounters with early death. And then, farewell.

It was beginning to get dark when they reached the ridge overlooking the loch. Peering cautiously over it, they saw, a hundred feet below them, a large herd of deer standing, heads erect, alert at some sign of danger. Even as they watched, the light changed again, and the whole landscape, from the snowy rocks up on Ben Rullig down to the silvery ribbon of the Buchat far below, was bathed in a deep rose pink glow. A stag roared, and James quietly pointed it out, a shaggy black dot standing out on the opposite ridge, across the march. Another answered the challenge from where the evening mist was beginning to shroud the foothills.

Reluctantly, they turned their backs on paradise, and started the long walk down towards Hepburnstoun, a welcoming white speck that just glinted among the black trees of its sheltering plantations, a thousand feet below them and nearly two miles down the valley.

'That's funny,' she said. They were coming back by the path from the ford, having leapt across the boulders to keep their feet dry.

'What is?'

'We should be able to see the top of the "Pride" from here.'

He stared through the twilight. 'Must be further than you think.'

'No,' she ran ahead. 'Oh God! James! It's not there.' He started to laugh. 'What's happened?' She turned frantically back to him. 'What's happened to it?'

'Keep calm,' he said, passing his arm round her waist and drawing her to him. 'I've had it cut down. Late this afternoon.'

'You can't have! But it's . . .' Suddenly the significance of what had happened dawned on her. 'But that's CHEATING!' she cried.

'It's called *politics*,' he said, smiling and pulling her to him. 'As practised at Westminster. We've got to stay together now. Here or St Andrews, London or wherever. You mustn't break your word. The future is so much more important than the past, especially if you'll agree to marry me when I'm free, of Susie, and of Hepburnstoun.'

She gazed up at him, aghast, but then, after a minute's thought, she too began to smile. 'Perhaps,' she said, 'but with one proviso.'

'Let's hear it.'

'Well,' she said, after a pause, 'IF I'm going to even *think* about being a step-mother, and I emphasize the IF, it's going to be here, at Hepburnstoun, where Sandy and Jennie feel secure. They're going to need a bit of safety with all the other upheavals.'

'The trustees want to sell.'

'But you're the tenant, aren't you? I doubt they'll

find a buyer if you sit tight. Or buy it back yourself if you have to. Didn't you say you'd got a lot of shares? That's what the children would want. I know it is!' Her eyes were shining with excitement. All her previous doubts had suddenly crystallized, and all but shattered. Of course his place was here. If his will was insufficient, she would add hers, and together they would outface his difficulties. 'What about this new lawyer? Can't he do something?'

He nodded. 'As it happens he can. His son rang me in the car this afternoon. Apparently I do have a right of pre-emption, and they've thought up a new angle, something to do with the capital gains tax liability, which has changed my accountant's attitude, it seems, but . . .'

'But what?'

'I told them it didn't matter.'

'You did *what*?'

'Well . . .' He gestured at the landscape which was shimmering round them in the fading purple haze, that magical gloaming unique to Highland valleys during the month of August. 'Look, Lucy. *Look* at this place! It's so *beautiful*. I love it, you love it, but it's hopelessly uneconomic. Surely you can see that?'

'So? Get that famous business brain to work. Start a deer farm. Build some holiday cottages. Bottle the water from the spring by the loch. I've got my degree to keep me occupied, but that doesn't mean you've got to sit on your haunches, staring into space. Less Celtic gloom and more Pictish action might be in order. Put some life into the place. It needs more people, not fewer. I know you could do it.'

'Do you really think so?' He was gazing at her, dreaming of putting life into her.

'Of course I do. I could still commute to St Andrews and do my degree, and you can get a part-time banking job in Edinburgh on the side. We could have plenty to do, if it worked. How could you even think of leaving this place?'

He stared at her. 'Where shall we start?'

'That's your third question in as many minutes. By planting another rowan of course. A pledge for the future. A renewal . . . *perhaps*.'

'You're on!' Together, they walked, very slowly, back to the house.

A SELECTED LIST OF FINE WRITING AVAILABLE FROM BLACK SWAN

THE PRICES SHOWN BELOW WERE CORRECT AT THE TIME OF GOING TO PRESS. HOWEVER TRANSWORLD PUBLISHERS RESERVE THE RIGHT TO SHOW NEW RETAIL PRICES ON COVERS WHICH MAY DIFFER FROM THOSE PREVIOUSLY ADVERTISED IN THE TEXT OR ELSEWHERE.

99565 7	**PLEASANT VICES**	Judy Astley	£5.99
13649 2	**HUNGRY**	Jane Barry	£6.99
99550 9	**THE FAME HOTEL**	Terence Blacker	£5.99
99531 2	**AFTER THE HOLE**	Guy Burt	£5.99
99421 9	**COMING UP ROSES**	Michael Carson	£4.99
99599 1	**SEPARATION**	Dan Franck	£5.99
99616 5	**SIMPLE PRAYERS**	Michael Golding	£5.99
99466 9	**A SMOKING DOT IN THE DISTANCE**	Ivor Gould	£6.99
99609 2	**FORREST GUMP**	Winston Groom	£5.99
99487 1	**JIZZ**	John Hart	£5.99
99169 4	**GOD KNOWS**	Joseph Heller	£7.99
99207 0	**THE WATER-METHOD MAN**	John Irving	£6.99
99205 4	**THE WORLD ACCORDING TO GARP**	John Irving	£6.99
99567 3	**SAILOR SONG**	Ken Kesey	£6.99
99542 8	**SWEET THAMES**	Matthew Kneale	£6.99
99037 X	**BEING THERE**	Jerzy Kosinski	£4.99
99595 9	**LITTLE FOLLIES**	Eric Kraft	£5.99
99569 X	**MAYBE THE MOON**	Armistead Maupin	£5.99
99603 3	**ADAM'S WISH**	Paul Micou	£5.99
99597 5	**COYOTE BLUE**	Christopher Moore	£5.99
99536 3	**IN THE PLACE OF FALLEN LEAVES**	Tim Pears	£5.99
99122 8	**THE HOUSE OF GOD**	Samuel Shem	£6.99
99546 0	**THE BRIDGWATER SALE**	Freddie Stockdale	£5.99
99547 9	**CRIMINAL CONVERSATIONS**	Freddie Stockdale	£5.99
99639 4	**THE TENNIS PARTY**	Madeleine Wickham	£5.99
99500 2	**THE RUINS OF TIME**	Ben Woolfenden	£4.99